White Bikini Panties

Books by Kelly James-Enger

DID YOU GET THE VIBE?

WHITE BIKINI PANTIES

Published by Kensington Publishing Corporation

KENSINGTON BOOKS are published by

Kensington Publishing Corp.
850 Third Avenue
New York, NY 10022

All Kensington titles, imprints and distributed lines are available at special quantity discounts for bulk purchases for sales promotion, premiums, fundraising, educational or institutional use.

Special book excerpts or customized printing can also be created to fit specific needs. For details, write or phone the office of the Kensington Special Sales Manager: Kensington Publishing Corp., 850 Third Avenue, New York, NY 10022. Attn. Special Sales Department. Phone: 1-800-221-2647.

Strapless and the Strapless logo are trademarks of Kensington Publishing Corp.
Kensington and the K logo Reg. U.S. Pat. & TM Off.

ISBN 0-7582-0698-4

First Kensington Trade Paperback Printing: November 2004
10 9 8 7 6 5 4 3 2 1

Printed in the United States of America

White Bikini Panties

Kelly James-Enger

Strapless

KENSINGTON BOOKS
www.kensingtonbooks.com

To my mom, my first fan.

Acknowledgments

Writers may spend much of their lives working alone, but if they're lucky, members of their "team" make their lives a whole lot easier—and happier. So thanks to my agent, Laurie Harper, and my editor, John Scognamiglio, for giving *Panties* a home. Special thanks also to my family; to my friends, especially Cindy, my favorite blonde, and Abby, who shares my love for the written word and tarot cards; Erik, my web boy, cute little monkey, and ceiling-holding-upper; and the fuzzy little pup.

Chapter 1
The Queen of Cups

A benevolent woman, eager to be warm and loving.

White bikini underwear changed my life. Really.

I've been thinking about underwear for a while. It's one of those things you don't expend too much mental energy on, at least most of the time. You wake up in the morning, shower, dry off, and get dressed. You pull on a pair of whatever panties happen to be in your drawer, grab a bra, and select the rest of your ensemble. Think about it. Could you tell me right now what panties you're wearing? I think not—unless you've got a new boyfriend, or you're going out and hoping to find a new boyfriend, or you have your period. All three instances require proper underwear for the occasion.

I was thinking about underwear as the traffic crept westward along the Kennedy on Tuesday morning. I tried to think positive—living in the city and working in a suburb, at least I had a reverse commute. It could be worse. Still, though, the traffic sucked. I'd been making this drive for almost two years, and during that time I'd cycled between phases where it nearly drove me stark raving nuts and shorter-lived phases where it didn't seem *that* bad. Lately it was one of the former. It was probably PMS, but lately the idea of climbing in my car to face the morning commute was almost more than I could handle.

The fact that it was mid-July didn't help. Running my Civic's air-conditioning tended to make it overheat, so I was forced to resort to rolling down my windows and breathing exhaust-laden air morning and evening, five days a week.

Of course, when your car isn't moving, the illusory breeze stops as well. I sat and fanned myself with the paper, and drank from the Diet Coke can that was sweating into my lap. I craned my neck but could see no reason for the holdup. There was no accident, no smoking car along the side of the road, no flashing police lights. That's what I hate about driving. It's the illusion of control. Traffic's light, and you're flying along at eighty mph, blasting Linkin Park and shouting along with the few lyrics you can make out, only to suddenly slam, meta-phorically speaking, into a backup of cars jammed bumper-to-bumper inching along at a speed slower than you *walk* . . . and then just as suddenly, the cars thin out and traffic accelerates and you cram the pedal down, realizing that you've lost pre-cious minutes in the day-to-day battle of getting to work on time. "Phantom accidents," I call them—those times when traf-fic slows to a stop and then speeds up again for no apparent rea-son. I counted three on the way to work—two on the Kennedy and one on the Eisenhower—but made it to work with four minutes to spare.

I'd been thinking about underwear because I'd been pon-dering vaginas in general. I'd seen *The Vagina Monologues* with Jane, at her insistence, of course, on Saturday. Jane's an ac-tress—well, an actor is the politically correct term now—and she'd wanted to see the production when Eve Ensler per-formed it here in Chicago several years ago. This time around, it was a group of three actresses, none of whom I'd heard of, but we went and Jane loved it. She laughed raucously through-out it, nodding her head and clapping frequently. I'd decided if she raised her fist into the air and yelled out, "Yeah, sistas!" I'd clear out of there, but she managed to stay in her seat.

To be honest, I was a little nonplussed by the whole thing. I wasn't shocked by the content—although hearing the word *cunt* bandied about over and over got a little old—but I just felt like I was missing something. The performance was simple. The actresses perched on stools on stage and engaged in casual conversation. Well, casual except that they were discussing women having different names for their vaginas, and what those names were, and what the best names were, and other thought-provoking questions like "What would your vagina wear?" "What would your vagina say?" and "What would your vagina eat?"

Women—I don't have to tell you it was 99.8 percent women in the audience, do I?—laughed, assumedly in recognition, but I left feeling that apparently I had not spent enough time pondering the potential name, clothing choices, and culinary preferences of my own vagina. I just don't think about it much. Sure, it's responsible for some sexual pleasure, and I'm happy for that, but most of the time I simply ignore it.

Several of the women I work with at the Coddled Cook had been scandalized that I had seen (insert hushed tone here) "that vagina show." I'd been peppered with questions yesterday. "What was it like?" "Did they actually talk about vaginas?" Rachel in particular had been fascinated.

"So what kinds of people were there? Were there any *men*?" Rachel is twenty-four, only four years younger than me, but often makes me feel *much* older. She has dark, curly hair, a sweet face, and laughs easily. I think what gives me the aging camp counselor feeling is that incredible earnestness she sports. She tries so hard—at work and with her boyfriend of the moment—to keep up on the latest look and lipstick color and love lives of her favorite celebrities, and she never expects to be disappointed. It always comes as a shock to her, you know? Like a five-year-old discovering that the tooth fairy is actually her mom. I don't want to sound too jaded, but I like to think of myself as a realist.

When I told Rachel that there was actually a variety of people in the audience—from college students to militant-looking (presumed) lesbians with aggressively short hair to white-haired old ladies (that really threw me!) to a handful of way uncomfortable-looking men (I counted exactly three), she was stunned. "Oh my gosh!" Her eyes widened. "I can't believe a guy would go to that! I don't even like to say the word"—she lowered her voice—"*vagina.*"

"Well, that was part of what she was talking about. How people think *vagina* is a bad word. How it's treated as profanity when it's simply the name of a part of a woman's anatomy." I spoke with all the authority of an OB-GYN who uses the word *vagina* as often as the rest of us bandy about the word *stress, diet,* or *chocolate.* I tend to do that with Rachel. She makes me act smarter than I know I am.

Rachel nodded. She was wearing a loose-fitting long-sleeved cranberry sweater and a black skirt that reached to her ankles. Rachel still dresses in the kind of clothes she probably wore in college, but it doesn't matter much at a company like ours. Unless you're a manager and expected to dress in more businesslike attire, you can—and many do—get away with nearly anything.

I'm a big fan of black pants myself. Jane says I need to experiment more with my wardrobe as a way to express myself. I'm continually waving her off. Black pants go with anything, they don't show dirt, and you can wear them forever. I have black flat fronts, black chinos, black wide-legs, black hip-huggers, black velvets for dressier occasions, black capris, and even black jeans. So sue me. I like black.

Anyway, Rachel and I were debating the whole vagina thing when Elaine sidled over. Elaine. She started here about the same time I did, but we've never really warmed to each other. Part of the reason is that I think she's happy only when someone else is unhappy. Everyone has someone like that at their office, no matter where you work. She's probably the biggest gossip in the whole department, and since there's close to forty of us if you include all the marketing, communications, and PR people, that's saying something. She's the same age as I am, but that's about all we have in common. She's tall, with streaked blond hair and pale, Nordic-icy-blue eyes. She's also thin as a stick and apparently puts a lot of time and money into her wardrobe. I doubt I've seen her wear the same outfit more than twice.

"Good morning, Trina. Good morning, Rachel." We both smiled and responded and waited. Elaine never stops by to just say hi. She's always got an agenda. "So, what's the latest around here?" She looked around, glancing toward the wall offices where the department heads were ensconced. It was still before nine, so most were presumably trickling in with their briefcases and giant portable coffee cups.

"Nothing major. Why? What's up?" I've learned to cut to the chase with Elaine.

"Did you hear Kirk just got canned yesterday? For porno on his PC?"

"He was looking at porn here at work?" asked Rachel. Like most companies, the Coddled Cook has a strict policy against using the web for personal reasons. And also like most companies, the vast majority of us employees just as strictly ignore the rule.

"No, he wasn't just using the Internet. He was writing nasty stuff and e-mailing it to women he met on-line. I hear it was plenty filthy, leaving nothing to the imagination."

"But he's married!" That would be Rachel. She believes that once you're married, sexual attraction to anyone other than your spouse sputters out like a damp candle.

Elaine rolled her eyes at me. "Rach, honey, he's a *man*. Please."

"How'd they catch him?" My heart sped up. I had to admit, I'd sent a few not-so-clean e-mails myself. Nothing that would qualify as porn, but Rick and I had done some of our early wooing on-line. I thought of one note I'd sent him after a particularly nutty night, and I cringed. What if someone was reading that stuff?

"He was having an on-line affair, I guess, and he broke it off. The woman was plenty pissed and sent all the e-mails he'd sent her from his work account to Jim." James Beckwith was the head of human resources, the person responsible for hiring and firing all of us. "And that was that."

"Geez." It seemed like a harsh punishment, but then again, it was company policy. I made a mental note to tame down any notes that I sent to Rick in the future. Not that our notes had been hot and heavy for some time—after you've been with someone for a while, that urgent sex stuff fades somewhat. And that's good because at some point you have to focus on the real world. Or so I told myself.

The truth was that things between Rick and me seemed stalled. We'd been dating for more than a year and a half, long enough to be past the first blush of infatuation and through a couple of bad arguments about his workaholic tendencies and occasional emotional unavailability. Rick can be the sweetest, most affectionate guy I've ever known, but when he's preoccupied with work, it's like I don't even exist. That was our biggest issue. That and his apparent disinterest in ever marrying me.

I'd sat down at my computer to start on the stories for the next newsletter when I got a "new mail" message. It was from Rick.

"Hey, babe. Can't meet U tonight. Got a cutover, last minute thing Roger just dropped on us. I've got meetings all day--maybe hook up tomorrow night? TTYL. XO R."

I sighed. I shouldn't have been surprised—Rick works as a network administrator downtown and most of his job seems to consist of putting out fires and dealing with technological emergencies—but I was disappointed. I'd promised him dinner and had been looking forward to seeing him. Maybe I'd just give Jane a call and see if she wanted to come over instead.

I replied to Rick's e-mail and spent the rest of the morning working on a story on selling techniques. The Coddled Cook sells kitchen products to people—women, mostly—through home shows modeled after Tupperware parties. Every season they come out with a few new products, and part of my job is to write articles explaining to our "Cook's Helpers" how to use and sell them to potential customers. This time around, I was describing a combination vegetable peeler/slicer/corer and listing as many possible uses as I could come up with. The test kitchen would no doubt have more suggestions, but at least I had a good start on it.

My phone rang just after lunch. I picked up without looking at the phone display that automatically identified the caller. "Hi, this is Trina. How can I help you?"

"Well, I have a problem. I have this turkey baster that I have to write about. Ironic, isn't it?"

I laughed. "Come on, Bobby. You know we just gave you that product to mess with your mind." Bobby is one of the few men in the entire department. He's a writer like me. He's also beautiful, funny, sweet, and gay. It figures.

"You're too cruel. Actually, I know a good use for a turkey baster, but I don't think our typical Cook's Helper in the Bible Belt would care to hear about how it's a great tool for lesbian inseminations."

"Seriously?"

"I even hear that our brand is one of the best."

"I thought that was just something people joked about."

"Nope. I know two couples who have used it, and both are the happy parents of a bouncing baby boy, and girl," said Bobby. "Maybe I could do a whole feature article on its advantages over our competitors."

"That might bring your career here to a screeching halt."

Bobby lowered his voice. "Don't even joke. You know how bad the job market is? One of my friends lost his job at Cahner's three months ago, and he hasn't been able to find anything. It's bleak, Trini."

Bobby had insisted on calling me Trini since he started working here a year ago. I kind of liked it. I'd never had a nickname—well, Trina is short for Katrina, but not even my parents use my full name—and Trini somehow made me feel fluffy and fun. Bobby and I had recognized something in each other almost immediately. He was the only one who knew how

I really felt about working there, and how disappointed I was in the way my Career was turning out.

When I majored in English, I hadn't thought much about what I'd do when I got out of school. Sure, I'd fantasized about writing poetry and wearing black turtlenecks and smoking cigarettes and drinking strong black coffee and exuding an air of mysterious sexiness. In these fantasies, I hadn't stopped to consider how I would actually support myself. My rude awakening started immediately after graduation. I lived at home, downstate, but set my sights on Chicago. Even then, it took me almost a year to find a job in publishing, and that was working for a horrible little women's magazine downtown. I was making the princely, or rather princessly, salary of $23,000 with no benefits except health insurance. I found an apartment out in La Grange—I couldn't afford to live anyplace decent in Chicago proper—and I took the train and then the el to get to work every morning. I stuck it out there for almost two years, and then took a job at a medical publisher in Oak Brook. The money was better, but the work bored me to tears. Writing about accreditation procedures, Medicare reimbursements, and hospital standards nearly sucked all of my life force right out.

So the job at the Coddled Cook had sounded pretty good. The money was decent, and the company offered good benefits, even money toward tuition if you wanted to take college courses. I'd moved to an apartment in Wrigleyville, but according to mapquest.com, this made for only a thirty-seven-minute commute. Ha! More like an hour, minimum. The work wasn't fascinating, but it wasn't nearly as bad as writing about hospital policies every day. During my tenure there, I'd become responsible for the copy in four separate monthly newsletters as well as some other writing projects. I'm a senior writer now while Bobby and Rachel are simply "writers." In theory, they're located under me on the food chain, although when you're this low in the hierarchy, I don't know that it matters. After Bobby and I agreed that the semen-carrying capacity of the Coddled Cook's latest kitchen implement should *not* be included in our next newsletter, I gave him the scoop on Kirk.

"What is with guys and porn, anyway?" I liked pumping Bobby for this kind of information, though he sometimes told me more than I wanted to know.

"You got me. I always thought there was something off with Kirk, though. I thought I was getting some gaydar vibes from him."

"Oh come on." Bobby is beautiful, but he's also vain. He thinks practically every guy wants him. Maybe he's right—I know most of the female employees had mad crushes on him when he first came to work here. He doesn't act swishy or femme, but his excessive well-grooming tipped me off. I mean, come on. How many straight men do you know who wax their eyebrows?

"Seriously. Some of those cockhounds are just in deep, deep denial. Believe me."

"I'll just have to take your word for it." After Bobby hung up, I tried to drag my attention back to my story. Ugh. I was bored. I checked my watch again. Only 2:03 P.M. Two hours and fifty-seven minutes before I was sprung for the day. I managed to occupy the rest of the day and called Jane before I left the office. I could have used my cell on the way home, but I don't like to talk and drive at the same time. That makes me an anomaly, I know. The truth is that I usually forget my phone, and on the occasions I remember it, the battery's usually dead. That's the kind of thing that drives Rick nuts. Being a techie, he wears a phone and a pager for work. I've teased him before about being able to track him down at a moment's notice.

Jane was up for coming over, and I was glad to have some company. By the time she arrived close to seven, I'd already made a big salad to go with the pasta and garlic bread. I can cook the most basic of dinners, but you won't find a lemon zester or any of the more obscure Coddled Cook tools in my kitchen. My family's another matter. My older sister, Jessie, has just about every product they make, and I get my mom discounts on whatever she wants. My younger sister, Missy, could care less, but she's still in college surviving on pizza.

After dinner, Jane dug in her bag for her tarot cards. She's into stuff like that—reads the *I Ching*, takes her horoscope seriously, thinks that there are spirits all around us. Rick thinks she's a flake and has told her so. I just try to keep the two of them apart.

"Come on." Jane drank a mouthful of wine. Her round face was flushed, and her hair—henna red this month—was held back from her face with little-girl butterfly barrettes. She wore a low-cut V-neck sweater that revealed impressive cleavage. I never think of Jane as fat exactly—she's way too confident and sexy for that—but she's not thin either. She says she's built for comfort, not speed. "You haven't let me do your cards in ages."

She pulled the deck out of a little black velvet pouch. Tarot cards are a little bit bigger than regular playing cards, but much more colorful. Each card has a little scene and a meaning attached to it. I'm always afraid I'll get the Death card—a skeleton on a horse—but Jane says Death doesn't mean actual death, it just means change. I have to be in the mood to let Jane read my cards—most of the time I don't feel like hearing what's going to happen, or may happen, or may not happen. Jane's readings include a lot of *possible*'s and *maybe*'s, and *it looks like*'s. Tonight, though, I was in the right mood.

"All right." I refilled both of our glasses. Jane had brought over a decent bottle of chardonnay. She temps to support herself while she's looking for acting gigs, and had been working as an assistant for a wine distributor for the past month. Her boss had let her bring home some free samples, and she was making the most of it.

Dutifully I shuffled the cards, trying to clear my mind. "What should I ask about again?"

"Anything. Just concentrate on what the future holds, if you want. Or ask about work. Rick." She wrinkled her nose. "Whatever."

Good enough. I tried to picture the future. I thought of Rick. I thought of the dreaded drive to Carol Stream every day. I pondered and shuffled, and shuffled some more.

"OK." I set the cards down.

"Do you feel comfortable with how the cards feel?"

"Yup."

"OK. Remember, now you cut the deck three times with your left hand." I always forgot that part. I did as Jane said and then handed her the cards.

"OK." Jane started laying out the cards. "This covers you." A woman sitting on a throne. "This crosses you." A scary-looking card with an enormous devil. It wasn't looking good. Jane continued setting the cards down, explaining the position of each, but I didn't pay much attention. She sometimes made little "huh" or "that's interesting" noises as she flipped each over, but I knew she'd explain them each in detail after all ten cards were down.

Jane looked at the cards for another minute or two. "Wow. You're going to have some changes. Big changes." She frowned and pointed at one of the cards. "See this? There's something going on you don't know about, and it's going to cause you heartbreak. Possibly." She pointed to a card that featured a bright red heart pierced by three swords. "The three of swords. But you have the capability to make the most of your creative abilities and reap benefits from it." She held up a card of a man using some kind of tool on a workbench. "There's a new man coming into your life, too. The Knight of Swords." She pointed at the card at the top of the reading. "He kind of storms right in. I don't know if he's good for you, though. You'll be very attracted to him, but the outcome card is interesting." She held up the card that read "The Hermit." "Hmm. Maybe you're going to have to retreat and figure out what it is that you really want. It may not be material things after all. Or maybe you wind up alone."

"Geez, Jane, thanks a lot! So what does the whole reading mean?"

Jane shook her head. "I don't know. It seems like the cards are telling you to be watchful, don't take things at face value. What did you ask about, anyway?"

"Nothing, really. Just what was coming up future-wise."

"Ah." Jane nodded and smiled. "Well, it seems that the future"—she paused for effect and then grinned—"is unknown."

Chapter 2
The Seven of Wands

Conflict will appear in your personal and professional life.

By the time I walked the short distance to Elephant and Castle, I was in major need of a drink. It had been a long week, and I was meeting Rick and some of his buddies at the bar. He likes to go out with his coworkers some Fridays, and this place was one of their favorite hangouts. We'd probably grab some dinner afterward, and I was hoping I'd be able to pry him away within a drink or two—he and his coworkers get talking about servers and network issues and firewalls and Ethernets and they might as well be speaking Greek. I love Rick, but he's a geek at heart. Around his buddies, he's a geek squared.

I maneuvered through the crowd, looking for someone I recognized. The crowd in here was aggressively, studiedly cool without trying—or at least that's the look everyone goes for. Lots of perfectly straight hair on the girls, poky, messy hair-cuts on the guys. The women mostly in their twenties, wearing hip-huggers slung low over flat bellies or minuscule minis with tank tops and strappy sandals. I felt like a frumpy suburban housewife in my neat little V-neck blouse and black capris.

I don't know what it is. Even when I buy trendy clothes, they never look right on me. I always feel like I'm playing dress-up. Maybe that's why I've kept my wardrobe so simple.

Those asymmetrical tops and gauzy hippie blouses and skirts would be out by next year anyway.

I finally saw Rick at a table, talking to some thin, serious-faced girl wearing a ratty-looking purple-striped shirt and—of course—low-slung hip-huggers that verged on obscene. Even sitting, her stomach was smooth and flat, not more rounded like my own. She was talking and gesturing with her hands, and Rick was laughing. That got my attention.

You know when you see your guy talking to another girl, and you automatically size her up? You compare her against yourself, and one of you loses. Rick was too much of a geek to even know how to flirt, but that was part of his charm. And this girl, on second glance, was a little too pretty. Even with no visible makeup, she sported the combo of perfect skin, nice teeth, good hair, and from what I could see, a pretty good body, too. I'd seen enough.

"Hi there!" I said brightly. Rick looked at me for a brief second before recognition flared.

"Trina. Babe." He stood up and leaned over to kiss me. "I was wondering what had happened to you."

"The usual nightmare. Traffic and then parking."

Rick pulled a chair out for me. "No problem. I'm just filling Jill in on the dirt at work. She just started last week." He gestured at me. "This is my girlfriend, Trina."

"Hi." Jill reached over and shook my hand. Shit. Close up, I could see she had delicate features, like a pretty china doll. I felt like an oversized peasant by comparison.

"So, you're new?" I was sure Rick hadn't mentioned her, but then again, he didn't talk about people at work so much as problems with DNS servers or system crashes or firewall issues. To be honest, I tune out that technology stuff most of the time.

"Uh-huh. I'm working the help desk."

Help desk? Rick had little to do with help desk people—his job had more to do with the hardware end of the job, I thought. Just then Toby, one of Rick's friends from work, si-dled up.

"Hey, it's the writing babe." He was carrying two Heinekens and what looked like a margarita. He set the drinks down on the table, pushing aside some empty bottles to make room.

Rick looked at Toby. "Where'd everyone go?"

"They took off. Milt and Rennie are going on, Web's on his way home to the wife." Toby looked at his watch. "I should be heading home soon, too."

Jill smiled. "Me, too. I've got to go soon." But she took a delicate sip of her drink and showed no signs of leaving. We made small talk—she'd just joined Rick's company after gradu-ating from DeVry a few months ago. She seemed incredibly confident for someone so new on the job. Self-contained. When I started at the Coddled Cook, I was a wreck for the first three months, spell-checking and proofreading every document three or even four times before I could bring myself to turn it in. Jill wasn't exactly standoffish, but she didn't act all that interested in me either. It bugged me.

After thirty minutes or so, I managed to extricate Rick from the bar. "Are we still getting dinner?"

"Yeah, I'm starving." Rick took his pager off his belt and looked at it. "Hang on. I've got to answer this."

I was used to this and didn't say anything. We wound up stopping for some Mexican food—nothing fancy but that was all right—and then he came home with me. My place on Hermitage was a twenty-minute drive, and Rick threw himself on the couch as soon as we came in the door.

"What a week. I'm bushed."

I was tired, too, but I felt like something was off. I sat down on the couch next to him. "So, what's happening with you?"

"You know how it is. It's just work, work, work."

"Uh-huh." I sat closer to him, and ran my finger down his neck. "Anything else going on in your head?"

He turned and looked at me. "Like . . ."

"Like . . ." I imitated his tone and kissed the side of his neck. Rick's pretty easy. He let me kiss him for a moment and then turned his face to mine, catching my lips with his own.

It was one of those times when I was amazed by my own horniness. It's kind of embarrassing, but sometimes I can be a guy—totally into my own pleasure, oblivious and unconcerned about whether my partner is even enjoying himself. To me, though, that's the sign of a good relationship—where you can lose yourself in sex and not be thinking about whether your breasts are flopping around or whether your vagina will make that horrible farting noise again or whether cellulite looks better when you're on top or on the bottom. (For the record, on the bottom—he can't see as much.)

Rick and I wound up having sex on the couch. I started off riding him, and what started as a teasing, friendly encounter turned into a hot-and-heavy session complete with carpet burns and sweaty backs. That's one of the things I love about him. In his daily life, he's this sweet, good-natured, somewhat boring tech-head. But strip his clothes off and give him an erection and he's a completely different person. That dichotomy is one of the reasons I fell in love with him.

"You want some water?" We were lying on the floor of my living room, and the specks of grime stuck to my naked back evidenced my lackluster housekeeping. I stood up, picking little bits of dirt off my backside. I seriously needed to vacuum.

"Uh-huh." Rick lay on his back, his arms sprawled. He grinned at me when I came back and sat down next to him, my back against the couch. "You are quite the dirty little girl, aren't you? Doing it right in the living room."

I shoved him. "That's what you like, though, isn't it?"

He took a sip of the bottled water and nodded, started to say something, and then stopped.

"What?"

He rolled to face me. "Nothing. That was great. You make me crazy."

"*You* make *me* crazy."

WHITE BIKINI PANTIES   17

"We make each other crazy." And that's what I loved about Rick. We had what I considered the best of both worlds—we commiserate about our jobs, go to a movie or out to eat or just hang out and watch *True Hollywood Story* together like buddies. But add a little sexual spark into the mix and things get really hot, really fast.

Jane found this hard to believe. "Still waters run deep, you know," I'd told her, but she claimed the idea of a naked, sweaty, groaning Rick was too much for her to handle. "TMI!" she'd say, waving her hand. Too much information.

After a while, we slid back into our underwear—I picked up Rick's shirt and put it on—and curled up on the couch. Nights we were together usually meant *True Hollywood Story* on E! We'd met at a Saturday Cubs game—I was sitting in the bleachers with Jessie and my brother-in-law, Ethan—and I'd tripped over him on the way to my seat. He claims I did it on purpose. I was so embarrassed that I bought him a beer to apologize, and we wound up half-watching the game while we exchanged various bits of personal data and history while I ignored Jessie's all-too-nonchalant eavesdropping. Even Ethan gave me the thumbs-up when Rick went to buy us a couple more beers. Since they're happily married, they figure everyone else should be, too.

After the game, he left with my number in his pocket. I thought it was so cool that someone would go to a baseball game alone. I'd never had that kind of self-confidence. Rick wasn't drop-your-panties gorgeous or anything, but he had nice eyes. Dark, soulful, puppy dog eyes, and brown hair just a few shades lighter. I'd noticed his forearms, too—they were muscular and moderately hairy, just what I like. Forget all those bare-chested models—I like my men to look like men, with a nice fuzzy pelt. I liked how he looked at me when we talked, turning his body toward me and propping one foot up, and how he'd stood briefly when I introduced him to Jessie and Ethan. He seemed . . . thoughtful. Attentive. Sweet.

He called me the next Tuesday, and we talked on the phone for almost two hours. It was then I discovered that we had the same strange fascination with this show, which invariably featured some has-been, or almost-was, or celebrity who had fallen from grace due to drugs, alcohol, bad sexual choices, or chronic lack of foresight. If the subject of the story was interviewed, he or she always waxed quite vitriolic about all the wrongs done to him or her during their usually brief, meteoric rise to—and fall from—fame.

"True Bitter Stories," Rick called them, and we'd devised a game to go along with it. If someone sounded jaded, he got an immediate "Bitter!" If someone was interviewed who had passed away, one of us would call out "Dead!" The idea was to label the person as rapidly and efficiently as possible. "Druggie!" "Dates prostitutes!" "Drunk!" "Has-been!" "Fake boobs!" were all frequent comments.

On the show featuring the untold story of the Drummond family from *Diff'rent Strokes*, that sitcom from the eighties that featured a rich old white guy and his daughter adopting two black kids, Rick killed me when he pointed at each of the former childhood actors in turn. "Dead!" "Bitter!" "Jailbird!" I laughed for ten minutes straight.

Still, Rick and I didn't share the exact same sense of humor. He thought the Jerky Boys were hilarious, and liked Howard Stern. "It's all an act," he'd say when I was repulsed by the way his female fans would reveal their breasts and bodies simply for the opportunity to be on the show. "He doesn't give a shit. But what a job."

"What's wrong? You don't have any users showing up in your office and flashing you? Telling you they'd love to screw your brains out?"

"Not that I recall." Their loss, I thought. In clothes, Rick looked quite average, but out of them, he had a strong, lean, well-proportioned body and a great ass. I'm shallow on some stuff, OK? And let's face it, when your guy is cute, funny, nice to you, and good in bed, you're willing to cut him a little slack on some of the other areas.

Like the fact that he wasn't all that into doing family stuff—

with either mine or his. And despite his Fridays out, he's not that outgoing—he has some friends from work and a couple of close buddies from high school, but that's it. As far as I can tell, his relationship with his dad has been strained. His mom died when he was in junior high—a few months after being diagnosed with ovarian cancer—but he never talks about that. His dad moved to the Florida Keys when Rick was in college, and the two talk only rarely. He's got an older brother, too—Jimmy—but all I know about him is that he's had an alcohol problem on and off for years.

It seemed like it might be a good time to hit him up for my dad's upcoming birthday. My mom wanted all three of us home—she's big on family stuff—and I was hoping he might come with me. I'd managed to drag him along for Christmas last year, and he'd met my parents a couple of times when they came up from Champaign. They both liked him, and I had the idea that if he spent more time with my family, he'd realize how cool it would be to spend his life with me. Not that I'd ever admit that to anyone. It's cheesy, I know.

I knew from experience that this was the best time to approach Rick—post-sex, when he was relaxed and more open to suggestions of any sort. But I was surprised when he agreed. "Sure, I guess. We can go down there if you want."

"Really?" I looked him. "You will?"

"It's not my first choice, but . . ." He let his voice trail off, teasing me. "You were pretty hot tonight. I suppose I owe you."

Like I said, good sex can pay off in more ways than one.

Chapter 3
The Empress, Inverted

Hopes may be dashed. Possible trouble ahead.

I could hear the sound of the television set as Rick and I walked up the front steps of my parents' duplex. Sounded like NASCAR. I rolled my eyes at Rick.

"Well, we know my dad's home."

I knocked as I pushed the door open. "Hey! Your middle child is here!" I called.

"Hi, honey!" I heard my mother's voice from the kitchen. "Come on in."

My dad pushed himself off his faded recliner. They'd "downsized" last year from the house we grew up in, but my mom still hadn't been able to force him to get rid of his favorite chair. Its scarred arms and worn cushions clashed with the tasteful cream-colored loveseats and ash end tables my mom had bought in what he called a menopause-inspired buying frenzy.

"Happy birthday!" I hugged him and kissed his cheek, waving his card. "I even brought you a card."

"You don't need to do that. Save your money," but he grinned all the same. "And Rick. Nice to see you, guy." He reached out and pumped Rick's hand. I knew he'd apply a little extra force. My dad's handshakes have always been legend among the guys the three of us have dated. It's some kind of testosterone thing, I suppose.

I left Rick talking about the sad state of the Cubs with my dad. Mom was chopping carrots for a salad in the kitchen. She'd gained a little weight in the past few years, but she was still pretty, with few lines in her face, and hair she kept dark blond. Jessica looked more like her; our baby sister Melissa, like my dad. I looked like no one. Like the mailman was the family's old joke.

"Trina." My mom held out her arms. I hugged her. I could smell her Chanel No. 5, the perfume she wears for special occasions. "I'm so happy to see you." She raised her eyebrows. "And Rick came!"

"Uh-huh." We smiled a complicit little smile. She knew that I was hoping for some forward motion in our relationship, but she knew me well enough not to ask, at least not now. Later in the day, when I'd had a few glasses of wine, she'd sneak in a question here or there, or better yet, get Missy to squeeze it out of me. She's eight years younger than me, ten younger than Jessie, and still quite the tattletale.

I heard Jessie and Ethan come in with Melissa. They'd swung through Bloomington and picked her up at summer school. She should be a junior by now, but she was still taking sophomore-level classes. She's changed her major at least three times, and is now in psychology or sociology or some other 'ology.

My mom and I went and hugged both of my sisters, and I gave Ethan a friendly shove. "Hey, bro-in-law."

Ethan grinned at me. "That's assault, you know."

"So sue me." I followed Jessica into the kitchen. She was pouring herself a glass of white zinfandel out of the box of wine in the fridge.

Jessie rolled her eyes at me. "Come on, Dad! What is with this boxed wine?"

"I got the *good* box! That's the expensive one!" my dad called. "For my birthday, you know! But us men will stick to beer." I heard Ethan and Rick laughing with him. I briefly wondered if he'd ever wished for a boy. With three girls and a wife, no wonder he watched sports all day long. I didn't know ESPN had four different sports channels until they got cable. He even watched the Golf Channel sometimes.

Jessie poured me a glass of wine, and we sat at the kitchen table. She was wearing a cotton lime green sundress in deference to the heat. It was in the mid-nineties, and I hoped we could talk Dad into eating inside. The kitchen was warm, but it was pleasant compared to the soupy air outside. Jessie fanned herself for a moment, then took a long swallow of wine and jerked her head at the living room. "How'd you get Rick here?"

"Hit him up after good sex," I admitted. Jessie and I didn't usually talk about sex, but this wasn't talking about sex. It was talking about men.

Jessie snorted. "What's that? I can't even remember anymore."

I watched her carefully. She was wearing her hair blown perfectly straight, the razor-edged cut fluttering about her shoulders, but her face looked puffy and the buttons on her sundress strained across her chest. I'd bet she'd put on about ten pounds, maybe fifteen, but I wasn't about to mention it. Both of us gain weight when we're unhappy—while that little twig Melissa has Dad's metabolism and is effortlessly thin.

"How's everything going?"

Jessie drank more wine and gestured at the glass. "Does that answer your question?" She and Ethan had been trying to have a baby for two years now. They'd tried on their own for more than a year, and now specialists were involved. I didn't know all the details, but I knew that she had been on some fertility drugs and nothing had worked yet.

"I'm sorry." I'd learned that if I tried anything else— "you've got plenty of time," "don't worry, it will happen," "at least you can still drink"—it was met with either hostility or anger. Jessie was the tough one of the three of us. She'd graduated at the top of her class from law school, and worked in a big firm downtown, putting in sixty-hour weeks. She thrived on conflict and rarely complained about anything. She also expected the same out of those around her.

"Yeah. Thanks." Jessie hung her head, and I realized she was crying. Shit.

"Hey. I'm sorry. I didn't mean to upset you."

She tossed her head back and wiped her eyes. "It's OK. I'm just having the period from hell and I feel awful. I didn't even want to drive down today, but you know how Mom is."

Mom and Missy came back into the kitchen. Missy had changed out of her shorts and T-shirt into a cute spaghetti-strap dress that flared out over her slim thighs. "Look what Mom bought me!" She twirled, grinning at us. Jessie and I both shook our heads.

"Spoiled. Very spoiled," said Jess.

"Must be nice to be the baby," I agreed.

My mom just shrugged. "I bought you girls clothes all the time when you were in school, too."

Missy squeezed my mom, sneaking a smile at the two of us. Her hair was shorter than before; with the new cut and her high cheekbones and large eyes, she bore a resemblance to Winona Ryder. "And besides, you love *me* the best, don't you, Mom?"

My mom waved her off. "You girls. I love all of you equally." She'd said that for years, but privately I knew Missy was her favorite. Even at twenty, Missy still talked to Mom every day. Jessica was probably Dad's favorite—he never stopped bragging about her, and for good reason. If you've been keeping track, well, that leaves me a little out in the cold. But I love my parents and my sisters, and I've seen enough dysfunctional families to know how lucky I am to have the one I do.

By the time we sat down for dinner—ham with all the trimmings—Jessie was a little drunk. Ethan didn't seem to notice—he was hitting up Rick for advice on his PC at home—and my dad was seriously involved in his food.

"Bonnie, this is excellent," he said between bites. "Isn't this wonderful?" he encouraged us.

We made all the right praising noises for my mom's benefit. She is a good cook, but her meals are heavy on the cream and butter and light on the vegetables. No wonder Jess and I gravitate toward the chunkier side of average. Jessie wasn't eating much, though—just mostly pushing her food around on her plate.

"Hey, are you going to finish that?" Melissa pointed at the pile of scalloped corn on Jessica's plate. She never seemed to get enough to eat.

Normally, that would piss Jessica off. She's territorial to the extreme about her food, her work, her husband. She lifted her plate and handed it to Missy. "You can have it," she said. "I'm not that hungry."

"Are you feeling OK?" My mom, oblivious as usual. Couldn't she see Jessie was half-crocked?

"Yeah, yeah, I'm fine." Jessica waved her hand in what was presumably meant to be a don't-worry-about-me gesture, and knocked over her wineglass onto Ethan's plate.

"Watch it!" He picked up the glass and my mom hurried into the kitchen for a damp towel.

"Sorry. I'm sorry." Jessie sighed and threw her head back dramatically. "Frickin' boxed wine."

"At least it was the good stuff!" I tried, but my attempt at humor didn't help.

Dad took this as his cue to leave the table. "Great meal, Bon," he said, returning to the safety of his recliner. Rick glanced at me and then back at Jessie, who was resting her head on her hand and looking damply miserable. We all waited for Ethan to do something, but he merely got up, carried his plate into the kitchen, and then returned to kiss my mom on the cheek. "Thank you for dinner. Delicious." Then he joined my dad.

OK. Mom glanced at me, nodding her head at Jessica. I

don't think any of us knew quite what to do. "Hey, Jessie, you want to go for a walk or something?" I asked.

"A walk?" Her voice was just this side of belligerent.

I glanced at Rick, then stood and walked over to her side of the table. "Yeah. Come on." I thought fast. "I need your legal opinion on something." Shit. Now I'd have to fabricate a legal issue, but at least I'd get her out of the house and away from the giant box-o'-wine.

"What about Dad's cake? What about the presents?" said Jessie.

"You go on, hon. We'll wait until you get back," said my mom, waving her hand at me.

The guys barely looked up from the game as we left. It was still hot outside, but the street was shaded with maple and oak trees and a light breeze played on my skin. Cicadas droned, and I could smell the cedar from the fence on the east side of the house. It must be new. "Come on, Jess. Let's walk."

Surprisingly, she complied. We walked for a couple of minutes, and then she turned to me. "So, what's your question?"

"Huh? What? Oh, that. Well . . . I know this woman at work who was dating this guy . . ." Shit. I was brain-dead. I could never think on my feet like this. I always thought of the great lines, the perfect comebacks, ten minutes after the appropriate moment of delivery.

Jessica shook her head. "Forget it. I know you were just trying to get me out here." She sighed and ran her fingers through her hair. "I'm not *that* drunk."

"Oh." I wasn't sure what to say. I'd seen Jessica upset before, and frustrated, and angry, but I hadn't seen this kind of dispirited helplessness. It scared me.

"Do you ever think that your life isn't turning out the way you thought it would?" said Jessie. We crossed the street toward the park where my mom liked to walk in the mornings.

"God, I don't know. I don't know that I had any idea of how it was going to turn out in the first place."

Jessie grabbed at a tree branch as we walked past, stripping it clean of its silvery green leaves. "That's because you don't have a plan." She shook her hand, scattering feathery little bits on the sidewalk. "You just fall into things."

"Not all of us have to schedule every five minutes of our lives. We can't all be anal retentive Franklin Planner drones." Jessie can push my buttons faster than anyone else. When we were in school, everyone told me how lucky I was to have such a smart, talented, pretty older sister. Believe me, you get tired of hearing that real fast. So what if she had gone to law school and I'd settled for a bachelor's? I wasn't exactly stupid.

"If you don't set goals, you won't get anywhere. It's as simple as that." Jessica was talking like she was reading a script, more to herself than to me, I thought. "You just have to set goals, and then work to achieve them." She suddenly shook her head, hard, and rubbed at her face. "*Fuck!* Fuck, fuck, fuck."

My polished, perfect sister appeared to be having a nervous breakdown before my eyes. "What's wrong?" I spoke slowly. "What's the matter?"

"Look at me. Listen to me. I'm full of it. 'Set goals. Work to achieve them.' That doesn't work anymore." She half-laughed. "Here's my big goal, Trin. Have a baby by thirty. Pretty simple, huh? Nope. Not even close."

"Jess, you're not even thirty-one. You have plenty of time." Major blunder.

"What would you know? Don't you know a woman's fertility peaks in her early twenties and starts sliding after that? By the time you're thirty-five, your chance of getting pregnant is twenty-five percent lower than it was at age twenty-five. And every year it gets worse."

"But you're not thirty-five! You're not even thirty-one."

"It doesn't matter. I'm not pregnant. Maybe I can't even get pregnant. I've been on Clomid and we have sex at all the right times, and I lie on my back for thirty minutes with a pillow propped under my back and nothing. Then I get to go and get poked and prodded again, and now we're supposed to do in vitro, and Ethan hardly even looks at me and the Clomid is making me fat and I'm having frickin' hot flashes for God's sake and Mom just keeps asking when she's going to be a grandma and I can't say anything at work and . . ." She was crying now, hard, wrenching sobs.

I didn't know what to do. I stood there awkwardly, unsure of whether to touch her. A woman in her thirties walked by, pushing twins in a stroller. She stared at us curiously, and I looked away from her. After a minute, Jessie shook her head, wiped her eyes with her hand, and forced a smile.

"I'm sorry, Trin. I shouldn't take it out on you. I just feel like I'm going crazy. I'm all messed up inside."

I reached over and rubbed her arm. I didn't know how she'd react to a hug. When I'm upset, being touched usually makes me feel worse. "It's OK. That's what little sisters are for, right?"

Then she surprised me. "Thanks." She embraced me awkwardly, and we hugged for a moment. "Oops, I almost got snot on your shoulder."

"That's OK."

"We should probably get back, huh? Let Dad open his gifts and all."

"If you're ready." We walked back to the house, not saying much. When we came in, all five of them were sitting in the living room. Ethan glanced at Jessie's face, and then got up and followed her into the kitchen. The rest of us sat and looked at each other. What's going on? my parents' faces asked me. Don't ask me, I tried to answer.

A few minutes later, Ethan and Jessie strolled back into the room like nothing was amiss. "I'm sorry about that. Sorry," she said to no one in particular.

"Oh, honey." My mom jumped up and put her arms around her, but Jessie stood there.

"Come on." Missy pushed herself off the floor where she'd been sprawled. "Aren't we ready for cake? I'm still hungry."

My mom recognized her cue and hurried into the kitchen for the obligatory cake (carrot—my dad's favorite) and vanilla ice cream. We ate, and my dad opened his presents. Jessie and Ethan had bought him a heavy Jersey Bears sweatshirt. He still dreams of the '84 Bears and insists they're prime contenders for the Super Bowl even this year. Missy and I had gone in on our gift—an old-fashioned bar sign and light, complete with water that appeared to flow when you plugged it in. Dad's been turning the garage into his "den" ever since they moved to the condo, stocking it with a minifridge, television, beer signs, and a dartboard. Probably a necessary escape after all those years of undiluted estrogen exposure, I figure.

I was touched when Rick handed my dad a couple of small boxes. Swisher Sweets, his favorite cigar. I looked at Rick.

"What?" he said. "I remembered he liked them from last year. No big thing."

I just smiled. I thought I knew him, but he could still surprise me.

Chapter 4
The Two of Swords

A temporary truce in family quarrels.

I was relieved when Rick and I left and headed up I-57 toward Chicago. Ethan and Jessica had left just before we did; Missy would stay the night and Mom would drive her back to school tomorrow.

"What was that whole scene about?" Rick looked over at me. He'd offered to drive and I'd agreed, relieved at the break. Driving to and from work five days a week, I try to avoid it when I can.

"What? With Jessie?"

"Yeah."

I gave him a brief rundown on the conversation. "What happened when we left? Did Ethan say anything?"

"Not really."

I wasn't surprised. I'd heard about sensitive men, read about them in magazines anyway. But, Bobby aside, I didn't know any men who found opening up and talking about their feelings anything short of agonizing.

I took a swallow of bottled water and passed it to Rick, who drank also. "What about you? Do you want kids?"

Rick glanced quickly at me. "What, like now?"

"No, of course not. Eventually. Is that in your plan?"

"I suppose. I guess I've never really thought about it." That is the difference between men and women—at least one of them, anyway. A guy can be twenty-five, thirty, even thirty-five without seriously considering whether he'll be a parent or if he even wants to. It's not high on their mental radar. Ask any woman of any age whether she wants kids and she'll know.

Sure, she might not be as definite as Jessica and have drawn a big red mark on her personal timeline at thirty, but she'll have an answer. "Eventually." "After I get my career established." "When I find the right person." "Absolutely not." I've known women who want kids and women who don't but never someone who has no idea whether she wants them or not.

I know I want to, but I still feel way too immature. It boggles my mind that my mom had two kids at my age. Of course she wasn't working either, but on the rare occasions I've held a baby, I've felt an overwhelming sense of panic. What if something suddenly happens? What if the baby chokes or stops breathing? What if I drop him? After I've made the requisite oohing and ahing noises, I'm relieved to hand the bambino back to his mother.

"Why do you want to know?" Rick's voice dragged me back to reality.

"I'm just thinking about Jessie. She's so desperate, you know, to have a baby. It's just strange to see her so out of control. And I can't imagine wanting a kid so much, I guess."

"Yeah. It'd be cool eventually. But not for a long time." Emphasis on *long*, I noticed.

Was he sending me a message here? We hadn't really talked about our Future together, preferring to live in the present. At first I'd had no trouble with that. Now I was starting to wonder where we were going. I knew we loved each other, we laughed at the same stuff, we had great sex. Rick's a nice guy, a hard worker, maybe a bit of a workaholic, but no major flaws like alcoholism, gambling, or narcissism.

But hey, I am a product of this society. Sometimes I let myself fantasize about getting married. I envision myself, fifteen

pounds thinner of course, my hair longer than I've ever managed to grow it, wearing an off-the-shoulder white gown,
walking down the aisle with my dad, who's telling me little
jokes to keep me from crying. After that, I'm not sure what to
expect. At Jessie's wedding four years before, I'd been over-
come by a sense of amazement. What an incredible risk to
take! I knew she loved Ethan and Ethan loved her, but the
thought of committing to only one person for the rest of your
life seemed like a high-risk endeavor. What if he changes?
What if you change? What if, let's face it, you get bored after a
while?

Maybe that's why I'd been content to let things shake out
with Rick. It had crossed my mind, though, that if he and I
weren't going to have a future together, we should probably
"cut bait," as my dad would say, sometime soon. I didn't want
to be like Dawn, one of the women who worked in marketing
at the Coddled Cook. She'd been dating the same guy for
eight years, living together the last five. One night, she came
home and he was packing. "I need some space," he told her.
"Time to myself, to figure out what I really want."

Here's the thing. When a man says he needs some space,
what he's really saying is that he needs to screw someone else
and doesn't want to have to feel guilty about it. Dawn suspected as much and staked out his new apartment. Turns out
that not only had he lined up a new girlfriend who was only
twenty-one years old and had a toddler to boot—but she was
pregnant with his baby now, too. The kicker? He married her
the next month.

I didn't want to be in Dawn's shoes. Eight years of her life
with this guy and she had nothing to show for it, except for
some cheap Christmas gifts and a newfound suspicion of anyone with a penis.

"So, does that mean you think about getting married?" The
question popped out of my mouth.

"First you ask about kids and now you ask about getting
married. What's on your mind?"

I sighed. It's not like I was fishing for a proposal, but that's what I sounded like. "I don't know. I guess I'm just thinking about all this stuff with my sister and it's got me thinking about us."

"Yeah?" His tone was noncommittal.

"I don't know. I'm not pushing you, Rick. Actually," I laughed, "I'm sitting here thinking that I don't know if I ever want to get married. Isn't that your line?"

" 'Cause what, the guy is the one who wants to screw around and the girl wants to settle down, right?"

"Sure. Women want love; men want sex. Women use sex to get love; men use love to get sex. Isn't that the way it works?"

"Mostly." Rick imitated Eric Cartman, a character from *South Park*, and we both laughed. That's what I really love about him. We can be talking about something serious, and he can immediately lighten the mood.

"Anyway, forget it. I'm feeling kind of introspective and funky, I guess." I didn't mention that spending any amount of time with my family usually produced a similar effect. I love them, but when I'm around them, I feel like I slide right back into that middle-slightly-neglected-nobody's-favorite-child role I've been playing all my life, or at least since Missy was born. And sometimes it gets a little old.

In my "real" life, I can be smart, funny, clever at work. Toss me home for two hours and I'm not as smart or pretty as Jessica and not as original or enthusiastic as Melissa. Since I felt like I'd been compared against Jessie most of my life, it's not that surprising that these inequities bother me. The fact that I can have that insight doesn't change its effect, though.

But at least I love my family and I know they love me—not like the screwed-up relationship Rick has with his dad and brother. He rarely talks to either of them, although I was at his apartment one night when his dad called. Rick spent maybe five minutes on the phone, then said he had to run out to pick up some beer. He was back thirty minutes later, and I could swear he looked like he'd been crying, but when I brought it up, he shrugged it off. Allergies, he said.

"Allergies? I didn't know you had allergies." I was trying for a concerned tone, but I must have come across as bitchy instead. At least that's how Rick reacted.

"Jesus, you don't know every single thing about me, all right? Can we just drop it?"

"Fine." I stood up. "Why don't I go home, then?" But it was an empty threat. I didn't want to leave, especially not with the way things were, all strained and weird between us. I moved in slow motion, waiting for him to say, "No, don't be stupid, stay here."

He looked at me for a long time without speaking. Apparently my plan wasn't working.

I picked up my keys. "Well, I'm here if you want to talk," I said. "About anything."

"What if I don't want to talk? Can you deal with that?"

I'd agreed, bobbing my head furiously. "I was just trying to help, you know," I said without looking at him.

Rick sighed and pulled me down on the couch next to him. "I know. I don't need any help, all right?"

And that's how we'd left it. I figured eventually he'd open up more, let me know what the real deal with his family was. Until then, he could always borrow mine.

Chapter 5
The Knight of Cups, Inverted

Beware of fraud, trickery, or rivalry.

It was nearly 3 P.M. on Friday. By this point, most of us barely bothered with the pretense of working. Weekend plans were under way, and people stood around talking in small knots throughout the floor. If a higher-up walked by, we worker bees darted back into our cubes, but popped our heads out like groundhogs immediately afterward. At this point in the week, little would be accomplished, but we were trapped here until 5 P.M.

Rachel was diligently proofing a story for the newsletter. "Trina, is it a serial comma or not?" she called over the side of our shared cube.

"No serial comma."

"Why can't I remember that? Thanks!"

"It's called a style book. You know, that text on your desk there?" Bobby called to her. He was leaning up against my cube, flipping through the Simpsons calendar Jane had given me for Christmas.

"Oh, hush. Trina's just as good and she's quicker."

Bobby turned to me. "Any festive plans for the weekend?"

"Not really. Doing laundry, getting groceries, cleaning my apartment. All the usual excitement."

"God, girl, how old are you?" Bobby lowered his voice. "That sounds like the weekend of one of the old marrieds around here." He pulled out several pushpins and then stuck them back into my corkboard in a more pleasing design. "Are you at least going to hook up with your man?"

"I don't know. They've got some big upgrade going on." Rick had mentioned it earlier in the week, and I was used to him working a lot of weekends. If it all went OK, sometimes I met him late at his apartment or he came over to my place. I liked it, actually. Once I'd waited for him at his place wearing nothing but one of his shirts and a black fishnet teddy I'd bought from Victoria's Secret. He'd wound up ripping it in his excitement to get it off me, which we'd laughed about later.

I listened to Bobby bemoan the state of his love life—apparently it's not just the good single straight guys that are already spoken for, it's the good single gay guys as well. He'd been going out with some older guy—Josh—who had too many weird hang-ups.

That got my attention. "Weird like what?"

"Trust me, you do not want to know. He's just been single waaaay too long and he's gotten the idea that what he wants is the only way it's going to be."

"Meaning what?"

"Meaning you get more rigid as you get older."

I couldn't help it. I snickered. "Uh-huh."

"Get your mind out of the gutter! I mean that you get too strict about your qualifications and what you'll settle for and what you won't. You've got to be able to give a little to get a little, but Josh doesn't see it that way. You know, 'It's my way or the highway'? That's Josh."

"Sounds like my sister."

Bobby examined a picture of the three of us from last

Christmas. "She is a gorgeous specimen." I swiped at him. "Not nearly as gorgeous as you, of course."

"Shut up. She's the pretty one." It was a fact, after all.

"Oh, come on. You've got the whole natural girl thing going for you. Though you could wear more makeup and do something with your hair."

Bobby was constantly after me to "do something" with my hair. I got it cut only once every four months or so, and had been wearing it in the same shoulder-length bob for four years. I'd see great haircuts on other women, but never thought that they'd look right on me. I stuck to the tried-and-true.

"Thank you so much. You really know how to give a compliment. That's like saying, 'Hey, you look great! You sure have lost a lot of weight!'"

"What do you mean?"

"You know, those compliments with a hidden criticism attached. It's like the opposite of a cloud with a silver lining. It's a fuzzy stuffed animal with a razor shoved inside."

"What a nice image. Any way you can work that into the next newsletter? But it would have to be a Cook's Collection Special Cutting Knife shoved inside."

"Enough." I glanced at my watch. "I should make an effort and pretend like I'm working for a while."

"Me too. Have a good weekend, Trini. Do something fun for a change."

So blame Bobby, or rather the too-rigid Josh. I thought about it and figured Bobby was right—it had been a while since I'd done something, anything, surprising. Saturday night, I knew Rick would be doing an upgrade that would force him to work late. "I don't know what time we'll finish, babe," he told me. "I'll just go home and crash."

I had a key to his place for occasions such as these, so I drove over about ten, made some tea and watched *Saturday Night Live*, and then slipped off my clothes and climbed into his bed. What a nice surprise he'd have.

I woke up to the sound of low voices in the living room. I glanced at his digital clock—it was after one. Who would he have over that late? Still half-asleep, I wrapped myself in Rick's blue comforter and padded out to the living room. Where Rick and Jill, his little help desk buddy, were sitting on the couch. He was surprised all right.

Chapter 6
The Three of Swords

Sorrow, tears, separation.

It had been one hell of a weekend. I could remember every detail of that moment when I saw the two of them sitting there. From the astonished look on Rick's face—his mouth actually hung up for a moment, just like on a bad sitcom—to the pink that slowly spread across Jill's dainty little face—to the fact that her blouse was two buttons undone and Rick's lips looked like he'd been kissing. I stood with the comforter wrapped around me, a slow nausea starting to build in my stomach.

"I thought I'd surprise you." Ladies and gentleman! Let me graciously accept this year's award for *Understatement of the Year*.

Jill was the first one of the three of us to recover her wits. She stood suddenly. "I should be going." Rick stared at her for a moment. I wouldn't have been surprised if he couldn't remember his own name, much less hers, at that moment.

"Uhhh . . . yeah. That's a good idea." His words were slow. She looked nervously at me once, and then moved hurriedly toward the door. Maybe she was expecting some Jerry-Springer-ish hair-pulling scene, I don't know. I probably disappointed her.

The only thing I could think of to do was to go back in

Rick's bedroom and start putting on my clothes. Underwear. Socks. Bra. Jeans. I was pulling my T-shirt over my head when Rick came in and stood by the door.

"Trina." He stopped. "Fuck. I don't know what to say. I'm sorry."

"Sorry?" I said brightly. "Sorry for what, exactly?" My voice was flat. I was cool. I was calm, I told myself. He wasn't going to see how much this hurt.

He looked at the wall behind my head. "Don't make this harder for me."

That's when I felt the rush of anger overtake my sense of hurt and that horrible sweeping sickness. "Harder for *you*? Harder for *you*? How is this hard for you, exactly?"

"I'm trying to apologize. I never meant—"

"You never meant what? To bring her back to your apartment? It's pretty clear what would have happened, isn't it? You would have gone to bed with her." I shoved my feet into my shoes. I could feel tears starting to prick my eyes, but damn it, I was not going to cry. Not in front of him. "You would have"— I paused—"fucked her."

"I don't know." He crossed his arms.

"Maybe."

I snorted.

"Probably."

"And at what point were you going to let me know about this, anyway? I mean, I am your girlfriend, right?" I grabbed my purse off the floor and stomped by him. "Oh, wait. I think I've got the tense on that wrong. I think I *was* your girlfriend. Until tonight." I was heading for the door, my body reacting faster than my mind. So I was sort of pleased that I could make a writerly joke out of the whole nightmare. Rick started to say something, but I was gone.

I drove home, found a place to park my car, and alternated between rage and despair for the better part of the night. I'd cry, then I'd punch my pillow, then I'd cry some more. I must have fallen asleep at some point—I woke a little after 9 A.M, lying on my stomach on the couch, my neck sore and my mouth dry. I had a tiny blissful moment when I didn't remember what had happened, and then it came rushing back in a blur.

Sunday morning crawled by. But Rick didn't call. The crazy thing was that I almost called him. How could he do this to me? How long had this been going on? Didn't he love me? All these were questions I wanted answered . . . or maybe not. I vacillated all day, and wound up drinking a bottle of merlot that Jane had left. Bad idea number 1.

Then I called him. Bad idea number 2.

God, I hate myself sometimes. But I hadn't eaten all day, and the wine went straight to my head, shutting off that section of your brain that keeps you from doing stupid-assed things. At least he wasn't home, and I wasn't so smashed to leave a message. That was the last thing I needed. Finally I called Jane. I started telling her the whole story, and when she realized what had happened, she interrupted. "Shut up. I'm coming over."

And she did. She let me cry and rage and cry and vent and cry some more. I thought I'd gotten most of it out the night before, but telling Jane made the emotions stronger. The thing was, I really hadn't seen it coming. Rick and I loved each other. We made each other laugh—I know that. We had really great sex—better than I'd had with anyone, except Joey anyway.

Of course, maybe the guys I had great sex with were destined to dump me. I'd met Joey at my first official-after-college-real-job. He worked in the design department of the crappy women's magazine I labored at and we became friends. Of course, I had a crush on him, but he was madly in love with his girlfriend, who was gorgeous, rich, and in her second year of med school. I knew nothing would ever happen with him, which made me comfortable around him. I treated him like a brother—if I'd have had a brother—and we amused ourselves by gossiping about the people we worked with and talking about what we

were going to do with our lives. I was still in future novelist mode
and Joey wrote music and played guitar in his spare time.

When his girlfriend dumped him three weeks before finals,
Joey came to work with dark circles under his eyes for a week.
We went out for drinks that Friday, and he came home with
me. I'd talked myself into thinking that it was innocent and
he'd sleep on the couch, but come on. You never invite a guy
home with innocent intentions. We'd been sitting there on the
couch, drinking Bud Light and burping (see, this proved I had
no ulterior motives), and after a particularly impressive belch,
he looked at me with interest.

"Donna would never do that," he said, squinting slightly.
"She doesn't even like beer. She says it makes her bloated."

"Well, sure, if you don't burp." It seemed obvious to me.
"Or fart, I guess."

Joey had laughed hard, his arms across his stomach. "You're
awesome, you know that?" He'd leaned over and kissed me, a
sort of friendly kiss, and then we were enmeshed in the kind of
raspy-breathing deep-tonguing make-out session I'd finally
gotten past fantasizing about. Thank God I actually had condoms around. We had sex four times that night—I'd never
known a guy who could get it up again so quickly (and again,
and again!). In the morning, I'd expected that things would be
awkward, but they weren't.

"Hey." He was lying on his back and rolled toward me.

"Hey." I felt completely comfortable. "So . . ."

"You want to go out and get some breakfast?" He grinned.
"I'm starving."

It was that easy. It was the perfect combination of friendship and great sex. For three weeks. Until Donna recovered
from finals and decided she wanted Joey back. It went on like
that for the next two years, I'm embarrassed to admit. I was
more or less the mistress waiting in the wings. Donna would
dump him; he'd show up in my bed within a day or two. Then
they'd get back together and we'd go back to being pals. I dealt
with it by developing a complex rationalization machinery—

you know, we were friends, after all, so an occasional romp wasn't that big of a deal, and I wasn't ready to get serious with anyone yet, so this was the perfect situation (seriously—I know, I'm pathetic), and that if something better, or someone better, came along, I'd simply cut out the sexual component of our relationship for good. But no one had. And then—surprise, surprise—they wound up getting married in Vegas before she started her residency. That's when I got serious about finding a new job. It had gotten too painful to "be just friends," and besides, I was ready to leave. (Rationalization machinery again.) I'd heard after I left that they'd moved to Atlanta for her residency, and I hoped they'd be happy. Really, I did.

But Rick and I had had more than an off-again, on-again relationship after all. He was the first guy I'd brought home to my family—I wasn't about to try to explain the Joey thing to my parents although Jessie knew the whole sordid story. Things had felt so right. Why had he wanted someone else?

"It's in their nature, sweetie." Jane poured herself another glass of wine. Between the bottle I'd drunk earlier and now the additional two she'd brought along, I was practically incoherent. "It's biological. They're programmed to spread their seed as much as possible. It helps ensure the survival of the species."

"That's bullshit." It came out sounding like bull-thit. "That's just an excuse to fuck around."

"Well, of course, sweetie. I didn't say they couldn't evolve. Some guys do." Jane took a drag on her cigarette. "At least that's the theory. I have yet to meet one of those evolved types, though."

I reached for Jane's cigarettes. "I thought Rick was one of those evolved types." I lit a cigarette, inhaled, and coughed. Jane watched me sympathetically.

"You are so not a smoker." She reached over and adjusted my fingers. "At least hold the ciggie properly."

"Thanks," I mumbled. I smoked about as often as I ate leafy green vegetables. But at moments like these—when you're drunk and you caught your boyfriend about to fuck another woman (one who is younger, prettier, and yes, even thinner than you) and you hate your job and you have no idea what you're going to do with your life—smoking seemed like an attractive option. Who cared if I was shortening my life with every puff? At this point, I wasn't sure I wanted a long life anyway.

I had debated telling people at work. Maybe Bobby, maybe Rachel. I didn't want to make a big sweeping announcement, but on the other hand, I knew people would notice. My fellow single coworkers (Bobby and Rachel) would express their sympathy, but people like Elaine would feed on whatever juicy morsels of gossip came her way. The married women I worked with would sigh with that peculiar married-people smugness, thinking, "I'm so glad I don't have to deal with this kind of thing anymore." And people would feel sorry for me. Ugh.

At least I was busy enough on Monday that I could lose myself in the world of the company's new Plenty-o'-Pans promotion. I was writing the copy that would be used to introduce the products to our sales reps throughout the country, and I was stumped.

Pans are good for . . . pancakes? Skillet suppers? Why would anyone need a set of ten pans, anyway? The pans ranged in size from a pan designed to cook one measly egg to two-egg pans to skillets of three different sizes. I thought that most people would probably manage with one medium-sized pan, and maybe a large one if you had a big family. But the idea was to sell people on the whole line.

Tuesday morning, Bobby strolled over. He'd been out the day before. He uses his vacation days as quickly as they accrue. "You eating in today?" Most of us ate in the lunchroom, a large room that housed twenty or so gray tables and dozens of gray and blue chairs. They provided refrigerators and microwaves for people who brought lunch from home, and a wall full of vending machines full of overpriced candy, chips, soda, and sandwiches for those who hadn't planned ahead. Sometimes I brought a sandwich, but I usually wound up eating the nutritionally balanced meal of pretzels, Diet Coke, and M&Ms.

"I don't know. I didn't bring anything."

Bobby handed me a story for the newsletter. "Here's the latest Selling Superstar story, by the way."

I took it and set it on my desk. "Thanks."

"You're not your sunshiny self. What's up?"

I didn't say anything.

"Oh no. That's a man trouble face."

I didn't even look at him, just nodded.

"Trini, what happened?"

"Actually it's your fault." I tried to joke. "You're the one who told me to do something"—I lifted my hands and made little quote marks with my fingers—" 'exciting' this weekend."

"OK, you've got me. Did the excitement get out of hand?"

I debated. I could see Elaine strolling our way, and she was the last person I wanted to hear about this. "I don't want to talk about it here. You want to go grab something at Jimmy John's?"

"Name the time."

"Let's go at twelve-thirty. I've got to make some headway on this first."

Over subs, I filled Bobby in on what had happened. "Don't say anything at work, though, OK? It's too humiliating."

"Come on." Bobby wiped his mouth with a napkin. "You've got to admit, it's a little funny."

"It is not funny! It was horrible. I'm standing there butt naked, wrapped in that nasty comforter, wondering why is Rick talking to Jill at, like, one-thirty in the morning? Then I thought, what is she doing here?" I shook my head.

"Ring ring! Clue phone! Call for you!"

"Pretty much." Despite everything, I started to laugh. "I guess it was pretty funny. The best part was the look on Rick's face. His face was, like, totally blank." I tried to arrange my features to show Bobby what I meant, and he laughed, too.

"And Jill practically sprinted out of the apartment. I wonder what he told her." I bit my lip, suddenly angry. "What the hell is her problem! She knows I'm his girlfriend. I met her! What was she doing?"

"And what was, uh, Rick doing?" Bobby said pointedly.

"Yeah, I know." I sighed and pushed the rest of my tuna sub away. "But it's easier to blame her. Maybe she bewitched him and he was unable to resist her."

"Mmmmm." Bobby made a noncommittal noise.

"But the fact is that he hasn't called me." Bobby handed me a yellow napkin and I wiped my eyes. "That's what hurts. If he still wanted me, he would have. He would have called. Shit, he would have come over, you know? Begged for my forgiveness?"

"This is all sounding like a bad chick movie."

"I'm aware." I blew my nose and then looked up at Bobby and took a deep breath. "Well, Mr. Laguna, I still hold you responsible for this nightmare. So how do you suggest I get out of it?"

"Best solution for getting over a man? Come on, Trini, that's easy. You find yourself another one."

Chapter 7
The Knight of Swords

Someone will rush headlong into your life.

Two weeks had passed, and I'd finally decided Bobby was right. It was time to get back on the horse, so to speak. So what if I still thought about him constantly? Since that drunken Sunday afternoon, I hadn't caved. I hadn't called him, I hadn't e-mailed, I hadn't even driven by his apartment on the off-chance I might see him. I avoided his two favorite bars (this of course was easy because, number one, there are a million bars in Chicago, and number two, I never liked hanging out in bars in the first place) and even told my mom and Jessie that we'd broken up. I knew Mom would pass along the news to Dad and Missy.

Mom got a sanitized version of the story, while Jessie heard the *True Hollywood Story* version. She was furious at him, which made me feel a little better. "What an asshole! I can't believe it." She was silent for a moment. "At least it happened now, before you were engaged or married or anything."

"Well, what difference does that make? He was still cheating on me."

"It's worse then."

"I don't think so. Cheating is cheating. I don't see how it's worse just because you're married."

"You make a promise, Trina. You take a vow to each other. That's what makes it worse."

"Yeah, maybe you're right." A thought occurred to me. "What would you do? I mean, if Ethan . . ."

"Are you joking? I'd cut if off and hand it over to him on a platter."

"Geez. Does he know this?"

"Sure. Seriously, Trina, that would be it. If he broke that promise, I'd know that he didn't want to be married to me. Our marriage would be over."

"Yeah, I see what you're saying. Hey, um, how's your medical stuff coming along?"

She sighed. "Nothing new to report. Thanks for asking, though."

I'd told her about my plan to reenter the world of dating, and she had invited me to a barbecue on Labor Day weekend. "Um, hello? Aren't all of your friends married?"

"Not all. We're inviting a lot of people from work, and Ethan says some of the guys from his office are coming."

"God, I must be desperate if I'm going after lawyers now." But I agreed to come. At least I was getting back "into circulation," a phrase that always made me feel vaguely like a library book.

So late Saturday afternoon, I scoured my closet, looking for something appropriate to wear. It was shaping up to be a gorgeous late summer evening. I briefly considered a strappy little sundress I'd bought from Victoria's Secret, then opted for powder blue capris, a blue-and-white-striped tank top, and white espadrilles. An outfit that said cute, available, not desperate. Or so I hoped.

I was also wearing new underwear. Jane had insisted. Like Bobby, she thought the fastest way over my broken heart was to distract myself with a new man. And new panties.

As part of her plan, she'd brought over a Victoria's Secret catalog and pointed out what she wanted me to buy. I'd fought her. "First of all, the guy isn't going to see my underwear. Second, this all looks sexy because it's on these perfect physical specimens." I held up the catalog. "OK, here is a woman who's maybe five-eleven, weighs a hundred and thirty, has fake boobs, a flat stomach, and no cellulite." I pointed. "Look! The panties just sit there. There's no bulging, no stomach sticking out, no ass hanging out of the back. These photos are not real! These bodies are not real bodies."

Jane considered the photo. "Okay, she's gorgeous. But so are you. And you still need something sexier. Underwear can change your whole mind-set."

I'd argued but given in. I'd agreed to two sets of matching bras and panties, silky fabric, one in cream and one in rose. Jane had rolled her eyes, insisting I buy at least one thong, but I'd refused, preferring to start out slow.

The drive to Jessie and Ethan's wasn't bad. Traffic was light. I rolled down the windows and cranked up the stereo, listening to Alanis Morrisette's new CD. Alanis was belting out "21 Things I Want in a Lover," and I was alternating between singing the words I knew and trying to memorize the rest.

Come to think of it, having a list wasn't a bad idea, but Alanis's inventory seemed a little too stringent. She sang about wanting someone who was funny, self-deprecating, and uninhibited in bed. All good. But thriving in a job that helps your brother? Against capital punishment? I figured if I was going to look for a new guy—and everyone around me seemed to think that I should—I'd be reasonable. Reasonably good-looking, reasonably funny, reasonably smart. And reasonably nice.

With such reasonable expectations, how could I lose?

Unfortunately I left out "reasonably single." And while I'd been at Jessie's for more than an hour, every man so far had been sporting a fat gold ring on his left hand and an attractive thin wife on his right. I was starting to get discouraged.

"Hang in there," said Ethan, who had been prepped by Jess about my ulterior motive at this gathering. "Some of the guys from work are due anytime." He took a swig of Heineken. "Come to think of it, you might like Derek."

"Details."

He ticked them off on his fingers. "Twenty-seven, out of law school a couple of years, doing traffic now. Nice guy. Funny. Smart, too."

Of course, Ethan didn't mention Derek was also vertically challenged, or rather, short. Not that I'm an Amazon, but at five-seven, I want to at least be able to look straight into a man's eyes, not down into them. Derek was maybe five-five. Throw my espadrilles into the equation and I had a good five inches on him.

He seemed nice enough, though, and we talked a little about his job and mine. It turned out his older sister was a Cook's Helper, so he was well versed in our product line.

"Do you ever get sick of writing about that stuff?"

I made a face to answer his question.

He laughed. "OK, sorry I asked."

"No, it's all right. It's just that I don't know what the next step is for me," I admitted. "It's a good job and it has good benefits and everything, but I'm not sure how much longer I want to write about ten ways to make women believe that they can't live without a vegetable oil spritzer!"

"What's a vegetable oil spritzer?"

"Don't ask." As we were standing there talking, several men about my age had joined the throng in the backyard. Must be more of Ethan's buddies from work—they weren't dressed conservatively enough to work at a firm as big as Jessie's.

One glanced at us, and then split off from the group, heading our direction. About six feet tall, dark brown hair worn in that slightly ragged cut twenty-something men seemed to prefer lately. Nice skin, dark complexion, brown eyes, a little too sexy in an Antonio-Banderish kind of way.

"Fielding." He greeted Derek by his last name in the way guys do.

"Rodriguez." They did a half-assed handshake. "How's it going?"

"Not bad, not bad at all." He smiled at both of us. Geez, dimples too. "I'm Javier. Javier Rodriguez."

"Sorry." Derek gestured at me. "This is . . ."

"Trina Elder. Jessie's sister."

Javier looked at me. "Younger?"

"Uh-huh. By two years."

He looked closer. "I see the resemblance. In the eyes and mouth."

Despite myself, I smiled. Jessie has the kind of looks that make men stop and stare after her when she walks by. Even with a few extra pounds, she's striking. My looks don't even slow men down. But still, he was sweet. I didn't need to point out the difference to him.

He nodded at me. "And what do *you* do, Trina? Are you a lawyer too?"

"God no!" I answered a little too emphatically and Javier raised his eyebrows. "No offense, I mean." Sure, why didn't I just start going off on lawyers—at a party filled with them. "I'm a marketing writer, actually. I write newsletters, brochures, stuff like that." Derek looked less than thrilled about hearing my job specs once more and nodded at his nearly empty glass as he walked back toward the house.

"What, do you have a journalism background for a job like that?"

"Yeah, actually. I went to U of I but couldn't get a newspaper job that paid more than about eighteen thousand a year. I worked for a couple of magazines and then wound up at the Coddled Cook a few years later."

Javier leaned up against the railing of the deck. It was starting to cool off, and the evening breeze stirred my hair. "Do you like it?"

"You're the second person to ask me that in ten minutes. My pat answer is sure. The longer answer is not really . . . but I don't know what I'd do instead," I finished. I tossed my head slightly, trying to get the hair out of my face.

Javier leaned forward and gently pulled a piece of hair away from my eyes, tucking it behind my ear. I watched him do it without speaking. What was *that*? It was the kind of intimate gesture that you'd make with someone you'd been with for a long time, someone you loved. I might do that to Jane, or to Jessie.

"Um . . . do you want another beer?" I gestured at his half-empty bottle. Great line, but I was stumped.

"Not yet. Why don't you let me get you another, though. Then I'll come back and we'll figure out what you'd *really* like to do." He smiled at me, letting his eyes linger on my mouth, then turned and walked into the house. I stared at his back for a moment. I felt that thrill, that sense of excitement when you meet someone you like, really like, the first time. At this point, there were no disappointments to be bitter over, no fatal flaws to spoil the illusion of perfection, no endearing personality quirks that grew less and less endearing as time went on. Now there was only potential. And I love potential.

I took a deep breath and closed my eyes, moving slightly to the chorus of "Red, Red Wine" that was playing. I was ready for the Next Man, I told myself. Maybe Javier was him.

The idea of a "Next Man" had been my friend Nikki's creation. We lived together the last two years of college, and during that time she must have gone out with at least ten guys, maybe more. Turned out that was just the warm-up for her post-collegiate years. Still, no matter how many losers she dated—and there had been plenty—she always seemed to shrug it off. "Next Man will be way nicer to me," she'd say. "Next Man will not screw around." "Next Man will not have issues with his mother."

The idea, of course, is that there will be a Next Man—you just don't know who he is yet. But if I could make a list of what Next Man would include, why not say dark-eyed, with dark wavy hair, smooth skin, and eyelashes too long to be believed? Maybe Javier was, in fact, my Next Man. The thought cheered me considerably.

Chapter 8
The Page of Swords, Inverted

An unprepared state; unforeseen events.

Jessie rarely called me at work. When she did, there was always a purpose for the call—she's not one to sit and while away the hours on the phone. She bills more than two hundred hours a month, and she doesn't produce those kinds of numbers by gabbing away with me or anyone else. Or so she tells me. So I knew something was up when she called me that Wednesday.

"So, did you have fun?"

"Yeah, actually I did! That Javier is a hottie. How come you've never told me about him?"

"Who? Which one is he?"

"Hispanic, gorgeous, cute butt . . ."

"Oh yeah, yeah. Well, good." Without stopping to share in my delight over Javier's cute posterior, she plowed ahead into the real reason for her call. "Trina, there's something I need to talk to you about. Something . . . personal."

"Sure. I've got a couple minutes."

My sister sighed. "No, not over the phone," she snapped. "Look, I'm sorry. I'm acting like a bitch."

"It's OK." But it wasn't. I was getting tired of this Jekyll and Hyde thing. I bet Ethan was, too.

"Let me make it up to you. Dinner someplace, my treat."

"All right."

She caught the lack of enthusiasm in my voice. "I'll make it good! How about Nine?"

I was tempted. I'd heard about Nine, but I hadn't been there. It had been billed as a sort of futuristic steak house for the elite. I wanted to see it for myself.

"You've convinced me."

"Meet me there at seven tomorrow, and then I'll just take a late train home."

I arrived a few minutes ahead of Jessie, which was rare, but traffic had been light. I told the blond twenty-something at the hostess desk I'd wait to be seated. Two minutes later, I told the brunette twenty-something the same thing. They were both easily five-ten, wearing tight black dresses that revealed lots of smooth skin and absolutely no spare flesh. They had straight, sleek hair like my old Barbie dolls. Barbie . . . and what was the brown-haired one called? I couldn't remember. All I could come up with was Skipper, Barbie's younger sister. I glanced over at the two of them, catwalking patrons to their tables, and felt pudgily short in comparison.

Jessie blew in five minutes later, checking her watch. She gave me a quick hug. After the brunette hostess seated us, Jesse ordered a Stoli with a splash, which surprised me.

"I didn't know you liked vodka." I took a sip of my chardonnay.

"I'm nervous." She took a sip, then another, and then pushed the glass aside. "OK, let's get right down to it."

"OK . . ."

"Let me finish before you say anything, all right? I have a proposition for you, but I want you to hear all of the details before you answer." She rubbed her hands together as if she were cold, then cleared her throat.

"OK." I nodded encouragingly. I had no clue what this was about, but I also had no doubt that Jessie would have prepared an outline and probably notes and references for this conversation. She was organized, even methodical, in her approach to every aspect of her life.

"You know that Ethan and I have been doing fertility treatment, IUIs, and everything." I nodded. "And nothing has worked." Jessie took another sip of her drink, started to set it down, then changed her mind and drained it. The waiter, who had been watching our table from afar, caught her motion and returned with a fresh one without being asked.

"Our RE now thinks that the problem is with my eggs. They're not 'high quality' "—she made little quote marks with her fingers—"for whatever reason. I'm only thirty but my eggs have a case of advanced age. Or something."

"Oh, uh-huh?" I knew RE stood for Jessie's doctor—reproductive something, but I couldn't remember which. It wasn't the right time to ask about this minor detail.

"Anyway, he wants us to try IVF. In vitro. But we'd have a much better chance of success, he says, if we were to use donor eggs. Instead of mine," she finished.

"Jessie, that's good! So you're going to take the next step? So, now what? How do you find an egg donor, anyway?" I looked at her and she said nothing, just bit her lip and looked back at me. Slowly, very slowly, realization began to form in my brain. "So, um, whose eggs did you have in mind?"

She didn't say anything, forcing me to say it.

"You . . . want . . . *my* . . . eggs?"

"Trina, it would be perfect, see? We're siblings so we share the same genetic material anyway. That way our baby would be as close to Ethan's and mine as possible."

"But they're mine." Not like I want to have a baby this minute—in fact, most of the thoughts I have about procreation at this point in my life involve the rigorous prevention of same. As I sat there, trying to take this in, the thought skittered across my brain. I have eggs! I thought, hearing that annoying voice that announced, "You've got mail" on AOL. And my sister wants them.

"It's not like we want all of them." Her voice was reasonable. I recognized her lawyer tone. "We'd just harvest a few, enough to try a couple of rounds of IVF."

"Harvest them? How exactly do you harvest them?" I was starting to feel like an expensive farm animal.

"Well, *harvest* isn't exactly the right word," said my sister, ever the lawyer. "I should say retrieve them. They put you on stimulating hormones, which cause your body to release more follicles—and then those become eggs. Then they go in, retrieve them, fertilize them, and then transfer the fertilized eggs inside me."

This was sounding way too sci-fi. "I don't know, Jessie," I said slowly. I drank some more wine. "I'm still unclear on the harvesting." Visions of miniature John Deere tractors ran through my mind.

"I told you, it's retrieval, not harvesting."

"Oh, great." Now I pictured fluffy golden retrievers bouncing around my ovaries, tails wagging as they snatched up my eggs in their mouths. That was worse than the tractors, definitely.

Jessie pressed her lips together and forced a smile. "It's not a big deal. They sedate you and remove them. In and out. It's an outpatient procedure, very minor." She looked down. "Oh, and you have to take some shots—some fertility drugs to make sure that you produce as many eggs as possible. But it's only for a week or two."

I opened my mouth and then shut it. I drank wine to stall for time. "Jessie, I have to think about this, OK?"

She started to say something, then stopped. "But—Trina, it's not that big of a procedure . . ." She bit her lip and shook her head, pulling her napkin out of her lap to twist it unhappily.

"I know it's a lot to ask," she said. "Don't say anything now, OK? Just think about it, and we can talk about it later."

"OK." I sat there for a moment. "You know, I really have to use the bathroom. I'll be right back."

When I came back, Jessie neatly changed the subject and didn't bring it up again. But I knew it was only a matter of time before she'd want to know my answer.

Chapter 9
The Two of Cups

The beginning of a love affair.

I admit it, I'm a little picky about guys' bodies. Women may not be quite as visual as men are, but we still have tastes and preferences. Me, I like a guy who's muscular without being overly big, lean without being scrawny. His chest doesn't have to be huge, and I don't care about bulging biceps, but he cannot have a pear-shaped body. A guy with broad hips and thick thighs is an automatic turnoff.

Fortunately, Javier did not possess scary womanly hips. In fact, his ass was even more adorable undressed—round, cute, with dimples on each side of his buns.

Of course, I knew this because on our first date together, we wound up in bed.

I know, that's a bad idea. I'd ignored the three-date rule—you know, you go out with a guy at least three times before you go to bed with him. The logic being that you get a chance to *know* the guy—at least a little—before you hit the sheets. And that you don't come off as too easy.

I had religiously ascribed to this theory through my entire dating life. (Well, except for Joey, but that whole situation wasn't really dating, after all.) With Rick, I'd managed to get through four dates before we hit the sheets. I had to admit that the whole sordid thing with him had addled my thinking. Jane didn't help matters. "The three-date rule is passé, sweetie," she'd told me. "That's about as trite as *The Rules*." But I'd read that dating classic when it came out, and I could understand its popularity. At least it gave you a playbook to follow, a set of instructions you could refer to instead of trying to negotiate the complicated world of coupling and uncoupling without a map, a compass, or even a clue as to how you were supposed to act when you really liked someone.

When Javier suggested we meet for a drink, my internal radar should have sounded. After all, "Want to meet for a drink?" is just another way of saying, "Would you like to screw my brains out?" A little alcohol, preferably mixed with a little loud music which compels you to sit in close proximity if you're to make out one single word of what he's saying—start with that. Then toss in this gorgeous specimen of masculinity whose eyes are so dark you can hardly make out his pupils, and who has a habit of watching your mouth when you speak—and when you're not speaking—well, blend that all together and you have the makings of a sexual encounter.

He should have asked me out to a movie, or for coffee, or even dinner. But he asked me for a drink, so I knew the score before I even showed up.

But I didn't care. I was still thinking about Rick, and that needed to stop. I wasn't obsessing, understand, but he was there, in the back of my mind, an ache as steady as a sore tooth. Every time I checked my e-mail, every time my phone rang, I felt that little hopeful twist that maybe it was him. It never was.

So, Javier and I met at Bin 66 that Tuesday, in Marina Towers just off the river. I'd wondered briefly why he'd asked me out on a weeknight instead of a Friday or Saturday. Does he have a girlfriend or what? Then, I decided I was being overly paranoid. People did do things on weeknights, after all. Not everyone came home from work feeling as if the life force had been systematically squeezed out of them, leaving them feeling like a dried, empty corn husk.

In deference to Jane, I wore my new rose-colored pushup bra and bikini panties under my usual work uniform of black flat-fronts and pink blouse. They matched! Javier and I met, selected a pair of seats at the huge oval-shaped bar, and drank three glasses of wine apiece. And had sex. There were a few other details, of course—we did talk, we did laugh, we did go back to his apartment (which was only a few blocks west of Bin 66 . . . hmmm . . .), we did take off our clothes.

But let's talk about the sex. On a purely physical level, it had to be the best I'd ever had. When you go to bed with someone for the first time, you expect a certain amount of fumbling and uncertainty. He can't quite figure out how to unhook your bra or you struggle with the button on his pants or your teeth knock together when you come in for a kiss. With Javier, there was none of that. It was effortless. The closest thing to what Erica Jong had called a "zipless fuck" back in the seventies. I'd read *Fear of Flying* in high school and that phrase had always stayed in my mind.

That's the best part about having sex with someone for the first time. You know how it will end up, of course—with tab A being inserted into slot B—but the steps that will be taken to create the end result can vary widely. Will he be a long, gentle kisser? Will he go right for your boobs like there's nothing else on your body worth touching? Will he tease you for a while, make you want him so much you can't stand it, or will foreplay be relegated to a few perfunctory kisses and maybe a dip-sticking finger to check if you're ready?

Javier followed the traditional sex steps. We had the kissing. We had the breast fondling. We had the genital fondling, and of course the penetration. It was the order he did things and the manner in which he did them that surprised me.

When we walked into his apartment, I was just buzzed enough not to be nervous. I'd also decided this was a necessary element of the items on my to-do list entitled "Get Over Rick." But I did feel a little awkward standing there, looking at the Dali prints over his couch. What happened now? Before, I'd always made out with a guy, going a little further each time, until we did "it." But Javier and I hadn't even kissed.

He squeezed my hand. "I'll be right back." He disappeared into his bedroom and then returned with a hairbrush. Visions of a spanking fest danced across my brain, and my expression must have shown my concern.

"No, no, no." He laughed. "Come here." He patted the couch next to him. "I want to brush your hair."

I stood there. "Brush my hair?"

"Uh-huh." OK, I thought, so maybe he's got a hair fetish. Maybe this isn't about sex. Maybe it's about getting his hands on my tresses.

Any doubts I had faded the moment he began stroking my hair. He brushed it slowly, evenly, with long, firm strokes. I closed my eyes. I couldn't remember the last time someone had done this for me. My mom, maybe, when I was little?

"You have gorgeous hair." I leaned against him.

"You don't think I should get it cut?"

"Huh-uh." He kept up his even strokes. My scalp was starting to tingle and I began feeling that little pull in my center, that sensation of wanting more. After ten minutes or so, he set the brush down, gently working his fingers into my scalp.

"Oh, man, does that feel good." I relaxed against him, shameless.

"That's the idea." His fingers kneaded down my neck, pressing firmly along the tops of my shoulders. I could feel my body temperature start to rise. As he caressed my shoulders, gently squeezing my arms, I pressed against him.

"I can do this better if you take off your shirt," he murmured.

So much for any sense of modesty. My shirt was off in a flash, and I settled back into my original position.

"You have amazing fingers." Problem was that I wanted those fingers to explore other parts of me as well. As if sensing what I was thinking, he tugged gently on my bra straps.

"You know, I can touch you even better if you take this off, too."

"It's new, you know."

"Very nice."

I hesitated for only a moment. Then, without looking at him, I unhooked my bra and slid it off my shoulders. I felt my nipples harden as I did so.

But even then, he ignored my breasts. He just kept massaging my neck, my shoulder, my arms, my back. He worked his fingers down my spine, and then trailed just the tips up my back, causing me to break out in goose bumps. I shivered. As he would trail his fingers down the outside of my arms, I'd tense involuntarily, waiting for him to touch "the good stuff."

After what—fifteen minutes? twenty?—of this, I was about to lose my mind. I was breathing harder, and every pore of my skin seemed open. I felt hyperaware, alert, alive. He was humming something under his breath.

"You have beautiful skin." Still nothing.

Finally I couldn't take it anymore. I turned around to face him. "What is going on here?"

He didn't even look at my breasts. What kind of man was he? "I'm giving you a massage. Do you like it?"

"Um, have you noticed that it's a topless massage?"

He smiled and looked down at my breasts intently, then back at my face. "I noticed. They're beautiful as well."

The expression on his face was having an effect on me. I was breathing even harder—geez, I sounded like Darth Vader or something—and I was definitely getting moist, as Rick would say. That thought interrupted me for only a moment.

"Um, thank you." I'm quite the little seductress, aren't I?

"Really. May I?" He waited for my slow nod, and then reached out and cupped them gently in his hands. It felt so good I almost moaned. I shut my eyes and arched my back. I didn't care. I just didn't want him to stop touching me.

"What are you doing to me?" My voice was low. I hardly recognized it as my own.

"Just a little teasing. You like that, don't you?" He trailed his fingertips over the tips of my nipples and I gasped. "Sensitive." Then he bent and took one into his mouth.

The sensation was so intense I grabbed his head and groaned aloud. I was out of breath, my panties were soaking, and I was so turned on I couldn't think straight. I knew I couldn't take much more of this.

"I can't . . . I can't . . ."

"What?" He lifted his head and reached out his hand to touch my face. "What can't you?"

"I can't take this. Kiss me," I said. "Please," I added. He slowly raised his head, his eyes never leaving my face, and gave me a soft, sweet kiss. I grabbed him and kissed him back hungrily. He smiled. His eyes were so dark I could see my own reflection in them. My hair was messy from the scalp massage and my mouth was open.

"Do you like being teased?"

I nodded dumbly. "Yes. No. I don't know."

"Do you want more? Or do you want something else?" He took my hand and placed it right on his crotch, where something hard was straining to escape. I'm embarrassed to admit that I actually looked at him with what I hoped was a sexy, come-hither expression and whispered, "Something else."

Chapter 10
Two of Swords, Inverted

Movement in affairs, sometimes in the wrong direction.

By the time Javier and I were finished rolling around on his sheets, it was close to 2 A.M. Since he didn't suggest that I stay, I thought it was wise to leave while we were feeling pleased with each other. I drove home in a fog of post-orgasmic bliss, which lingered through the drive into work the next morning.

"Oooh, someone got laid last night." Bobby, leaning against my cubicle wall.

"What? What are you talking about?" But I had that slowed reaction time, that lazy air that only good sex can provide.

"So, he came back, huh? I thought he might." He took a sip from his Starbucks cup.

"Ummm, no, not quite."

"What? Then who were you kicking it with?"

"That guy I met at my sister's. The Cook County state's attorney."

"You little ho!" Bobby swatted at me. "I didn't know you had it in you."

I raised my eyebrows. "Oh, I did, all right." We both laughed, then I looked around. "Don't say anything, though, OK?"

"Who am I going to tell? Anyhow, I'll only agree to that if I get all the details at lunch. Let's go to the Tavern."

"I hate that place!" The Tavern was a dimly lit, smoky neighborhood pub down the road. It staunchly resisted the influx of the Chili's and Friday's and Bennigan's chains that sprung up all around it. The place did have good burgers, but the main attraction as far as I could tell was that people who needed an alcohol fix could grab one over lunch. "Can't we go somewhere else?"

"No, I've got a craving for grease. Besides, no one else from work will be there, so you can spill your horny little heart out."

I told Bobby most of the story over Cokes, burgers, and fries seasoned with vinegar and pepper. I omitted the details that revealed how simultaneously turned on and frustrated I'd been at Javier's approach to sex.

"So, are you going to see him again?"

"Um, I'm not sure. He said he'd call me." But I smiled to myself. He would. You can't have sex that intense and that incredible with someone without feeling a sense of connection. Javier was sexy, charming, and smart—what had my list of attributes included again? I couldn't remember if he was funny. Once my sex drive kicked on, it was like those afterburners on jets that take off and land from aircraft carriers. Everything else gets drowned out in the resulting noise and power.

Jane got the entire story that weekend. One of her shows— she had had a small part in a production at the Viaduct Theater— had just finished its run and she was left without anything to do on a Saturday. Neither of us felt like going out, so I'd agreed to come over to her place. We watched *Chocolat*, which I'd been wanting to see on video.

"Man, is Johnny Depp the hottest thing you've ever seen or what?" I shifted positions on Jane's somewhat lumpy sofa.

"Ummm-hmmm. 'How about I come get that squeak out of your door?'" she quoted from the movie and we giggled.

"He kind of reminds me of Javier." I couldn't help myself.

"Yeah, he has that sexy Latin guy thing going on." Jane reached for her cigarettes. "But he's short, you know? All those guys. Tom Cruise, Mel Gibson, Sly Stallone. They're shrimps. The camera just shoots them so that they look taller than they are."

"Like how short?"

"Like Tom Cruise is five-seven or something."

"No way!"

"Yup." Jane exhaled. "It's a lot of fancy camera work."

"Hmmm." My mind was elsewhere. I was wondering what Javier was doing. He'd said he'd call but it had only been, what, four days? He didn't want to look too eager, I decided.

Jane stubbed out her cigarette. "I hate Saturdays. I don't feel right without a show."

"I know." Jane belongs on stage. Put her in a role, any role, and she gets this air of excitement about her. She's charged up, hyper almost, bubbling over with enthusiasm. That energy can carry her through hours of partying afterward—and then she goes home and crashes, recovering in time for the next performance. It's a schizophrenic way to live, but that's what she wants.

"Did I tell you Jason called me?" She rolled her eyes. "Said he'd been thinking about me, and how much he misses me."

"What did you say?"

"I said, 'How can you miss me when you're banging that bimbo?' That shut him up."

I was silent. Jane and Jason had had a weird on-again, off-again relationship for the last several months. Jane called it a love-hate relationship—"I love him and he hates me," she said dryly. He was an actor, too—they'd met during her last production—and that was also the problem.

"Actors are the vainest men there are. Worse than models. They can't go anywhere without checking themselves. What's my body language saying? What kind of impression am I making? What am I emoting? What's my motivation?"

I had noticed that about Jason, but had never said so to Jane. You could be talking to him, and he'd be standing there listening to you, sipping from a bottle of water, all raised eyebrows and watchfulness. But halfway through your conversation, you'd sense that he wasn't paying attention at all. He'd be off in his own mind, thinking about something else. Himself, most likely. And he could turn from cheerful to truculent and then just as quickly back again. It was unsettling. I'd attributed it to some kind of mental disorder or split personality, although I eventually came to believe it was simply a by-product of his chosen profession.

Jason was built on a small but perfect scale. Nicely muscled body, silky dark hair worn to his shoulders, charmingly crooked teeth, and lots of moles. Not as moley as Matt Damon but close.

Jane had maintained a crush on him before they'd started going out. "That beautiful boy" is what she called him. Then he'd been sleeping with another actress in the same production. After a noisy breakup, the way was clear for him and Jane, but that had proved temporary. Then he'd started up with yet another actress, a fairly well-known one in her mid-thirties. And yet Jason had called to say he missed her. I thought of Rick and pursed my lips together. I wasn't going to cry over him anymore.

Besides, I had Javier to take my mind off Rick. "Should I call him?"

"Which one?" asked Jane. "If you're talking about Rick, absolutely . . . not. Javier? Sure, why not? What's he like, anyway?"

"Gorgeous, sexy, with the warmest hands you've ever felt." I sighed. "And his skin is so beautiful and smooth. It's this coffee-with-cream color. I felt pale and pasty next to him."

Jane rolled her eyes. "You already told me about the sex. I meant what's he like? You know, his personality?"

"Oh." I thought a moment. "He's relaxed, I guess. He didn't

talk that much about himself—asked me a lot of questions." I paused. "He listens. He's polite. And he's just incredibly sexy."

"Yeah, I think you covered that. So call him. What's the big deal?"

"I don't know. I feel kind of weird about the whole thing. First, I go to bed with him after maybe three hours and that's including the whole topless massage. He probably thinks I'm a ho."

"You, a ho?" Jane laughed. "Hardly."

"Hey, I could be a ho if I wanted." I stuck my chest out. "See? I got it going on."

"It's not your chest size, sweetie. I mean you're too emotional. You get involved with guys when you go to bed with them. A ho doesn't care. She'll screw anyone, it doesn't matter who." Jane got up and used the bathroom. "Come to think of it, maybe you should try the ho approach. Don't get into this guy so fast, Trina. You hardly know him."

"Um, I've seen just about every square inch of his naked body, remember?"

"Which has nothing to do with knowing him."

Jane was wrong. When you have sex with someone, there's an intimacy there. To take a man into your body is the most personal thing you can do, isn't it? When a man is inside you, and you're brave enough to look into his eyes, you can feel that bond. It's sex and desire and connection and need and comfort all at once. I'd had that feeling with Javier on Tuesday, when he first got inside me.

"Open your eyes," he'd murmured, and I had. He was propped up on his elbows, watching me. I'd felt a flush of embarrassment. He was too close. I didn't want to be reminded that I was with him and not Rick.

"You're very desirable."

I hadn't known what to say. "Thank you" might have been appropriate, but it didn't seem right. "You, too"? "Obviously, because you're inside me right this minute"? Maybe he hadn't expected an answer.

"Well, are you going to call him?"

The sex had been incredible, after all. And maybe we could get to know each other better the next time. And I needed to get over Rick. So I called.

Chapter 11
Seven of Pentacles

Cause for anxiety over money or career.

When my mom wants something, she usually gets it. My dad's recognition and acceptance of this fact is one of the reasons they've managed to stay married for going on thirty-three years. The only thing he ever controlled in the house was the remote—but now she's even begun forcing HGTV on him. Growing up, it was bad enough with four television stations. Now my parents have hundreds, and they haven't agreed on a program for years.

When you're little, you don't think of your parents as having a relationship with each other. You think of them only in terms of yourself. But at some point in your teens—or at least your early twenties—you realize with a shock that they have lives completely independent of you and your siblings (unless you're completely self-absorbed).

I'd never thought of my parents as having a "good marriage" or a "supportive relationship" or anything along those lines until I got into college. Then, everyone I met had divorced parents or stepparents or still-married-but-seriously-dysfunctional parents or absent parents or parents who were screwed up in the extreme. I'd listen to my roommates and boyfriends talk about their families and feel a twinge of regret that my parents weren't as interesting. I certainly had the requisite amount of teenage angst growing up, but my mom didn't flirt with my boyfriends and my dad wasn't a drunk or unable to keep a job for more than three months at a time. My parents hadn't beaten me or abused me or messed with my head. For a while, I despaired of the fact that my parents were normal, solid, stable (read: boring), reliable adults. But the older I got, the more I appreciated them—and wanted to understand them.

What made their marriage work? As far as I could tell, it was simply that they got along. I'd seen my parents yell at each other—Dad still got worked up about the amount my mom spends on those idiotic Beanie Babies—but they just seemed to like each other. My mom might be constantly trying to get Dad to do things he didn't want to—like come up to Chicago and spend the weekend at the Drake, see a show, shop, and eat out—but he liked to be home, watching sports and working in the yard. My mom had learned to compromise—several times a year, she and several women friends would go to Chicago for the weekend, eat too much, spend money on clothes, and get their hair done at expensive salons. My dad got to stay home and watch as much television as he wanted—his idea of paradise.

Anyway, Mom had her heart set on a grandchild, and had decided that I was the only obstacle in her way. She was more subtle about it than Jessie was, but the end result was the same.

"So, how's everything else going? Have you heard from Rick?" She didn't know the whole sordid story—just that we'd decided not to see each other. I couldn't really say I'd decided to surprise him at his apartment and discovered him there attempting to bed another woman. My parents know I have sex—they know all three of us do. But they want to operate under the illusion that we progress no further than hand-holding and chaste pecks until our wedding nights.

"No, nothing." I kept my tone neutral.

"Well, at least if this had to happen, you know now. Better now than after you're married." This was one of my mom's favorite refrains. She operated under the assumption that any man—in fact, every man—I dated could possibly become my husband. Come to think of it, so did I.

"Yeah, uh-huh." I checked my watch. *True Hollywood Story* was about to come on. "Mom, I have to get going here in a minute." Might as well get this over with.

"Trina, there is one more thing. Have you thought about, well, Jessie's, uh, request?"

I sighed. "You mean for my eggs?"

"Well, yes."

"Mom, it's only been a week! I haven't had time to think about anything." I was surprised Jessie had even told her. Or maybe she'd thought enlisting her help would sway me.

"I'm sorry. I'm not meaning to pry. I just thought if you wanted to talk about it, I could listen. I know it's a big decision."

"It is, Mom. And I need some time to think about it and decide, OK? Without anyone pestering me."

"You're right, honey. I'm sorry." She didn't say anything for a moment. "It's just that they want a baby so badly—"

I interrupted her. "Mom. I know that. OK?"

"Of course you do. Well, as I said, if you want to talk to someone about it, I'm here, all right? I'm always here for you."

"I know, Mom. I'll decide soon, OK? And I'll let you know."

The truth was I hadn't thought about it at all. Every time it surfaced in my head, I just as quickly pushed it away again. The whole issue seemed unreal. Why did it have to be me? Why not Missy, for example? I wondered if Jessie would ask her.

It wasn't just the medical part of it, although that was scary enough. If we did it, and it worked, they'd be raising my child. My baby would also be my niece or nephew. I knew I wanted to have kids eventually—at least one of them—and how would I explain that their cousin was actually their sibling? The more I thought about it, the more complicated it seemed. Underneath it all, I could feel the unspoken assumption that I would do it. Jessie's my sister, after all. Why wouldn't I?

The next morning at work, Elaine startled me in my cubicle.

"Good morning, Trina!" Elaine's voice trilled at me. "Oh, what a great color. That looks wonderful on you!"

I looked down doubtfully at the teal Gap hoodie I was wearing along with my standard black pants. Elaine had a way of saying things so that you were never sure whether she was simply overly enthusiastic or whether the words were drenched with sarcasm.

"Thank you." It seemed like the best bet.

"So, did you hear?"

I was sure I hadn't. Bobby was off again today, and he was my conduit to the gossip train around here. I shook my head and tried to arrange my face into a please-tell-me-but-make-it-brief expression. I was rewriting the *Cook's Helper Handbook* and I still had three more chapters to finish by week's end. Without interruptions, I could have cranked the thing out in a couple of days. As it was, I'd spent more than three weeks on it already.

"Word is we're going to reorganize. Apparently they had an efficiency consulting team come in and now they're going to streamline operations."

"What? How streamlined?"

"I don't know." She pretended to ponder. "But I'm sure your job will be fine. You're always so busy!" Her tone implied that I was unable to handle my workload. Or maybe that was just me.

"Geez. When is this supposed to happen?" I forgot my rule about never letting her see how I really felt about anything. She practically whooped with delight.

"Right away, I hear. They're going to have a departmental meeting later this week."

"How do you always know all this stuff?"

"I'm connected, my dear. I keep my ears open for this kind

of thing. It never hurts to know what's going on. You should probably do the same." She checked her watch. "I'd better let you get back to work."

She sashayed off. It wasn't until that Friday afternoon that the scope of the "optimization" was revealed. The marketing, public relations, and communications departments were going to merge. Up until now, the three had all worked independently. Now we'd be "under the same umbrella," explained Robert Kinney, the vice president in charge of communications. They'd be conducting interviews with everyone in each department over the next six weeks, and then the new structure would be announced.

"We appreciate your cooperation during this time of transition. Your job title and responsibilities may change slightly, but you'll still be an integral part of this team," said Robert, spreading his arms open. "We are, after all, a family. Think of this as simply switching bedrooms with your brother or sister. Changing bedrooms."

He was trying a little too hard with the metaphor, and his words didn't seem to offer any comfort. I could see other people exchanging glances with each other. Not surprisingly, we were all sitting in delineated little groups—PR at one end of the table, then the marketing people, and finally us communicators. As in any corporation, each department considered itself the hardest-working and most underappreciated. We were loyal first to our own and to the company itself afterward. It was the same at lunch, even within our own department. The designers sat together, the copy editors sat together, the writers sat together, and the PR department took up a table of its own. I couldn't imagine how we were going to cross all those unwritten boundaries, even in the name of greater efficiency.

I tried explaining the whole thing to Jane later that night. She temps occasionally at companies, but she's never at any one place long enough to get a sense of the low-level angst that overwhelms even the most dedicated workers. Let's face it—some days, work just sucks.

Certainly this job was better than my last one, though, where I was writing about the snooze-inducing world of hospital regulations. But after two years, writing about kitchen implements had lost its appeal. There was only so much room for creativity. Most days I felt like I was putting my brain in a stifling little box, working within the prescribed parameters of the company's rules.

But what else was I going to do? An overabundance of writers—highly educated, quick-thinking, well-versed scribes—flooded the job market every year. New grads were lucky to nail a salary in the low twenties. I was making in the upper thirties now, which wasn't bad for a writing position. Salaries at consumer mags were notoriously low, and newspapers were worse.

When you were in school, you liked to read. You liked to write. You'd become a writer! It was that simple. And it was not. Writing is one of those skills that no one appreciates because everyone writes. It's not like being a lawyer or a doctor or a brain surgeon or even a mechanic. Everyone writes letters, e-mails, Christmas cards, shopping lists, so how hard could it be?

I'd started a novel when I started working at my first job out of college. I'd learned the writing skills I needed in college. Now it was just a matter of applying them. Or so I thought. I floundered for months, trying to craft a literary piece of fiction that explored the meaninglessness of a young woman's early twenties. Gee, I wonder where I got the idea. Then I met Joey and got distracted for the next two years. In between trying to obsess over him, rationalizing our strange relationship, and trying to act nonchalant and detached at work, I didn't have the mental energy for writing fiction. I'd tried to pick it up again after I left the magazine, but I didn't like what I'd written. I didn't even know where the book was now.

Besides, I didn't think I had the motivation to write fiction anymore. After a day of sitting at my computer, churning out how-to articles, tightening headlines, and using every positive adjective in my arsenal to describe the latest in cookware, my brain felt vacant. I still liked to read—I usually had a stack of books I hadn't gotten to yet—but writing the great American novel wasn't in the cards.

I wasn't a real writer anyway. A real writer was someone like Renee. In college, Renee and I had shared the same dream—to become Writers. We'd met during our sophomore year in a fiction class and I'd been wowed by her guts. She wrote a short story that included a graphic, blow-by-blow (if you'll pardon the pun) description of giving a blow job and read it aloud without even flinching. After that, everyone in the class was somewhat in awe of her, especially the guys. (It was a really long, detailed description.) I felt chosen when I ran into her at the student union and she bummed a dollar for coffee. Soon we were hanging out, sharing short stories and talking about authors. I thought I was so radical and cool, liking Margaret Atwood, but she introduced me to writers I'd never heard of like Tom Robbins and Charles Bukowski. Eye-opening stuff.

Renee was never afraid to express herself in her writing, and I knew that's what separated us. Even when I talked about moving out West to work in a bar and write fiction and poetry in my spare time, a little voice in my head said, "How are you going to pay your bills? That doesn't sound very responsible." Renee never got sidetracked by pedestrian thoughts like that, and now she was living in Manhattan. She'd moved there with no money and no job when we'd graduated. She'd lived in the YWCA, found a job at a small women's magazine as an editorial assistant, and now was an editor at a big fitness magazine. We still talked occasionally, and I was careful to keep the jealousy out of my voice. But she'd done it—moved to New York when I was scared to even go there. I'd been convinced I'd be mugged as soon as I got off the plane.

Renee was part of the publishing scene and had already published a novel to some critical acclaim. And me? I was writing articles about colanders, for God's sake. Sure, I'd managed to get a job in a writing field, but I was working in the suburbs, not midtown Manhattan. The thought depressed me.

"I don't know what to do," I said to Jane. "I guess it's time to update my résumé."

"What do you want to do?"

"That's the problem. I have no idea."

Chapter 12
Temperance, Inverted

Possible loss of self-control.

When Javier called me, I was a little surprised. It had been two weeks since our, um, date. Enough time had elapsed that I didn't expect to hear from him. At least I'd left him only one message. I may be horny but I'm not desperate. I tried to play it cool—well, as cool as I know how, anyway.

"How's your week going?" I could hear the smile in his voice.

"Fine, I suppose."

"So, what are you writing about this week? New and exciting potato mashers?"

"Nope, that was *last* week," I said pointedly. I thought it was rude for him to wait a whole two weeks to call me. After all, we'd gone to bed together, hadn't we?

As if sensing my feelings, he spoke. "It's been nuts here. I've had trials every morning for the past ten days. All of a sudden these mopes don't want to plead anymore. I don't know why."

"Oh, so you've been busy."

"Very. But not so busy that I haven't thought about you." He lowered his voice. "And you?"

I practically squirmed in my chair. So much for making him pay for not calling. "Oh, I've thought about you a little bit."

"Only a little bit? Is that all?"

It wasn't, but I wasn't admitting that, either. He laughed. "Don't like to reveal much, huh? Maybe you should be a lawyer."

"I don't know. I've got this honest streak in me that might hurt my chances." But I was only teasing. I was thinking about those dark eyes, those long lashes, that coffee-colored skin, and the way he had made me forget about everything except how good his fingers and mouth felt.

"You have plans tonight?"

"Boy, you don't believe in planning very far out, do you?"

"Guilty as charged. I just like to keep my options open until I know what my night looks like and how I feel."

Actually I could relate to that. I was the same way. I'd much rather call Jane on the spur of the moment and decide to see a movie or hit a festival or cook dinner together than agree on a Tuesday afternoon that I'd be up for something on Saturday. I mentioned that, and we agreed to meet for dinner. I suggested Café Luciano—I'd been craving good pizza margarita and it was a gorgeous day. We could sit outside and people-watch, but he hedged, saying he'd prefer to meet in the Loop. "Closer to my office," he said. And to your apartment, I thought. So we settled on 312.

By eight forty-five, we were back at his place. I was wearing my standard black pants, with a black-and-blue-striped scoop-neck top and black slides. Javier sat down on the couch.

"Take off your shirt."

"Excuse me?"

"You heard me." His voice was low. "I want to look at you."

I felt ridiculous. "What are you going to take off?"

"We'll get there. You go first."

I pulled my shirt over my head. Of course, I was wearing an old, white, stretched-out bra with elastics popping out all over. I was more embarrassed by the sad state of my bra than standing there with my shirt off. I revealed this much at the gym, after all.

"Now your pants."

I looked at him. He said nothing, just hooked one finger over his lips, gently resting his hand on his chin. He looked calm, serious, in control.

I did as he said, kicking off my shoes and pulling off my socks for good measure. He looked at me. I could feel goose bumps pop out along my skin. I was starting to feel a weird mix of anxiety, discomfort, and arousal. I wasn't sure if I liked it or not.

Javier shifted in his seat. He leaned back and spread his legs a little, and I could see he had an erection. The sight bumped up the arousal percentage of the emotional blend I was experiencing. I was breathing a little heavier, and I stopped worrying about him noticing my tummy pooch—no matter what I do, I never have a flat stomach—and wondering instead what he'd tell me to do next.

"Take your bra off. Slowly."

I reached around, unhooked the horrible bra. My nipples immediately got hard—the room was chilly—and I found it hard to look at him.

"Now your panties." My underwear were a slight improvement on the bra, cotton bikinis with a pattern of little pink hearts. I reached down and slipped them off, wondering when I'd last waxed. My timberline, as Jane called it, needed some attention, but he didn't seem to care.

"Now, get down on your knees." Whoa, Nelly. It felt like a splash of cold water.

"What?"

"You heard me." He unzipped his pants and took his cock out.

"Ummmmm . . . no." I wasn't getting on my hands and knees for any man. This game—or whatever it was—had started out like an interesting new experience. I could write it off as experimentation. Now it was starting to seem creepy and humiliating.

I bent down and reached for my underwear. "You know, I think this has gone far enough. I think I'll be going."

"Trina." I didn't look at him. "Trina." He sprang from his chair and walked over to me. I had my back to him and was struggling to hook my bra. He placed his hands on my upper arms, and I shrugged him off angrily.

"I'm sorry. Look at me."

I did.

"You're angry."

"No shit, Sherlock." God, where had that come from? I hadn't heard that one since junior high.

"I'm sorry," he repeated. "We were just playing, and I apparently crossed a boundary."

"What does that mean?" I crossed my arms over my chest.

"Sex is—sex is like play for adults. There are always rules to go along with it, whether unspoken or explicit. Sometimes you only discover the rules when you break one."

I still didn't say anything but I let him pull me gently toward the couch.

"Sit down, please. I don't want you to leave. Come on. Please."

I let him keep touching me, let him kiss me, but I couldn't enjoy it the way I had before. I felt outside myself, watching us together. I closed my eyes and thought of Rick, then immediately forced him from my mind. The whole idea is to get over him, I thought. This was the prescription for heartache and I needed to take my medicine.

Chapter 13
The Six of Cups

May signify memories and looking back on the past.

It had been five weeks since I'd planned to surprise Rick at his apartment and succeeded. And I still had heard nothing from him.

I'd read about the stages of grief back in college. Denial, anger, bargaining, depression, acceptance. I'd plowed through denial and battered my way through anger. The problem was that I missed Rick. I still watched *True Hollywood Story*, but now there was no one to say "dead," "jailbird," "druggie," or "bitter" with me. I'd been used to that before I met Rick—my *THS* obsession predated him, after all—but now I'd gotten accustomed to watching the show with him.

That's the hardest part about a breakup. You get used to each other when you date someone for a while, settle into a comfortable groove. You share your own inside jokes. He knows when you throw your legs across his lap and wiggle your toes at him that you want a foot massage. You know when he asks, "So, how tired are you?" that he's really asking for sex.

Rick knew more about me than anyone except Jane and Jessica. I'd thought I'd known about him, too. But I'd obviously been missing something. How could I be so gullible? So stupid? Half the time I was pissed at him, the other half pissed at myself. Oops. Careful. I was trying to get through the bargaining phase but kept sliding back into anger instead.

The thing is, Javier wasn't helping. My sexual recovery plan was backfiring. The orgasms were great, but if anything, the sex made me miss Rick more. It was all physical, nothing more. I wasn't sure I even liked him that much. But I couldn't talk about it with Jessie or Jane. While they were opposites in many ways, they were definitely on the same side when it came to Rick.

"You deserve better," said Jessie.

"You need to get past him, sweetie," said Jane. "Talking about him all the time will only make things worse." She'd started holding up her hand when I'd mention his name. "Think before you speak!"

I knew she was right. I needed to focus on the rest of my life and forget about Rick. I'd be all right. I'd survive. It would all work out. I soothed myself with these thoughts whenever I felt particularly desolate, and tried to focus on all the things about him that had driven me crazy. The way he couldn't go anywhere without his pager. The way he would shut down and not talk to me when he had a bad day at work. The way he'd refused to come to the holiday party with me last year.

There's good and bad in every relationship and focusing on the bad was helping me get over him, I reasoned. I made a list of his negative qualities to refer to when I felt weak or lonely, and carried it in my pocket. Repetition is a powerful tool, and it worked. I believed I was at the point where I thought I'd be OK. We just weren't meant to be. That was sad, but I could live with it. Woo-hoo! I'd congratulated myself. I'd successfully transported my heart from denial to acceptance in just a month's time!

Then I saw him.

Jane and I were having a drink at the Hungry Brain. The place is one of those bars that has old ratty-looking couches and chairs, furniture that looks worse than what you owned in college, scattered throughout. It tries so hard not to be trendy that it is. Jane hangs out there occasionally with people from her acting company, and she waved at a pair of men sitting very close on a beige couch. "Tony and Leo," she said to me.

She brought me a glass of wine, and a margarita for herself. We'd been there less than an hour, and the bar was now half-full. The cigarette smoke—everyone here smoked—was getting to my eyes.

"I'll be right back." I used the bathroom and was walking back when I saw him with her.

For God's sake! How many bars are there in Chicago, anyway? Out of all the bars in all of Chicago, he has to walk into mine. Well, not mine, but Jane's. At least sort of. And shouldn't it be mine as well by proxy?

Forget the fact that I was just a hair away from being over him. As soon as I saw him, my heart squeezed, hard. I felt excited and nauseous simultaneously. He was standing at the end of the bar, ordering drinks. I recognized Rennie from Rick's firm, next to him. Then I saw her, standing very close to him.

That did it. I strode past him, head high, staring straight ahead, hoping that he wouldn't see me. Of course he did. Or at least I think so. Out of the corner of my eye, I saw his head move suddenly, and his body turned in my general direction.

Then she said something, tugging on his arm, and I kept moving, and made it to Jane, and said, "Come on, let's get out of here."

Jane turned her face to mine. "What? Why?"

I sat down on the edge of the chair and gestured with my head. "See?" I hissed.

She squinted and I saw recognition cross her face. She settled more deeply into her seat. "We're not leaving."

"What?" I shut my eyes. "I can't stand to be here."

"Look. We were here first. We are not leaving. He can leave." Jane spoke slowly, enunciating every word as if I were a slow-witted child.

I made a face and picked up my wine. "Why?"

"Because if you run out of here, he'll know it's because of

him. Why give him the satisfaction?" She pulled out a cigarette. "Living well is the best revenge."

"Which means what?"

"It means be cool. Ignore him. If he has any balls at all, he'll come over here. If not, then I guess we know he doesn't."

I sat in my chair and tried to appear cool, calm, in control of myself. I resolutely ignored Rick and the entire quadrant of the bar where he sat. I sat and drank my wine and Jane brought me another glass. "Be cool, sweetie."

I drank some of my wine. I am never falling in love again. I'll just screw Javier when I need sexual release, have a sex buddy instead of a boyfriend. Meaningless, albeit very good, sex is the answer. I'll simply become a man.

I'd been *this close* to getting over Rick. I had! In the space of less than a second, though, I'd been catapulted back into depression and only a tiny shred of self-respect kept me from sliding all the way to the bargaining phase. If he'd only come and talk to me, I'd thought on Saturday, maybe things would be OK. Maybe there had been some huge colossal misunderstanding. I wanted to make things right, to fix things. I had to grip the arms of my chair to keep myself from getting up and walking over to him. I hated the feeling. I hated still wanting him. And I hated myself for feeling that way. Ooops—there I was, back in Angerland. I sat there clutching my glass, my stomach twisting, until I caught a glimpse of Rick and Jill. Leaving, thankfully. Without talking to me. I was at once relieved, furious, and heartbroken.

Life would be so much easier if there were an on-off switch in your heart. Things are going well with your boyfriend? Great. Leave the switch in the on position. Once things start to sort of suck, you simply switch it off. What could be easier? No heartache, no disappointment, no five stages of grief to deal with. Then, when you met a guy you thought you could be interested in, you'd turn it on again. Forget emotional entanglements. Love, lust, need, desire, sexual attraction—it would all come down to one simple question. Was your switch on or off?

I pondered this theory. Maybe I needed to start doing yoga, take a more Zen-like approach to life. I thought about this at the Coddled Cook when I should have been editing Bobby's story. He came over to see what was taking so long, and I explained my idea about the heart switch to him.

"It makes life too easy," he said. "Besides, you can't know true happiness unless you know true heartbreak."

People only say shit like that when they're happily snuggled in a tight little couple. It's easy to talk about heartbreak when you're not in the midst of it. I shook my head. "That's bull. It'd be easier if you'd only fall in love—and stay in love—because you wanted to. Because you made a conscious decision to do it, see? Then, if he turned out to be a jerk, you'd simply flip the switch."

"And?"

"And that would be it. No pain, no agony, no wondering what you did wrong and how could you fix it and what's wrong with you"—I was rambling now—"and will you ever find the right person and—"

"When did you see him?" he interrupted.

"What?" I frowned at him and then covered my face. "Saturday! At Hungry Brain. I thought I was over him, really!"

"Come on, it's been how long? A month? Give yourself a break."

"I know. But he still looks so good."

"They always do right after. Just wait. You'll know you're over him when you can see him and think, 'That's what I was so hung up on?'" Bobby picked up his story to look at his edits. "It'll happen, really."

"If you say so." I looked at him more closely. He looked tired today—he had faint smudges under his eyes, and I could see a few small strips of razor stubble he'd missed when shaving. "So, how are you? You look beat."

"I am. I was up late again."

"I won't ask."

"It's not what you think." He looked around. "Keep this to yourself, OK?"

"Like who am I going to talk to around here? Elaine?"

He nodded. "True enough. I've been working on a screenplay."

"You're kidding! For how long?"

"Couple of months now. It's really coming together. It's about a firm of gay lawyers. Kind of *Queer as Folk* meets *Ally McBeal*."

"Bobby, that's great! How far along are you?"

"I've finished the first draft; now I'm cleaning it up as I go along." He looked away from me. "I don't know. I'll probably never sell it."

"Come on. I'm sure it's great."

Bobby grinned, his confidence immediately restored. "Actually, I think it's pretty damn good myself. I'm just trying to be modest."

"Not your strong suit, you know."

"Modesty is overrated, Trini." He motioned to the clothes I was wearing—a black-and-gray-striped sweater and black chinos—and deftly changed the subject. "You know, the whole time I've worked here, I don't think I've seen you wear anything but black pants."

"That's not true. I have some other pants. And some skirts," I added.

"Uh-huh." He looked skeptical. "Are you done with this?"

I grabbed it back and glanced over it. "Yeah, take it. Sorry it took so long."

"No prob. Just want to hand it on up." We had five different layers of "approvers" who had to read any written materials we produced, which meant that we spent much of our time chasing down pieces and begging for higher-ups to read them so we could actually publish the things.

Maybe Bobby was right. Or maybe it was PMS, or low blood sugar, or the position of the planets, but when I went to get my hair cut later that week, I gave the woman carte blanche. I'd only come here a couple of times ago, always insisting on a trim.

"Not too short, but I want a different look." As she cut, I closed my eyes, peeking out to see four- and five-inch strands of hair dropping into my lap. I flinched, but I didn't say anything.

When she'd finished, I opened my eyes in amazement. My straight, shoulder-length hair was gone. In its place was a haphazard mess of short spikes and tendrils waving out from around my head, which felt strangely light. I was speechless. I turned my head and touched my hair the way every woman does after a cut, and managed not to cry until I made it to my car.

My new shearing made me feel awkward and exposed. When I walked across the parking lot toward the office the next morning, I could feel the sun on the back of my neck for the first time in years. The rest of the day was spent nodding cheerfully, and pretending to love my radical new look.

"Oh, look at you!"

"A nice short cut. So much easier in the summer."

"It looks . . . good!"

I knew they were all lying. It took only one look at Elaine's face to know I'd made a terrible mistake, but it was too late now.

"What a cute cut!" sang Elaine. "Reminds me of the pixie I used to have when I was a little girl." In other words, my hair made me look childish, or dated, or elfish, or all of the above. Or maybe she meant nothing by it. Maybe I was simply paranoid.

That was my problem. I always had trouble picking up on what Jane called the second layer of conversations. As an actor, she was an avid student of body language, vocal inflection, and gestures and tics that most people wouldn't notice. She said she'd figured out that Jason was screwing that other actress by the way he handed his script to her at rehearsal.

"He held on to it for just a fraction of a second too long, and then they made eye contact," Jane had said. She lifted her shoulders and raised her arms, palms up. "And I just knew."

I thought this kind of thing verged on paranoia, but then again, Jane would be able to thrive in a corporate environment like the Coddled Cook. If you know someone's primary motives, you can act accordingly.

In every conversation there's the text and the subtext— what's spoken and what's unsaid. Under Jane's tutelage, I'd grown more adept at reading people. Sometimes we'd practice in bars and restaurants.

"OK. Who likes who more out of that couple?" Jane gestured toward a couple in their mid-twenties sitting two tables away from us at Cousins. She was petite, with perfectly cut dried-spaghetti-straight blond hair, green-and-gold-patterned capris, and a low-cut moss green V-neck sweater. The guy with her was wearing those horrible low-rider baggy chinos and a wrinkled black Tool T-shirt. He was smoker skinny although I hadn't seen him light up.

I watched them. "I don't know. They don't really go together, though, do they?"

"First date?" asked Jane.

"No. Come on, you'd think he'd at least wear his nonwrinkled T-shirt."

"Uh-uh. Watch him." Unaware of our attentions, he said something to the woman and she laughed. He leaned closer toward her and picked up his glass of water and took a drink.

"See? He put his glass out to the side. He doesn't want there to be anything between them. And see how he's reaching toward her? Trying to get emotionally as well as physically closer."

"Maybe." The girl reached over while she was talking and touched his arm.

"Ooh." Jane reconsidered. "She's making contact. And look. See how she just tossed her hair like that? That's called preening behavior. It means, 'Look at me, notice me, pay attention.' "

It seemed to be working—he didn't take his eyes off her. I had to admit that Jane was good at decoding people, but reading body language was easier in bars than at work. At work, I didn't see a lot of preening behavior. I was starting to become more aware of people's tics or unconscious habits, though.

Like the way Bobby would rearrange the thumbtacks on my cube wall whenever he'd stand there and talk to me. Or the way Rachel twirled her hair with her left hand. Or even how Elaine sniffed a lot—delicate little inhales that were still exceptionally annoying—when she talked to you. But noticing the habits was only half of the game. The tricky part was to figure out what they meant. I'd decided to try out my new talents when I went over to Jessie's. Mom and Dad were coming up for the weekend, and we were having a family get-together. I wasn't sure if Melissa was coming, but I was expected to make an appearance.

I'd thought about asking Javier, but we'd never done anything except meet up, talk briefly, and screw. Introducing him to the family proper seemed like a stretch, even if he did work with Ethan. Besides, I wasn't sure if we were actually dating. We seemed instead to be friends who had sex. I wasn't sure how this had happened. I liked Javier, but I didn't feel particularly interested in him. We exchanged work stories and then exchanged fluids, although with condoms, of course. I was starting to feel a little bored. I missed Rick, or at least I missed the way we'd been able to talk about anything. I wanted a guy who I felt I never had to make conversation with.

Everyone was out in the backyard when I arrived that Saturday. Dad and Ethan were practice-putting on the grass, and Mom and Jessie were sitting at the round molded glass table on the deck.

"Hi, Mom. Hi, Jess." I hugged each of them and waved at Dad and Ethan.

"Your hair!" My mom touched it uncertainly. "It's so . . . short!"

My hand stole up to my head. I liked the way the little bits poked my fingers. It made me feel punk, but now I wondered if I was trying to hard. "I was sick of the same old thing."

Jess looked at it critically. "I like it," she said. "Whose idea was it?"

"Mine, all right? I wanted something different. Is that so hard to believe?"

"Lighten up!" said Jess. "I'm just teasing. It looks good on you. Really."

"Thanks." Her opinion still means more to me than most people's and I knew she would have told me if my head looked like a giant pumpkin. I can always trust her to be honest.

"What do you want to drink?" Jess was having something clear—maybe 7-Up, I thought—and my mom was drinking wine.

"I'll have wine. What is it, white zin?"

"It's that blush your dad likes. From the box." Jess and I grinned at each other. Some things never change.

"So when did you guys get up here?"

"Early this afternoon. We went to Bed Bath and Beyond and Home Life while the guys went to Home Depot."

"We're going to redo that upstairs bath next," explained Jess. "We've been looking at fixtures and vanities and everything." They'd bought this house when it was only five years old, but she still managed to find something wrong with nearly every room. So far they'd repainted the downstairs, installed new kitchen cabinets, and totally redone the living room. Apparently she was now moving on to the upstairs.

"Come on, I'll show you the paint colors we're looking at." Jess got up and went into the house to get them.

"How are you, honey? How's work?"

"It's fine, Mom. Busy as usual. Nothing new to report."

"And Rick? Should I ask about him?"

"You can ask. I haven't spoken to him." I left out the sighting on Saturday.

"I just can't believe that. He seemed like such a nice young man. I guess you never know, though, do you?"

"No, I guess not."

"Are you dating anyone now?"

"Um, not really. I've gone out with a guy who works with Ethan a few times." Sometimes giving a little bit of information is the best strategy. I'd learned that she was often satisfied with a morsel, but if I tried to keep everything from her, she'd badger me or, more likely, squeeze it out of Jessie or Missy.

"Oh, another lawyer. What's he like?"

"He's nice. Good-looking, smart, um, nice, you know." And incredible in bed, I did not add.

"Well, good. I think that's the best thing you could do right now."

If only she knew. "Yeah, I think so."

Dad and Ethan came walking over. "There's my girl." My dad gave me a hug and a kiss while Ethan squeezed my shoulder.

"Nice 'do," said Ethan.

"How's everything at work?" asked my dad, his standard conversation opener. I waited for him to comment on my hair, but then realized he wouldn't. He knew from years of experience what a minefield the simple act of getting a haircut could be for any woman. He probably thought if he mentioned it, I'd burst into tears.

"Fine. Nothing too exciting. What about you?" I said. Dad had worked for the university's grounds department for nearly twelve years now. His degree was in biology but he'd worked as a landscaper in college during the summers and went full-time after he graduated. By the time he met Mom, he'd decided he'd rather work outside than in an office or a lab. He'd run his own landscaping business for years and then got a job with the college because it offered benefits and health insurance. He was now a supervisor, and as far as I could tell, he liked what he did. When I was in college, I'd see him on campus sometimes and we'd stop and talk for a few minutes.

"This is my daughter—she's a student here," he'd say proudly. I was proud of him, too—he'd stayed in good shape, and he kept a year-round tan. My roommates all thought he was hot, which had been weird. One of them had even flirted with him when I brought her home with me one Saturday afternoon. He was embarrassed, and my mom thought it was funny. I was furious.

Ethan went inside to get Dad another beer, and he told me about the trip they were planning. My mom had wanted to take a cruise for years, and the two of them were going to go next month.

"We're going, too," said Jessie as she emerged with a bunch of paint samples in her hand. "Trina, why don't you think about it? It'd be fun."

Hmm, let me think about it. My parents. Jessie and Ethan. A bunch of blue-haired old people playing shuffleboard and drinking fruit concoctions with little umbrellas in them. "Umm . . . I don't think so."

"It's only a week, and it's not that expensive," said Jessie. That was a switch. Usually, she assumed I couldn't afford anything she could. Just because I don't make $200K a year must mean that I'm barely eking by.

"Um, it's not the money. I just don't know that that's how I want to spend my vacation." That's the truth—I get ten precious vacation days each year. I'm not spending over half of them trapped on a ship full of shrimp scampi, bingo players, and the smell of suntan oil mixed with BenGay.

Why would Jessie want to go on a cruise, anyway? I couldn't imagine her lying by the pool doing nothing. She'd probably have an itinerary hammered out for poor Ethan as soon as they set foot on the dock. My mom would no doubt make a handful of new friends—she can talk to anyone—and my dad would hang out in the bar, watch sports, and drink beer.

"Well, if you won't consider it, would you mind watching the house for us?"

"Why? What's it going to do?" God, I'm a bitch sometimes.

Jessie sighed. "Forget it."

"No, I'm sorry. If you need me to house-sit, I'll do it." It'd mean a longer commute, but that was OK. I felt so guilty about the whole egg thing—which she hadn't brought up again—that I was willing to do almost anything to ease my conscience. Staying in Geneva for seven days seemed a low price to pay.

Chapter 14
The Knight of Wands

A fair-haired man capable of creating conflict.

I'd noticed a definite sense of foreboding at work ever since the reorganization—excuse me, optimization—was announced. The Coddled Cook is one of those places where you can work as long as you want—unless you're stupid enough to be caught downloading porn on your computer. But very few people get fired. Sure, lots leave in search of greener pastures or better benefits or a shorter commute, but most people stay awhile. While the marketing and communications departments were full of more recently hired employees, there were people in departments like shipping and order fulfillment who had been there for five, ten, even fifteen years. The idea freaked me out. Weren't they bored? Didn't they want a new challenge after a while? Some days I felt like if I had to write the words "Boost your bookings" or a scintillating headline like SIX NEW WAYS TO SUPER SALES one more time, I might scream.

But that's what the working world is like. I don't think I know anyone who likes their job, with the exception of Jessie. She complains about the hours she puts in, but she likes the challenge. Even Ethan has said he's sick of practicing law. "You see the same kind of mopes, day after day," he'd say. "Mopes," I'd learned, were the habitual offenders who were either too stupid, too lazy, or too slow to avoid arrest. He'd recently switched to a different division—I think he was doing misdemeanors now—but he still didn't seem thrilled.

I'd noticed that Ethan had lost some weight. His shorts were baggy on his butt and his face looked leaner, more defined. Like many guys, he'd gained weight right after he and Jess got married. In addition to working sixty-hour weeks, she cooked dinner most nights. Insane. I get home by six-thirty or seven every evening and still can't be bothered to prepare real food. It's sandwiches, cereal, popcorn, pizza, or whatever's in the fridge.

Ethan wasn't particularly athletic—he had one of those skinny-guy builds with a little pot belly—but he'd started lifting weights. "Three days on, one day off," he'd said before launching into a discussion of split routines and muscular failure.

Come to think of it, I should get back into a routine, too. Exercise and I have an uneasy relationship. I'll go to the gym—I maintain a membership at Bally's although I sometimes wonder why—for several weeks in a row. Usually I get motivated by seeing one of those ads on TV and think, OK, that's it! I'm really going to get in shape this time.

Then after three or four weeks, I start to lose interest. I can't seem to make that transition from couch potato to fitness buff. I don't look *that* bad, after all. Sure, I could lose ten pounds, and my upper arms tend toward pudge, but so what? I just don't wear sleeveless shirts. Besides, whenever I managed to lose some weight, the first place it went from was my chest, and I didn't want to lose anything from there.

But Ethan definitely looked better. I'd never considered him sexy before—I mean, he's a lawyer, for God's sake—but lately he had seemed different. More relaxed. He was even letting his hair grow—it touched his collar now—while Jessie was more tightly wound than ever.

She called me on Wednesday to remind me about the house-sitting.

"I know! I told you I'd do it."

"I'm just calling to confirm."

"I'll be there! Relax."

Jessie snorted. "Yes, boss. You sound like Ethan. I'll relax when I get on the ship, all right?"

I seriously doubted that, but my opinion wasn't wanted. "Leave a list of what plants need to be watered when." I didn't need to tell my sister this—she'd have a detailed agenda for me to follow. I'd house-sat for them before and made the mistake of overwatering the spider plant, which had turned brown and died by the time they returned from their vacation. I'd hidden it in the garbage, but she'd called me two days later to ask what had happened to it. I think she was angrier about me trying to hide the results than the fact I'd killed it.

This time, though, I'd follow the plant instructions to the letter. I was looking forward to the chance to sit outside in their hot tub, watch the enormous TV, and sample some interesting food. Jessie does leave the fridge stocked with everything from Kalamata olives to brie to three brands of sparkling water, so each night is like dining at Whole Foods.

The first night, I made dinner from an exotic selection of cheese, crusty French bread, grapes, and strawberries, and poured myself a glass of merlot. I put on one of Ethan's Jimmy Vaughn CDs and the music poured out of speakers that had been built into the house. I had to admit having a home like this would be nice, but it was also impossible with the money I made. Unless I married someone who made a ton of money, that is.

It's Jessie's income that pays for this place—Ethan makes around $50,000, I think, but she makes at least four times that. She'll double that when she makes partner—she'd told me so. It's weird, though. She doesn't exactly brag about it. When Jessie talks about money, she's businesslike, matter-of-fact. I don't think she realizes that most people her age aren't worried about sheltering their earnings or trying to decide whether real estate is a smarter investment than the market. The whole paycheck-to-paycheck mentality is foreign to her.

My entire apartment could fit in what Jessie called their great room, and the furniture in this room alone would have paid my rent for a year. I didn't know why she was so into material things. I wasn't like that and neither was Melissa from what I could tell. But she'd always been driven to be at the top of her class, get the best job, and make a lot of money.

While Jessie was scaling the ladder of success, I was just hoping to find a job that I liked. I've never been that motivated by money, but I would like to have a place of my own at some point. My apartment is OK, but I'd been fantasizing about buying a condo, or maybe a little duplex. How I was going to afford this, I hadn't figured out yet.

The phone rang. I thought it might be Jane—I'd told her where I'd be this week.

"Hello?"

"Say, Jess, it's Pete. Ethan around?"

"This is Trina, her sister."

"Sorry. You sound just like her." He paused. "Oh, that's right. They're off on their cruise, aren't they?"

"Uh-huh. They left this morning."

"So you're holding down the fort while they're gone?"

"Pretty much."

"This is Pete Trippiani, Trina. I think we met last summer."

I tried to match a face with his name. If it was the guy I was thinking of, he was big, broad-shouldered, with ruddy skin and a loud laugh. A little too high on the testosterone meter for my taste.

"Oh, yeah. You guys went to high school together, right?"

"Yup and now we're practically neighbors. I've got a place in Naperville, and sometimes I come up and we play some pickup b-ball on Saturdays. Hey, you interested in a game?"

"I don't think so. My eye-hand coordination leaves something to be desired."

"Aw, come on. Half of every sport is mental anyway. Take golf."

God, another golf fanatic! Time to go. I made some not-that-interested noises, hoping he'd get the hint. He did not.

"So, if not sports, what do you do on weekends?"

I hate questions like that. If I tell the truth—clean my apartment, catch up on errands, do laundry, hang out with Jane, read, for God's sake—it makes me sound like the biggest loser of all time. Twenty-somethings are supposed to be out hitting cool nightclubs, shopping at trendy boutiques, and lunching at expensive restaurants. I did none of the above. "Ummm . . . it depends. Sometimes I go shopping, run errands, you know."

"With your boyfriend?"

He lost points for being so obvious, but hey, who cared. "I'm boyfriend-less at the moment, actually."

"Well, how 'bout you and I get together tomorrow? You want to check out some estate sales? I'm furnishing my place and I'm always looking for antiques."

"Um, well, OK. Sure."

"We'll have to get an early start. There's a couple of sales out in Oswego and Morris I want to hit."

"How early?"

"Pick you up at six-thirty?"

"Geez! I thought this was a weekend!"

He laughed. "Got to get there early for good deals. Come on, I'll buy you breakfast, too. You'll have fun."

Pete honked at six twenty-eight. I didn't know what to wear for a day of antiquing. The ubiquitous black pants seemed too dressy, but maybe jeans were too casual. I settled on jeans and a dark blue knit sweater with loafers.

Pete was wearing khaki shorts and a light blue button-down shirt. Now I remembered that he dressed a little preppier than I liked. Not that I like the whole grunge look, either. Now it seems like half the guys I see wear pants so baggy they could fit two guys in there. Or they swing the other way and go for Dockers, which are just as bad.

I was still groggy, but Pete was cheerful. "Hey there! How you doing?"

"I'm good, thanks."

Pete handed me a large Starbucks cup. "Thought you might want a latte. I picked it up at the drive-through on the way here."

I took it gratefully. "Thanks." Wow. This wasn't starting off too bad.

I'd wondered what we'd talk about, but making conversation was surprisingly easy. I'd met Pete even before Jessie and Ethan got married. He and Ethan had known each other in high school and then gone to U of Wisconsin–Whitewater together. Pete had that Wisconsin lack of pretentiousness about him. It was like hanging out with Ethan.

We wound up visiting three different estate sales, one in Oswego, one in Plainfield, and one in a little town called Marseilles. I'd never been to an estate sale before. It was like a garage sale but held inside. Every piece of furniture, every knick-knack, every piece of china and silver and candlesticks and even paperback books were labeled with a price tag.

It looked like all three estates had formerly belonged to little old ladies. Even their jars of hand cream, their knitting needles, half-finished needlework kits, and antique perfume atomizers were up for grabs. It made me depressed, seeing people pick up items, glance over them, and then frown at the price before setting them down.

The first sale didn't offer much, but the last two had lots of furniture, including a dining room set that Pete liked. He showed me the price tag.

"Eight hundred dollars? That seems like a lot."

"Not for what you're getting. This is solid oak." He pointed out the grain and lifted a chair. "Feel how heavy that is? You'd have this for a lifetime."

"Yeah." I looked around the crowded little room. We were the youngest people there, surrounded by women and men in their forties and up. The men favored T-shirts and jeans; the women, patterned blouses and pull-on polyester pants in pastel shades.

"What's wrong?" Pete looked at me.

"I don't know. It seems sad, I guess." I gestured. "This is someone's whole life, you know?"

"Yeah, I thought that the first couple of times I came. But look at it this way. This furniture, even these little gewgaws"—he handed me a mint green marble turtle to admire—"were all part of someone's life. If you find something you like, you save it from becoming garbage. Isn't that what this woman would have wanted?"

"Maybe." I looked around the tiny dining room, which was lined with miniature animals of all shapes and sizes. Someone had spent a lifetime amassing this collection, and now it was being sold off for a dollar apiece. "Still sad, though."

It turned out Pete wasn't positive about the dining room set. The chairs were a little smaller than what he wanted. He sat in one experimentally and dwarfed it. "People were built on a smaller scale then," he explained. "That's the hardest part—finding something that fits me, too."

By this time it was past noon, and I was starving. Driving back east on Route 13, Pete gestured at a tavern alongside the road. EATS AND DRINKS, read the sign.

"What do you think? Want to give it a whirl?"

"Sure." We went in and sat at the bar. A waitress in her forties—thirty pounds overweight, with a chest that spilled out of her V-neck T-shirt, wobbly arms, and whitish-blond permed hair—walked over.

"How you all doing?" We weren't eighty miles from Chicago, but it seemed like a different world. "Get 'choo a beer?"

"Um, actually I'll have a Diet Coke." Pete ordered a Miller, and we both got burgers. "You know what? A beer sounds kind of good," I told the waitress. "Do you have Amstel Light?"

"Miller, Miller Lite, Bud, Bud Light, Old Style." She recited the list, staring at me.

"Miller Lite. Please."

Pete grinned at me. "Amstel Light? What you doing, ordering up a foreign beer in this here establishment?"

"It only sounds foreign. It's domestic, I think. I read the label."

The bartender set our beers in front of us. She didn't bring me a glass or ask if I wanted one. "Oh well." I lifted my bottle and tapped it lightly against Pete's. "I guess I'll never get married."

"Huh?"

"Oh, it's this book one of my roommates in college had. Have you heard of *Thin Thighs in 30 Days*?"

Pete looked blank.

"Oh, that's right. You're a man. Well, it was this stupid book that sold like a million copies. Then the author came out with another one, called *Get Married in 30 Days* or something like that." I took a sip of beer. "Anyway, it was full of things to do and not to do to catch yourself a husband. And the big one was 'Do *not* drink beer.'" I quoted from the book as best I could remember. "'A man drinks beer with his buddies. He does not want his ladyfriend to drink beer. When out, order a glass of wine or a cocktail. But if you must, if you insist on drinking beer, by all means, drink it out of a glass!'" I took another long swallow and set the bottle down. "'Because there's nothing less feminine than a woman sucking beer out of a bottle.'"

"Do women really believe that kind of thing?"

"Oh, come on, Pete. You're what, thirty-one, right? You've got to know by now that we fall for all kinds of stuff. Look at all the pop psych books. *Men Who Hate Women and the Women Who Love Them. Getting the Love You Want. Men Are from Mars, Women Are from Venus*. And who buys them all? Women!"

"You sound awfully familiar with those books, you know."

The bartender came back with our burgers in red plastic

baskets, a heap of steaming, curly French fries by each one. "Man, that smells awesome." Pete set the top of his hamburger bun on his burger and took a bite. Some juice ran down his chin. "Oh man, is that good."

It was delicious. The burger was hot and greasy, and I wiped my mouth with my napkin.

"Sorry." He ate a couple of French fries. "What were you saying?"

"Ummmm." I ate more of my burger. "I've been distracted by this food. This is the best burger I've ever had!"

"You can't go wrong with these little holes in the wall." Pete motioned for two more beers. A guy wearing a heavy black motorcycle jacket came in and sat at the bar a few seats away.

He nodded at Pete. "Shot and a beer." The bartender obviously knew him and brought him his drink order.

"I don't know. I've always liked psychology. Thought about majoring in it in college, and then stuck with journalism. Really, though, being a writer is sort of the same thing. Trying to figure out why people do the things they do, you know?"

"Is that what you do at that company? What is it called? Kitchen Crap?"

I laughed. "The Coddled Cook. No, I don't do anything like that. I come up with new and creative ways to basically say the same exact thing day after day."

"You don't sound too thrilled about it."

"Maybe not. It's a job, you know? With the economy, I feel bad even complaining about it."

"Yeah, I know what you mean. When I started at Peterson's, I was psyched. Thought I'd found the right place. But it's just another paycheck."

"Yeah, you're a sales manager, aren't you?"

"For now. Until something better comes along."

"Don't you think we're promised too much? In college it's

like, 'Decide what you want to do and find the right job and you'll be happy.' No one says that all jobs basically suck."

"Yeah, maybe. That's why you've got to have more in your life than your job. Work is all right, but I'm there for the pay-check. Gotta do something to pay the bills."

I felt depressed again. "What an uplifting attitude."

He lifted his hands. "What? Gotta be a realist. I've got a de-cent job with good benefits, decent money. But I can't say I love going to work. Hey, did you know more people have heart attacks on Monday morning than any other time of the week?"

"Really?"

"Yup. Makes you think, huh?"

"I guess." I pushed my basket away.

"You going to finish those?" He pointed at my fries and I pushed them toward him. "Like I said, I've got other stuff going on. I'm renovating the place I bought, so I've got to make enough money to pay for the repairs. It adds up fast, be-lieve me."

"That's right, you bought a place. I'd like to see it."

"Really?" He looked at his watch. "Speaking of, we should hit the road."

I raised my eyebrows.

"Maxie. Didn't I tell you I have a dog? My neighbor's kid comes over and lets her out for me, but I hate to leave her cooped up all day on a Saturday. I'd like to show you the place but I've got to put some time in on the half-bath today. Another time?"

I agreed. I wouldn't have minded if he'd suggested I stay for the remainder of the day. I liked hanging out with him. I liked how he'd held the door for the pair of old ladies behind us at the estate sale in Marseilles. "Ladies," he'd beckoned. Then, when they'd thanked him, he'd said, "My pleasure." I liked the way he'd nodded at the biker in that unspoken language men

have. I liked the way he'd left a twenty for the bartender when
our bill was fifteen and change.

He dropped me off at Jessie's and didn't get out of the car.
"Say, I had a great time. Thanks for coming along and keeping
me company."

"Are you kidding? It was great. Thanks."

"How 'bout I give you a call?"

"I'd like that." I bounced up the front steps of Jessie's house
and turned and waved as he drove off.

Chapter 15
The Three of Pentacles

Insecurity regarding financial matters.

I have to admit, I daydreamed about Pete quite a bit over the next week. I couldn't get over the fact that I'd known him for years yet had been oblivious to his obvious dating potential. He'd seemed too big, too unformed, too much of a guy's guy. What in the world would we talk about?

The answer appeared to be anything and everything. I'd spent nearly eight hours with him on Saturday and had never experienced one of those awful lulls where you scour your brain for some interesting conversation-starter. I hadn't felt that kind of comfort with any guy—well, except Joey, at least early on before the second or third go-around with the magical girlfriend (Now you see her! Now you don't! Wait, she's back again!), and well, Rick.

Maybe Rick and I simply weren't meant for each other after all. Maybe it was Pete who was my soul mate. Maybe all this had happened to bring the two of us together.

I debated these thoughts. There's still something of the romantic in me, even if around Rachel I act jaded and blasé about everything. With Bobby, though, I could share my excitement. He's been swimming in the dating sea as long as I have, but he's managed to hang on to that same idiotic hopeful streak that I have—the one that lets you sparkle with uplifting maybe-this-is-it-after-all-this-I've-finally-found-him feelings you'd promptly deny to anyone but your closest of friends.

I admit, I gushed a little at work on Monday. "He's . . . I don't know. He's just big, you know?"

"Big how? Big bones? Big muscles? Big all over?" Bobby raised his eyebrows.

"I have no idea. Not yet anyway."

"Still, estate sales?" Bobby frowned. "Are you sure he's not playing for my team?"

"He's straight. I'm sure of it."

"You never know. Bring him in here; I'll use my gaydar on him."

"No thanks. I know you'd try to convert him anyway."

Our conversation turned to our new boss, Petra Taylor. She was a new hire from Tupperware, where she'd played an integral role in helping the company's reps sell more plastic food storage bins in a variety of shapes, sizes, colors, and uses than any of her predecessors. She was tall, and very thin, and had brittle, straight dyed-black hair that looked like it would snap in half if you bent it in your fingers.

"She's been reviewing all the copy and she's pissed. Says it's not nearly the caliber it should be."

"So what's she going to do about it?"

"I don't know. Elaine says she's going to handpick a couple of people to be her right-hand people, and then the rest of the reorg will shake out."

"Two right-hand people? Shouldn't she have one right-hand person and one left-hand?"

"I don't know, Trini. All I know is what I hear." He lowered his voice. "But it might be safer to be one of those people."

I'd thought the same thing. "Keep your friends close, your enemies closer?"

"Too true. Just be aware that Elaine is pushing hard for one of those jobs."

"She's not even a writer! She does PR, for God's sake."

"Just telling you what I hear."

Elaine had said nothing to me about it, but that wasn't surprising. She'd only tell me if it suited her purposes. Come to think of it, though, she had been asking me a lot of questions about how things worked in our department, and of course, I'd been a font of information. I could be brainless sometimes.

I thought I'd done a good job of preparing for my meeting with Petra. I'd reviewed my job description and my actual responsibilities—not exactly the same thing, of course—and made a list of ongoing projects she'd want to know about. I hurried to the bathroom and took a preemptive pee before I walked down the long hall to her corner office and knocked on her door at exactly three twenty-nine that afternoon.

"Come in." Her voice carried no hint of friendliness. She didn't look up from her computer screen. "I'll be with you in a moment."

"Sure. No problem." I perched on a leather chair, setting a notepad and pen on my lap. I looked around her office. She had one large window that took up most of the eastern wall. A dozen or so framed certificates, awards, and other commendations hung about her desk. I saw no personal photos, no knick-knacks, nothing to give a clue about her life outside the office.

She finished whatever she was working on. "All right. It's Trina, right?" She stood and reached over to shake my hand.

"That's right. Nice to officially meet you."

"And you. How long have you been at the Coddled Cook?"

"Two years."

"Mmmm." She looked at a folder in front of her. What, did she have my employee file, too? "And what would you say your most critical task is here as a senior writer?"

"Well, writing, of course." Great. Way to impress her.

"Writing what, specifically?" She smiled a businesslike smile.

"Well, just about everything. Newsletters, special promotions, stories for the website, training materials, you name it." I felt like she was looking for an answer that I wasn't providing.

"And of those pieces, which would you say the most important is to the company as a whole?"

"Well, they're all important..." I was stalling for time. "But if I had to say one, I suppose it would be the newsletters."

"Why is that?" She picked up a fountain pen in her left hand and cocked her head.

"Well, because it's how we keep in touch with our Cook's Helpers. And they're really the heart of the company." I scrambled, trying to produce the mix of words she was looking for. Somehow I found it.

"Exactly. The Cook's Helpers are the backbone of this company. Their success is what creates the company's success. And the job of the marketing and communications department is to provide the information, the inspiration, and the motivation to make that happen."

I nodded. Petra continued, and I tried to pay close attention. She was talking about how communications played a vital role in the health and viability of the company. "I get the sense that this department's value may have been overlooked in the past," said Petra, leaning forward. "But I'm here to change that."

I nodded and tried to get a better read on her body language. Her movements seemed calculated to me. The way she picked up a pen to make a point, the way she steepled her fingers together when she waited for me to answer a question. I couldn't shake a certain uneasiness, though.

"As you know, we're going to be making some changes in this department. Change the reporting structure, maybe shift who reports to whom, that sort of thing. I welcome your thoughts regarding potential changes." Petra stood up. The meeting was over and I hadn't even had a chance to explain what I actually do all day! Crap.

"I'll keep that in mind." I stood, smoothed the front of my pants, and walked back to my cube. My phone rang as soon as I sat down.

"What did she say?" It was Rachel. I'd passed her cube on the way to mine.

"Nothing really." I lowered my voice. "Just what we already know—they're reorganizing the department, yadda yadda yadda."

"Did she say whether anyone's going to be laid off?" Rachel whispered. She had been there for only six months and was one of the newest employees in the department.

"No, Rach, but don't worry. We're too busy to lose anyone. How could we get the newsletters out without you?"

"I hope so."

"Don't worry. Everything will be fine."

We hung up and I wished briefly I was Rachel. I'd like to have someone comforting me instead of doing the comforting.

That's what sucks about being single. You can only get that kind of support from a guy who you've been with for a while, long enough to have a sense of each other's hang-ups and fears. Like the way Rick engaged in an ongoing power struggle with Roger, his boss. Roger routinely hassled Rick about projects that weren't his responsibility and would expect him to come in at the last minute to bring a server back up on-line, even if he wasn't the one on call. I'd told Rick he needed to stand up to his boss if he wanted things to change, but he'd wave off my concerns. Over time, I'd realized that Rick was repeating with his boss much of what he'd done with his father.

Rick spoke about his family only rarely, but when he did, I tried to glean insightful nuggets from anything he said. His dad had been one of those emotionally absent parents, finding it easier to criticize Rick and his brother than praise them. Now he worked for a boss who filled that same role. Rick's dad had played football and thought his sons should too. Of course, Rick had had no interest in offensive lines or scrimmages and had chosen to run cross-country instead. He'd qualified for the state meet, and his dad hadn't even come to watch. He'd mentioned that offhandedly when we were watching a Bears game last fall. I'd waited for more but he hadn't added anything else.

The difference, of course, was that Rick couldn't alter his parentage but he could change his work situation. When I'd mentioned that, though, he'd dismiss it.

"Every boss is like that. Besides, I like the guys I work with." That had frustrated me. Rick was too like me in that respect—we're the kind of people who complain about something but have a hard time taking action to change it. At least I'd realized that about myself. I didn't know if Rick ever would. But that wasn't really my problem anymore, was it?

Chapter 16
The Six of Cups

A new horizon is imminent.

Jessie and Ethan's vacation seemed to have helped her. They got home late that Sunday morning. I was packing my stuff and doing some last-minute cleaning. Not that I had made that much of a mess, but Jessie's fanatical about the house.

"Yoo-hoo! We're ho-ome!" I heard Jessie's voice as I shut off the vacuum cleaner. I leaned over and unplugged it, wrapping the cord back around the unit, and carried it to the hall closet.

Jessie was standing at the kitchen counter, riffling through the mail. Ethan stood behind her and slid his hands around her waist, bending to kiss her neck. He murmured something to her and she playfully twisted away.

"Trina's here!"

"So?" I heard him. "I'm not ready for this vacation to end."

"Oh, hi!" Jessie saw me and shoved Ethan.

"Hey, sis!" I hugged both of them.

"Wow, two bronzed bodies. You guys look great."

And they did. They practically oozed sex, too. I stared at both of them for a second.

"What?"

I shook my head. "Good trip, huh?"

"It was fantastic." Jessie grinned.

"Definitely." Ethan opened the refrigerator and pulled out a bottle of water. "Jess?" he said, offering one to Jessie. "Trina?"

"Thanks, hon." She opened the bottle and raised it to her lips, and Ethan watched her, grinning. She caught him and shook her head.

I'd seen the whole thing—how could I miss it?—but I didn't comment. I had a pang of jealousy. They'd been married almost five years and he still had the hots for her. Why did I find that so amazing?

I made excuses and drove home. I figured I could catch up on the details of the trip later. I was right—she called me at work late the next afternoon.

"Thanks again, Trina." She sighed, a long happy sigh. "That was exactly what I needed."

"Which part? The trip or the sex?"

She burst out laughing. "How'd you know?"

"Are you kidding? I thought you were going to get it on right on the kitchen table. It was all I could do to leave."

She giggled. "Sorry about that. It was great, though. It was so much fun."

"I'm glad. You needed it."

"I know. Would you believe this was the first time in at least two years we have had sex without trying to get pregnant? I think we'd both forgotten that it can just be fun." She lowered her voice. "And I think Ethan had forgotten that I can still give a good blow job."

I almost fell out of my chair. Jessie doesn't talk like that. Sure, we'll talk about sex in general terms, but she's always been more uptight than I am about stuff like that. For details, suggestions, new techniques, I go to Jane, not my sister. But I acted cool.

"Well, that's good, I guess."

"It's one of the keys to a happy marriage. I think I'd forgotten that."

"For your marriage or for anyone's?"

"Oh, come on. For anyone's! Men are easy when it comes to that. You know that."

She had a point. I did. It's just I hated giving oral sex. First you had some guys who wanted to grab your head and shove it all the way down your throat. That was Joey. Then they insisted you swallow. That was Joey again. Ugh. I'd never liked the taste, and once an overly enthusiastic guy (yup, Joey!) had triggered my gag reflex. Puking on someone's penis is not considered sexy, believe me. That happened only once, but I have a miniphobia about it now. Still, I didn't really want to know about Jessie and Ethan's sex life. Once you got married, sex ceased being kinky and fun and became something you did out of obligation, didn't it?

I didn't voice these thoughts to my sister, though. They made me sound way too immature. "Well, actually I have some news. I went out with Pete while you guys were gone."

"Pete? You mean Trippiani? You're kidding! How did that happen?"

"He called when you guys were gone, and I wound up talking to him. And we went antiquing last Saturday." Listen to me. Antiquing. Jess and Martha Stewart had nothing on me.

"Where?"

"Oswego and some little town down by Morris. It was wild. A whole other life, you know? But it was fun. He's nice. Really nice."

She considered. "Yeah, I've always thought that too. He was engaged for a while, but I only met her a couple of times. A real nut bar."

He hadn't mentioned being engaged, but then again we hadn't talked about that much serious stuff. I swallowed. "What happened?"

"I'm not sure. She had a lot of issues. I always thought she was majorly eating disordered or something. They'd come over and she wouldn't ever eat anything. Not even take a plate. Just stand around and sip Diet Coke and look pained."

I started to laugh. "I can tell you're her biggest fan."

"Well, come on. It's a party. Eat something!"

Jess was just like our mother that way. To not eat food that was offered to you was a rejection of your host. Pete seemed way too normal to get hung up on someone like that, much less propose to her. Obviously there were things about him I didn't know.

That made him more interesting to me, actually. I'd always been intrigued by the intricate workings of the male mind. What made a guy fall in love? Women liked guys who were good-looking, funny, sweet, nice to them, right? So why did so many guys pick neurotic or unbalanced or demanding or just plain mean women to fall in love with? And then stay slavishly devoted when there were plenty of good-looking, funny, sweet, nice, normal women out there who would have done their best to make their man happy? It was a mystery I had always wanted to solve. And the fact that there might be more to Pete than met the eye intrigued me. Not enough for me to actually call him, you see, but I decided if he made the effort, I'd go out with him again.

Chapter 17
The Lovers, Inverted

Beware of making the wrong romantic choice.

I couldn't believe I'd done it again. I'd blown the three-date rule and slept with Pete. What was I thinking? Apparently I wasn't. Sure, we used condoms and everything, but I wasn't sure what had come over me. Once Pete kissed me—and he wasn't even that good of a kisser—I thought, what the hell. Why not? Let's get this over with.

For the record, "why not" isn't a good reason to go to bed with someone. You should crave them, desire them, lust after them, want them with every fiber of your being. Or at least most fibers. It shouldn't be an on-the-bubble thing where you could sleep with him, or not sleep with him—no big deal either way. I'd made that mistake a couple of times and had always regretted it. If the chemistry isn't there—at least enough chemistry to get some serious juices flowing—the sex wouldn't be good.

But the before-sex and the after-sex parts with Pete were great. It was the sex part that was lacking, but he didn't seem to pick up on that fact.

He kissed a little too fast, a little too much probing tongue action. I didn't like the way he touched, or should I say manhandled, my breasts. And his idea of intercourse was ramming it into me as hard as he could.

I tried murmuring, "Could you slow down a little, please?" but that worked for only twenty seconds. I was just beginning to find my own rhythm when it was back to the fast-and-hard show. I gave up and faked an orgasm, but I didn't fake a very good one. Once the sex was out of the way, however, it was wonderful. He got up and ordered a pizza, and we ate pizza in bed and watched a movie on HBO. I felt totally comfortable with him.

Pete and I went out a few more times, and the result was the same. I had so much fun with him when we weren't copulating, I started to wonder how important sex was to me. But that was because I hadn't heard from Javier in several weeks. When he called, I came running to him like an obedient dog, and then spent most of the evening whining and sweating and panting for more of his affection. I felt crappy about it afterward driving home.

Why couldn't I just have great sex and not feel guilty? Why couldn't Pete kiss and touch me the way Javier did? Or better yet, why couldn't I just combine the two of them into one funny, sweet, sexy, long-term potential boyfriend?

LTP—that's how Jessie had referred to it when we were in college. "I admit he's hot, but no LTP," she'd said about several old boyfriends. Of course, she'd been right, but not about Rick, who had had "definite LTP," she'd told me after meeting him for the first time.

"How do you know?"

She ticked the reasons off with her fingers. "Steady job. Has had girlfriends before you. Not obsessed with his appearance. Doesn't have huge major ego issues." She'd considered. "And the way he looks at you. He's whooped."

I'd flushed with pleasure. I'd thought so, too, but hearing it from Jessie just made it more real. Or so I'd thought. My problem was that I didn't give enough thought to LTP, letting my hormones make all the big decisions for me. I needed to start thinking with my brain instead.

I decided to stick it out with Pete. He had all the basic ingredients for LTP except the skills in bed. And those can be taught, Jane and I decided. I'd told her of my problem, and after extracting most of the story from me, she'd sat for a moment, considering.

"OK, be more specific. Would you say it's more of a coming-too-fast thing, or more of a clumsy thing, or more of a weird thing, or what?"

"More of a weird thing? Like what?"

"Like he talks dirty or wants to come on your face all the time or only has sex from behind, stuff like that?"

I stared at her. "What? No! Nothing like that." I made a face and shook my head. "No, no, nothing like that. Geez, have you been with guys like that?" Jane was more experienced than I was—come on, she's an actor—but maybe I was just woefully inexperienced when it came to the kink factor.

"I'm speaking from my experience and the experience of others," said Jane. "Guys complain that women have hangups, not liking oral sex or not being comfortable in bed, but you know what? The men are the ones with the outrageous things. Read the ads in *The Reader*. Men who want to be diapered or spanked or masturbate on your feet or whatever. You never see women requesting that kinky stuff."

"I feel out of it, Jane. I thought it was kinky when Javier touched me for an hour without kissing me."

Jane laughed. "I know, sweetie, but I love you anyway. All right, back to the matter at hand. What's the problem? Start with the kissing."

"Too hard, too fast, too wet, too much tongue."

"And the rest of it?"

"It's like he doesn't know what he's doing. Not that I'm some sexual expert, but come on. I feel like he's groping about with no real sense of what he's doing. Like trying to get dressed in the dark, you know? And then once the actual sex starts up, it's welcome to jackhammer land. And shortly thereafter, it's, well, over."

Jane stretched out on her couch. I was sitting on the floor cross-legged, sipping Diet Mountain Dew. Jane had the windows open—it was in the mid-seventies outside, a perfect fall day. I heard a plane overhead.

"First question. Are you attracted?"

"Yeah, sure. Kind of. I don't know," I finally admitted. "He is good-looking, in a big and beefy kind of way. And he's so nice! I'm just starting to feel like there's no spark." I sighed. "I've been faking orgasms with him."

"Oh, sweetie! You should never, ever fake. Why give the guy the satisfaction? If he's lame in bed, he should know it."

I had to admit that faking orgasms wasn't going to help matters. But I'd never been able to talk about sex very easily, at least not with the person I was having it with. "I feel like it's expected, though. What am I supposed to do otherwise?"

"Well, what did you do before you had orgasms?"

I had to think. It had only been with Rick that I'd been able to have orgasms on a fairly consistent basis. But we'd never talked about the mechanics of how or why. We just seemed to like having sex the same way. I'd taken that for granted. I thought back to my pre-Rick days. "Just tried to get into it, I guess."

"Can't you do that now?"

"I'm trying! But it's hard when I'm barely turned on and he's already about to finish." I thought about it. We'd gone to bed only three times, but the idea of doing it again repelled me. I couldn't take much more of this scenario.

"I think you need to take charge."

"Meaning what?"

"*You* take control. You show him what you want him to do."

"I cannot do that, Jane. I'm not like that!"

"Trina, look at us. Who has had more experience? I've slept with twenty-two men. And you?"

I thought. "Six. No, seven."

"And which of us is in a better place to give advice?"

"You are."

"So. Here's what you do. Make it fun. Invite him over to your place. You need to be on your home turf. Set the stage so that you're the boss."

"Sounds reasonable."

"Then, you make him dinner. Get him buzzed. Just enough to be more open to what you're going to do."

"Dinner. Check." I nodded my head.

"Oh, I almost forgot. You're going to wear something sexy but not over the top."

"Like . . ."

She considered. "That red long-sleeved shirt, unbuttoned to the third button. Underneath, black panties, black bra. Oh, make it a thong. Guys love those things."

"Hello! I've never even worn a thong!"

She shook her head. "I forget how sweet and innocent you are. Gotta get the thong. Guys love them."

"OK. Thong, check."

Jane pursed her lips. I drank more Diet Dew and waited. "Then, you make your move. Tease him a little during dinner. Flirt with him. Touch his arm when you're talking. Make a lot of eye contact. Be very interested in everything he's saying. Laugh a lot."

"This is starting to sound more like manic depression than seduction here."

"Hush." She waved her hand. "Then, when the moment is right, stand up, take his hand, and tell him you've got a surprise for him. Lead him into your bedroom and tell him just for tonight he's yours." She squinted her eyes and made her voice sound throaty. "You get to do everything you want to him and he just has to lie back and enjoy it."

"Jane, there is no way I can say something like that. Please."

"Well, figure something out. Because unless you can fix whatever's going on in the sack, you've got no future with him." She reached for her cigarettes. "It's bad enough when the sex *eventually* gets bad. If you start off and it's bad, where is it going to go?"

She had a point but still I resisted. It seemed like I had to exert too much effort for something that should be natural, easy. I wanted it to be like it was with Rick, where we slid easily into sex and just as easily back into real life.

I had a sudden pang. I missed him. I loved Jane, and hanging out with her helped, but it wasn't the same as having your guy in your bed, waking up in the middle of the night to wrap your arms around him and feel him shift and sigh in his sleep. I'd let him become my biggest source of comfort, and now I missed that.

But hey, what about making lemons out of lemonade? Pete did have a lot of what I wanted in a guy. Maybe there was still hope. I was willing to try.

So I did. I invited him over and chose a clingy-but-not-sleazy red sweater and crushed velvet black pants I wore only for dressy occasions. Underneath I wore a black lace bra and matching thong with red trim that Jane had picked out for the occasion.

"It's got to be black and red," she said, holding up a flimsy-looking thong the size of my palm. "Those are the two colors most likely to turn men on."

"Geez, I guess I've been doing my part all along with my pants then, haven't I?"

Jane rolled her eyes. "In lingerie, you goof. White is good, too, but only for guys who like that whole I'm-a-virgin-and-I've-never-done-this-before thing. What we need is lingerie that says, 'I'm in charge and I'm gonna rock your world.'"

The thing is, it worked. When I slipped on the lingerie, I suddenly felt a sexy new edge. The bra did put my usual plain white Warner's numbers to shame, and the thong looked pretty good. It felt creepy when I pulled it on, but Jane was right. It was like wearing a tampon. Once it was in, you forgot it was there. So what if my butt was hanging out of it? I'd just try to make sure I was always facing him.

With my newfound self-assured sexiness, I was actually able to pull off the seduction of the century—or at least the decade. I teased, I giggled, I flirted. I complimented Pete on his quite ordinary L.L. Bean button-down, and leaned closer to him to close my eyes and whisper, "You smell goooood."

He must have thought I was nuts. I caught him watching me several times with an expression between bemused and stumped. After dinner, which he had seconds of, I cleared our plates. I came back and put my hands on the back of his chair.

"Are you ready for dessert?" I tried to make my voice sultry. It sounded like I had a frog in my throat.

"Yeah. What is it?"

I leaned down and kissed the side of his face very gently. "Me," I murmured. Part of me was thrilled I'd even been able to say it out loud without bursting into laughter. Part of me was thinking what a moron I must sound like. And part of me really liked it.

Pete turned his head a little in his chair. "What's gotten into you tonight?" He had an uncertain smile. I could see the hamster in his brain running full-tilt, scrambling to figure out exactly what I was doing.

"What do you mean?" I practically purred. I ran my hands across his shoulders and down his arms. I loved how solid and big he was. Even my hands looked tiny on his forearms.

"Come on," I whispered. "Let me take you into the bedroom. I want to show you something."

"Sounds good to me." He grinned and stood up, and I led him to my bedroom, trying to sway my hips in what I hoped was a feminine, alluring motion.

In the bedroom, I gently pushed him down on the bed. "Your job," I said, starting to unbuckle his pants, "is to relax and let me do all the work."

He didn't say anything, just slung his arms behind his head and watched me.

"Can you do that?" My voice seemed a little thicker.

"I suppose." There was a note of something—teasing? laughter?—in his voice, too. I wasn't sure what.

I pulled off his shoes and then tugged at his socks. It was more difficult than I'd expected, and I almost lost my balance tugging on the second sock.

"Oh, shit!" I rocked back suddenly and then caught myself. Then I realized I was going about the seduction all wrong. I was supposed to have taken my clothes off first, so my hot thong and push-up bra would mesmerize him. Crap. What was I supposed to do, start over?

I stood up and bit my lip. "OK, hold on a second." I started pulling my sweater off over my head and then remembered that I was supposed to be seducing him with my actions. Too late now. I unbuttoned my pants and pulled them off, trying to keep my stomach sucked in as I did so.

"OK!" I said brightly. "Now I'm ready for the next step."

He just smiled. I could swear I saw an erection in his pants, but I didn't want to assume too much.

"And that," I said, straddling him, "is the removal of these pesky articles of clothing."

I carefully unbuttoned his shirt and he obediently leaned forward so I could remove it. Then I undid his belt and pants. I grinned to myself without letting him see. I'd been right about the boner. A very good sign indeed.

I pulled his pants off him but left his underwear on. "Now, I'm going to touch you the way I want to touch you, and you're going to go along with it, all right?"

He nodded. He was breathing a little harder.

"And your job is to just do what I tell you. That's it. Do you understand?" He didn't answer. "Say yes."

"Yes." His voice was choked, low. He raised his eyes to look at me, and even in the half-light, I could see how huge and dark his pupils were. I had him where I wanted him. Now the question became what would I do with him now that I did?

The answer shocked me. I did everything I wanted, and I loved it. I kissed him the way I wanted to be kissed—softly, and lightly at first with a minimum of pressure. He immediately brought out Mr. Tongue but I stopped.

"Uh-uh." I shook my head. "I don't want to kiss like that. I want to kiss like this." I showed him. After a moment, he responded with the same kind of teasing, gentle kisses I'd been giving him. Suddenly my body went into overdrive. I could feel my heart rate increase, my breathing quicken, and my skin flush. Before I'd been mildly turned on, but also had the sense of being outside myself, watching what I was doing. That second self slid away, though, and then it was only me and Pete and my plans in the room . . . and then only me and him.

Chapter 18
The Eight of Wands

Movement in affairs, possible travel.

I squeezed my eyes shut for a moment and then opened them again. Nope. It hadn't helped. The same pathetic copy appeared on my computer screen. Rambling nonsense about the benefits of participating in the company's latest sales incentive. The highest achievers would receive an expense-paid trip to Orlando.

Why would anyone want to go to Orlando, anyway? It wasn't on my list of top ten destinations. I'd received an e-mail note from human resources several days ago telling me that I had three days' worth of vacation that I needed to use in the next month; otherwise it would be lost. At the Coddled Cook, you can amass only up to four weeks of vacation and that's only if you've been here for something like five years. Relative newbies like me got only two weeks' worth. If I didn't use it, I would simply start the third year of my employment without having made full use of one of my benefits.

But where would I go? Not Orlando, that was for sure. I wasn't sure I could afford to go most places anyway. I rewrote a sentence, trying to inject enthusiasm into the story. So far, though, all I'd done was scatter exclamation points throughout, which made the copy read not so much enthused as manic. I could fix it later.

I was still pondering the vacation trip as I drove home. It seemed too early to ask Pete if he wanted to take a trip. All that time alone—I wasn't sure we were ready for it. I liked him, but I also liked the fact that we hadn't slipped into a comfortable groove together. He still called me to ask if I wanted to go out; there was no assumption that we'd see each other on Saturday nights. The drive was getting to be a pain, though. It was at least an hour in either direction, often more, and I didn't see either of us moving at any time in the future.

"Could be geographical incompatibility," I'd commented to Jane.

"For God's sake. First it was the sex. Now this." She rolled her eyes. "It's not him and it's not the drive, sweetie." She pointed her finger. "It's you."

"That's not what I'm saying! I just mean I wish we lived closer, that's all."

"Uh-huh." Jane shifted on the couch to make room for me. I tucked into the end of it and pulled my feet off the ground.

"What?"

She smiled. "Tell me again about the sex."

I pursed my lips. "OK, it was pretty good. Great," I amended. It had been. Under my spell, or my command, or call it what you will, Pete had proved remarkably compliant. He'd let me boss him around, for lack of a better phrase, and I'd found that as long as I could control the pace and demonstrate what I wanted him to do, he was a remarkably fast learner. I'd also discovered that being in charge gave me an erotic thrill that nothing else ever had before, but I wasn't going to share that with Jane, at least not yet.

The trouble was that our relationship had now been split into two separate, distinct parts. There was the sex and there was the nonsex—and never the two shall meet, as the saying goes. We were either joking around, hanging out like siblings or otherwise sexless pals, or we were screwing our brains out in his bedroom. After sex, we immediately reverted back to the jokey, casual relationship I'd enjoyed so much at the beginning. It was reminiscent of the relationship I'd had with Joey, and I knew I didn't want that again. I wanted something . . . I don't know. Meatier, more substantial. But there wasn't anything else there, nothing under the sex to cement it or propel me forward into something like love.

Usually when you start dating someone you really like, you can feel that slippery sensation, that whispered hope that this might lead to something more. The sense that you could love this person, a slight loosening of the strictures around your heart. I didn't believe that you could fall in love in one sudden swoop—it was more a series of little warning bells that chimed along the way. But I wasn't feeling any of those with Pete, and that bothered me.

I'd noticed that absence before, with a few other guys I'd dated casually, but that's all it had been—casual. A few dates here and there, maybe a dinner or two, but no real sense of connection. The older I got, the harder it seemed to be to find someone I really liked. Jane said I was too picky. Maybe I was. But I couldn't shake the belief that if I was meant to be with someone, I'd know almost immediately. I might not believe in love at first sight, but I do believe in attraction.

Jane was a bad influence as well. She swore she could tell within the first two minutes of meeting a man whether there was any romantic possibility there. "Less than a minute if I'm really on," she bragged. "Sometimes twenty seconds."

"Well, it's easy to rule people out," I argued. "If some guy has a nasally laugh or is rude or pretentious or racist or stupid, sure. But what about the hordes of not-so-bads? How do you know about them?"

"You just pay attention, sweetie." Jane sighed. "I worry for you."

"OK, fine. But what about Rick? I felt that with Rick. There was something there with Rick." I lowered my voice. I was at my cubicle during my lunch. Without the usual hum of conversation, fingers tapping at keyboards, and ringing phones, the room was unusually quiet.

That was the trouble with working in a cube environment. You had the illusion of privacy, but you never knew who might be listening. Short of standing on my desk to survey the immediate environment, I was stuck speaking in a whisper about anything important. Technically we weren't even supposed to use the phone for non-work-related calls, but that rule was even more flagrantly ignored than the one about e-mail.

"I don't get it. What's your point?" said Jane, whispering as well.

"My point," I hissed, "is that we're not together anymore. So obviously your theory has flaws."

"Nope. Wrong again. My theory only deals with attraction. It doesn't have anything to do with whether it will work or not. That's a whole separate matter."

"Which can only be answered through the use of tarot cards, correct?"

Jane laughed. "Now you're getting it. You're about due for another reading, aren't you?"

"Yeah, well, I don't know if I'm up for one."

"Trina! The cards were right on before, remember? Don't you want to know what's next?"

"I don't know. I think I'm afraid to."

"Those who do not respect the lessons of the past are doomed to repeat them, you know."

"What?" I propped my feet up on the desk. If Petra or anyone else important saw me, she'd flip, but she was out on some luncheon with a bunch of the other VPs. I figured I was safe. "What are you talking about?"

"Oh, it was some quote. Some Greek guy, I think. Or maybe some American general. Basic idea being that you'll repeat the same lessons over and over in your life until they sink in."

"And the tarot cards?"

"They just give you an idea of what's coming. Foreshadow your future. Let you prepare for it a little better, that's all."

She had a point. Life might be a great adventure and everything, but I was wishing I could be better prepared for whatever was going to be thrown at me. Certainly I might have handled the Rick thing better with some advance notice, a low-key warning of some sort.

So that night, there I was again, shuffling the cards and trying to focus on my question. I tried to concentrate, but my mind was whirling. Should I ask about Pete? Should I ask about Rick? Should I ask about work? Then there was the whole egg-donating thing. Jessie had called me earlier that week and taken only forty seconds to cut straight to the heart of the matter.

"So, Trina, I don't want to push you, but have you thought about what we talked about?"

She was trying to be delicate, I thought. I wasn't going to make it any easier for her. "About what?" I asked.

She sighed. "Egg donation. You know."

"I do. I'm sorry." I paused, then took a deep breath. "Look, honestly the whole idea just kind of freaks me out, actually. I don't know if I'm ready to participate in something like that."

I was expecting her to explode or start pointing out how selfish I was, but she didn't say anything. I stumbled on. "I mean, I know I don't want kids yet, but I don't feel right about it. I just don't think I can do it." The words were out of my mouth before I could stop myself. It's true, that's what I had been thinking—but I hadn't planned on telling Jessie that.

She still said nothing. I waited, stringing together a line of paper clips. "Jess . . ." I ventured.

I thought I heard her sniffle, but her voice sounded controlled. "I understand. It is a lot to ask. Ethan says the same thing. He says we'd be better off with a stranger's eggs. I'm sorry. Thanks for thinking about it, anyway." Her voice sounded flat, monotone. I shut my eyes and leaned my head back against my chair. Her apparent acceptance of the situation was only making me feel worse.

"Jessie, I'm really sorry; I am."

"I know. Don't worry about it." She cleared her throat. "Everything will be fine." I heard papers rustling. "I've got to get going. I've got a motion in thirty minutes. I'll talk to you later, all right?"

She hung up and I put my head in my hands. I was making the right decision, wasn't I? So why did I feel so guilty?

I laid out the tarot cards and Jane looked them over carefully. "Much better!" she said, pleased.

"Gee, thanks."

She caught the sarcastic tone in my voice and glanced up at me. "What? What's the problem?"

"It's not like I had anything to do with the cards, after all."

"You have everything to do with the cards. They pick up on your energy." I didn't say anything. We'd been over this ground before.

According to Jane, things were going to be looking up for me. She saw acknowledgment at work and at least two men competing for my affections. "And you're either going to travel or you're going to receive messages of love," she said, picking up a card with twigs on it.

I snorted. "Well, sure. Travel. Messages of love. Practically the same thing. Maybe some guy will come on to me on the plane."

Jane takes the cards seriously, though, and she waved me off. "Remember this. I'd say this is all going to come to pass in the next few weeks."

I hate it when she's right.

Chapter 19
The Page of Cups

A fair young man; may be the bearer of good news.

So maybe this was what Jane's mystical tarot cards had predicted. As trips go, it certainly wasn't spectacular. One of my friends from high school was getting married, and I'd been invited to the wedding. Terri and her intended, Brian, still lived in Champaign. She worked for the U of I, and I wasn't sure what he did. In fact, I knew nothing about him, which wasn't that surprising since I hadn't spoken to her in, what, three years? We still sent Christmas cards—one of those habits my mom instilled in me that I've found impossible to break—but I could barely consider her a friend anymore. The fact that I'd received the invitation a mere week before the wedding made me assume I'd been on the B list—hell, probably even the C list—of invitees.

But I wouldn't mind visiting my parents, and maybe the wedding would be fun. I called to let them know when I'd arrive.

"Who is it, again?"

"Terri Thompson, Mom. Remember? She was kind of heavy, reddish hair; she had three younger brothers?"

I could hear my mom rattling dishes. "Oh. Oh! That girl who smoked," she said, the disapproval clear in her voice.

I had to laugh. If Mother Teresa had smoked, that would have completely negated her worth as a person according to my mom. Her mother—my gramma—had smoked her entire adult life, and instead of growing used to the scent of cigarette smoke, my mother had detested it, more with each year as far as I could tell. It was kind of a joke with all three of us, and we'd learned to use it to our advantage. Take Missy, who had dated a guy last year who my mother had adored. When Missy had dumped him, my mom had been disappointed.

"He was so polite, helping me with the dishes!" she'd said. "And he was smart, too. And handsome."

Melissa had rolled her eyes at us. Usually our mother didn't think any guy was good enough for her baby. Now that she'd found one who might be, she wasn't going to give up.

"He's weird, Mom. He never wants to do anything with anyone but me," Melissa had said.

My mom waved off any potential stalking or abusive tendencies with her hand. "So, he's attentive. That's good, honey." My mom gestured at Dad, who was glued to some college basketball game. "There are certainly worse things."

"And he's cheap. He thinks fast food is a date." My little sister already had decided that she wanted a guy who would spend money on her. It seemed shallow to me, but what did I know? Maybe I'd been going at things all wrong.

"He's frugal. What's wrong with that?"

Finally, Missy played her ace. "I didn't want to say anything, but he smokes, Mom."

"What?" My mom stopped what she was doing. "I didn't smell smoke on him."

"Because he wanted to make a good impression." I couldn't tell if Missy was lying. Then I caught the slight smirk on her face.

"Oh. Oh. Well, forget him!" My mother waved away Mr. Potential Right with a quick, airy motion. "Plenty of other fish in the sea."

So, I was coming home for "that smoker's" wedding. Driving

down, I started suffering from low-level dread. Before, I'd been thinking the wedding would be fun. Now I wondered what had possessed me. I should have talked Pete into going, but he claimed to be working on his house all weekend. Which, come to think of it, was all right with me. I really didn't want to get into that whole parental introduction thing until I was sure there was some kind of future between us. I knew they'd like him, and then if we broke up, I'd have to explain why.

I took Thursday and Friday off to use up two more vacation days. Thursday I caught up on laundry and did some early Christmas shopping downtown with Jane. I hate to wait until the last minute with stuff like that. Friday afternoon, I drove down to Champaign and spent the evening with my parents. It was the same as always. Dad asked about work; Mom asked about my love life. Dad offered me a glass of wine—out of the box, of course—and I explained about the reorganization and my new boss. He listened carefully.

"You've got to prove that you're valuable," he said, setting his beer down. "Show her that the department can't get along without you."

The truth was, I was as expendable as any other writer in the department. Anyone could learn the style book. And any recent J-school grad could interview Cook's Helpers and write two-hundred-word new product blurbs. I told him so.

"There's your problem, Trina. Your attitude."

That stung. "What does that mean?"

"I've been managing people for thirty years. You know who my best employees are? Hell, anyone can drive a truck or operate a trimmer or spread seed. My best workers—and the ones who work with me for years—are the ones who don't bitch and moan about work. They do a good job, and they're proud of the work they do, and it shows."

I didn't say anything. He continued.

"What, you think we're all just a bunch of grunts out there?"

"No, Dad. I would never say that."

"Work is work, Trina. It doesn't matter whether you're digging ditches or driving a bus or a lawyer like your sister. I don't even care how talented you are. It's your attitude that makes the difference. Believe me."

I thought about what he'd said. Ordinarily he wasn't a big advice giver. That was my mom's role in the family dynamic. But when he offered something, it often made sense, even when you didn't want to admit it.

I suddenly had a flash to ten, eleven years ago. Jessie had been a freshman in college, and she was home for Thanksgiving. I was still in high school and absurdly grateful to have her home again. I'd missed her. Sure, she had that know-it-all thing going a lot of the time, but I was starting to clash with my parents over the usual things—the way I dressed, how late I stayed out, having friends who were smokers—and she'd already dealt with the same issues. Well, some anyway. I couldn't remember her ever staying out past curfew or drinking in high school, both of which I'd been nailed for.

For the first time in her life, Jessie was overwhelmed by the workload. She'd gone from being number one in her high school class to merely one of a cast of thousands. She was tired all the time, she said. It was too hard. As she whined on about how her roommate didn't respect her space, the girls on her floor were loud and obnoxious, her professors were too hard, her classes were too far apart on campus, the curriculum was too difficult, we all listened attentively. I'd thought she'd come home from the University of Chicago with exciting stories of funny professors, cute college guys, and the excitement of being on her own. Instead, it sounded like one big drag.

My dad listened along with the rest of us and then raised his finger. "Hold on. Do you think it's your roommate, and the girls on your floor, and the classes, and the professors, and the schedule, and the curriculum . . ." He ticked them off on his fingers. "Do you think it's all of those things that are the problem, or do you think maybe, just maybe, the problem is *you*?"

Jessie had stared at him and then pressed her lips together.

She'd hung her head. "I'm sorry." She looked at our dad. "It's just hard. Really hard. Harder than I thought it would be."

"You're making it harder," Dad had said, more gently. "You can do it, Jess. You're probably the smartest student there."

She wiped at her eyes. "That's not true, Dad. Everyone there is smart. It's not like high school, where it's easy to stand out."

"Well, that doesn't matter," my mom said firmly. "You can do anything you want to. You know that. We believe in you."

I looked across the table at her and smiled. "Yeah," I said softly. Missy, who was sitting next to her, had been watching Jessie carefully, her fork left forgotten in her hand. Now she leaped up and threw her arms around Jessie's neck.

"Yeah, Jessie. You're the smartest! Don't cry!"

Jessie let Melissa hug her and shook her head. "I wasn't even going to come home," she said, kissing Melissa's cheek. "Thanks, Dad. Mom." She looked at me and Missy. "You guys. I love you."

"Where's Norman Rockwell when you need him?" It threw me to see Jessie so upset, so I made a joke out of it. We all laughed, even Melissa, who then said, "Norman who?"

I thought about what Dad had said as I drove to the wedding at a Lutheran church way over on the east side of Urbana. I got there a few minutes late and sat near the back.

The wedding progressed the same as they usually do, although the bridal party exuded a certain seediness I hadn't seen before. The bridesmaids were wearing teal green sleeveless low-backed dresses that did nothing to conceal the tattoos several sported. One of the groomsmen had a shaved head; another was still wearing a mullet. I saw a few people who looked familiar, but Terri was the only one I recognized. She actually looked radiant, truly happy. She was a little thinner than I remembered, and of course she had the whole bridal beauty thing happening as well.

I made it through the receiving line intact. Terri seemed

genuinely happy to see me. I admit, I felt a twinge of jealousy. It wasn't that I wanted *him*, after all—her husband looked like he was already nearing two hundred and sixty pounds and wouldn't see his fortieth birthday—but some man had loved her enough to want to make that commitment. That was way further than I'd gotten.

At the reception, held at the Round Barn, I consoled myself with the thought that they had a fifty-fifty chance of divorcing. Geez, what was happening to me? Couldn't I just be happy for them? I wished that Pete would have come. At least he'd stand around and mock people's outfits with me. He wasn't as good as Jane—no one is—but he was a lot better than nothing.

"'Scuse me." A short, squatty guy built like a wrestler banged into my left side, sloshing my chardonnay. Thirty minutes into the reception and he was drunk already. I made a face and picked up my glass.

"Hey, dude, take it easy!" A guy a few years younger than me, with blue eyes and sun-bleached hair, grabbed his buddy. "You almost knocked over her drink."

I rolled my eyes and started to walk away. "Don't worry about it."

"Wait. Wait a sec! Aren't you Melissa's sister? Tracy, Trixie, no, Trina, right?"

I looked at him again. "Yes . . ."

"I'm Matt. Matt Jacobsen."

I still was drawing a blank. "And . . ."

"I worked at the pool with Missy. I think my brother Randy was in your class, right?"

Randy Jacobsen. Oh, yeah. A skinny guy with curly hair and glasses who had been on the chess club and had nailed a 31 or something insane on his ACT. I remembered him now.

I smiled and looked at him more closely. "I'm sorry. You guys don't look anything alike."

He picked up his glass and took a sip. "I'm adopted," he said matter-of-factly.

"Oh my God. I'm sorry!" Way to put my foot in my mouth.

"You don't have to be sorry. No big deal. It's just the reason we don't look alike."

"Is Randy adopted, too?" I tried to remember if I'd ever seen his parents.

"Nope, he's their biological child. My family did it backwards. Usually you adopt a kid and then have a bio one. My parents had him but my mom couldn't have any more . . . welcome me."

I didn't remember Matt, but that didn't surprise me. Jessie and I knew most of each other's friends and classmates because we'd been only two years apart. With Missy, though, it was a whole different age group. I forgot that her little friends eventually grew up as well.

"So, why are you here?"

"I work with the groom."

"Doing what, again?"

Matt and I had stepped back from the bar a little ways, which was a smart idea. The reception hall was nearly filled with people. The bridal couple still hadn't arrived, but the DJ was already cranking out wedding standbys like "Celebration." *"Celebrate, good times, come on!"* But no one was dancing yet. More alcohol needed to be served.

"He's the manager at Jiffy Lube. I'm a service tech there."

"Oh." I couldn't think of anything to say. Personally I couldn't imagine a more boring job, but it would be rude to say so.

"It's not that bad, you know." Matt laughed. "Besides, I play bass in a local band. The Ubiquitous Jakes. That's just my day gig until we take off."

I had to smile. He sounded so . . . young. But enthusiastic, too.

He nodded at my glass, and stepped back to get us another drink. "Where are you now? Chicago, right?"

"Uh-huh."

"Man, that rocks. I'd love to get a place up there. This town feels way too small after you get out of school, you know?" He grinned. "Although the college girls make it worthwhile. My band does have quite a following."

It didn't surprise me. He was cute in a scruffy, younger Brad Pitt kind of way. And his eyes were very blue.

"Do they throw their panties on stage or what?"

"If I'm lucky."

He was so cute and so appealing, I couldn't resist. He steered me to a table and we sat down to talk more. "So where do you live? Dogtown? Lincoln Park? What neighborhood?"

"Wrigleyville, about six blocks from the field. For those of us without great jobs or trust funds."

"Yeah, I know how that goes." He sighed. "I'd love to move up there, but the cash, man, the cash just isn't there. If I didn't live with the folks, I'd be screwed."

"How's that working out for you?"

"It's all right. My parents aren't bad. My dad gets on my case, but I do stuff around the house. And my mom likes having me around. I'm kind of a momma's boy, you know."

"I believe it."

He grinned. "What can I say. Women love me."

She laughed. "So I suppose modesty isn't your strong point, huh?"

He ran his hand through his spiky blond hair. "Modesty is overrated. I say if you've got it, flaunt it."

I just laughed. "Well, I guess at least your youth isn't wasted on the young, huh?"

"Huh?" He missed the reference. We were distracted by the DJ.

"Ladies and gentlemen, please welcome . . . at their first public appearance, Mr. and Mrs. Brian Cardoff!" The crowd broke out into applause, and Terri and Brian paraded into the room, followed by their wedding attendants. I was again struck by how different Terri looked in her wedding finery. She looked radiant, truly happy. Sure, her groom was maybe eighty pounds overweight, and was already displaying evidence of his male pattern baldness, but did it matter? Today she was the bride, and he was her groom.

After they'd taken their places at the head table, Matt nodded his head at me. "So, what do you think? The marriage thing is wild, huh? Man, one person for the rest of your life? I couldn't deal."

I didn't want to admit that I'd fantasized about this very idea not too long ago. Matt seemed to think I was so . . . hip. Cool. Sexy. The thought struck me. What was he, twenty? Twenty-one? Why did that seem so young to me?

"What do you think? You're still single, right? Doesn't that seem just way too much for you?" He motioned me to a table. "Let's grab a seat."

"Ummm . . . I don't know. It has its appeal." I thought of my parents, of Jessie and Ethan. "I actually think having a happy marriage is a valid goal." Geez, I sounded like a Presbyterian marriage counselor. So much for being hip and cool.

"I don't know." Matt picked up a roll from the bread basket the waitress had deposited on the table and began chewing on it. "My parents, man, they've been married for almost thirty years and all they do is bitch at each other. Who would voluntarily sign up for that?"

"I suppose," I admitted, "people probably stay married for the wrong reasons. But that doesn't mean the whole institution is flawed."

"Maybe, maybe not." Our conversation was overshadowed by the unmistakable sounds of "YMCA."

"Young man . . . there's no need to feel down . . . I said, young man, 'cuz you're in a new town . . ."

"Dude!" Matt jumped to his feet and grabbed my hand. "Come on, let's rock!"

I followed him onto the dance floor. I hadn't had enough wine to get out on the floor and jack my body, but I let myself be dragged. Within twenty seconds, I forgot about any self-

consciousness. How could I be self-aware when I was dancing—dancing being a relative term—with a boy who had no
qualms about throwing his limbs spasmodically? A line came
back to me—something Jane had said about one of her old
boyfriends.

"He wasn't a good dancer," she had said. "He was a *fun*
dancer."

And Matt was fun. We danced to "Love Shack," "The
Safety Dance," "We Are Family," and even, though I protested,
"The Macarena." We ate the tasteless meal of roast beef, scalloped potatoes, and green beans together, and then critiqued
the wedding party when they joined the bridal couple after the
first dance.

"Dude, check her out." Matt elbowed me. "See that heifer?"
He pointed to one of the bridesmaids, who was doing a rough
interpretation of the twist to "White Wedding." "She's a ho,
man! She did one of my buddies and then tried to play it like
she was knocked up with his kid when she'd been doing someone else all along."

Matt was proving to be a bigger gossip than most of the
women I worked with at the Coddled Cook. I couldn't figure
him out. I wondered if Melissa had ever had a crush on him.

He brought us back drinks. "I can't have any more," I said,
pushing mine away. "I'm driving."

"Come on." He grinned. "I'll drive you home."

"That would present the same problem, wouldn't it?"

He shrugged. "I'm fine. I've been way worse than this and
driven home!"

By this time, people were starting to straggle away from the
reception. I felt a rush of fatigue. This had been fun, but the
smoke and the noise and the alcohol were taking a toll. "Matt,
this has been really fun, but I'm going to get out of here."

"What? Come on! We'll go out. Hit the bars."

"Are you even old enough?"

He snatched his wallet out and showed it to me. "Fake ID."
Oh my God. Now I really did feel old. "That's great, but

I've got to get going. I'm getting up early," I lied, and stood up. "It's been really fun, though. Thanks a lot." And it had. I hadn't felt uncomfortable or out-of-place—I'd been too busy dancing and laughing.

He grabbed my hand. "I wish you didn't have to go. We could hang out awhile longer."

I smiled.

"Man, sometimes the whole living-at-home thing sucks bad," he said, gazing into my eyes. "We've got no place to go." He caressed the top of my hand with his finger.

It took a long moment before I caught on, and I laughed. "Oh, right." I smiled at him in what I hoped was a chaste, maiden-aunty kind of way. "I'm way too old for you."

"I like older women." But he couldn't help grinning. "Hey, it never hurts to ask."

Chapter 20
Three of Pentacles

Skill and mastery in a trade; material increase.

I was sitting at my desk on Tuesday morning when my phone rang. The caller ID revealed that it was Petra. I cleared my throat before I picked up the phone. "Good morning; this is Trina of the Coddled Cook," I sang.

"Good morning, Trina. This is Petra."

"Hello. How are you?"

"Fine, fine." She rushed past the preliminaries. "Can you come to my office at eleven-fifteen A.M. this morning? Or do you have a meeting scheduled?" Her tone made it clear that I was expected to clear my calendar.

"No, no, that's fine. Today is clear."

"Eleven-fifteen then."

"I'll see you then." I hung up, feeling a sudden surge of nausea. What had Bobby said? That this was the week the ax would fall? Tears sprang to my eyes. I was going to be fired for my bad attitude. My dad was right. I picked up the phone to call Jane, and then set it back down. Then I dialed Jessie's number.

"Jessica Elder Gentry's office," I heard Jessie's secretary's voice. Crap. I could never remember her name.

"Hi, is Jessica in, please?"

"Who's calling?"

Give me a break. Surely she knew my voice by now. "It's her sister, Trina."

"One moment."

A long pause, and then Jessie's voice came on the line. "Hi, Trina. How was the wedding?"

Wedding? What wedding? "Fine. It was fun." I lowered my voice. "Jess, I don't know what to do. I think I'm going to get fired."

"Fired? Why? What'd you do?"

I scowled. "I didn't *do* anything. Thanks a lot. It's that reorganization. The VP just told me to report to her later this morning. What do I do?" My voice broke, but I was still whispering.

"All right, hold on. First of all, you don't even know that you're going to get fired. Maybe she wants to see you about something else."

"Doubtful." But I could hope, couldn't I?

"All right, so worst-case scenario. If she does fire you, ask her why you're being terminated. Get specific reasons. Make sure you know what the company's position is going to be."

"Why?" I frowned at the phone.

Jessica sighed. "To see if you have a case. Wrongful termination, discrimination, that kind of thing."

"What, a case against the company?"

"Sure, if they're firing you for an illegal reason."

I didn't say anything. I hadn't thought that far ahead. I was still trying to figure out how I'd find another job . . . I hadn't updated my résumé since I came here. What could I do, anyway? I supposed I could look for another corporate gig, but the job market was really tight.

"Trina. Trina." Jessie's voice brought me back to reality. "Calm down. Maybe it's nothing. And if it is something, you'll be fine. Maybe we need a PR writer or something here."

Ugh. "Working with lawyers all day? No thanks."

"I'm only trying to help. Look, call me after the meeting.

Getting fired isn't the worst thing in the world. I'll help you with your résumé if you want. You'll get another job."

God, why couldn't I be as calm, as practical, as my sister? She really would be a good mom. I felt a tiny twinge of guilt. Then again, she wasn't the one on the chopping block. She could afford to be relaxed.

"OK. You're right." I sighed and shut my eyes briefly. "Thanks."

"No problem. Call me after; let me know how it goes. I've got depositions this afternoon, so leave a message with Paige if I'm out."

Paige. That was her secretary's name.

"OK." I hung up the phone and sat there blankly for a minute. The usual hum of conversation and fingers on keyboards swirled around me. I had a sudden pang. Not that this was the best job in the world, but it wasn't that bad.

I pulled a pad of paper off my bookshelf and started making a list of my accomplishments since I'd arrived at the Coddled Cook. I'd go into this meeting armed and ready, prepared to prove my value to the company. Then again, if the decision was already made, this list made me look pretty pathetic. Like listing all your positive attributes to a guy who's told you that he only wants to be friends. What's the point?

The minutes crept by, but finally the chosen hour arrived. Petra was at her desk, her door partly open. I knocked.

"Come in, Trina. Have a seat."

I sat down on the edge of the seat. I would not cry. No matter what, I wasn't going to break down. I had my pride after all.

"Is something wrong?" Petra turned her head to the side a bit. She was wearing a blood-red blouse, chunky gold earrings, and a gold watch.

"No. No. No, nothing." Great, I sounded like an idiot. Or a maniac. Or a maniacal idiot. Something.

Petra smiled briefly. "Trina, I'm sure you're aware that we're undergoing some major changes to our corporate structure. Combining the marketing and communications divisions, for example. And as part of that, we're shifting some people around to help facilitate the reorganization."

"Uh-huh." I nodded.

"As part of that, we're creating a new position. Manager of U.S. publications. And we think that you'd be a real asset to the company in that position."

I stared at her for a moment. "What? You want to make me a manager?" I thought suddenly of Elaine. She'd been gunning for one of these new positions.

"Yes, with a commensurate increase in pay, of course."

I nodded. "Ummm . . . how commensurate?"

She looked down at an open folder on her desk. "You're making thirty-eight thousand currently, correct?" Without waiting for my response, she continued. "As of next week, your base salary will be forty-three thousand."

Wow. Five thousand dollars more a year might not mean much to my sister, but it was a nice raise for me. "That's great. Thank you. Thanks a lot."

She stood and offered her hand. "Thank you, Trina. We look forward to seeing what you can do for us in this new position."

I walked back to my desk in a daze. Manager of U.S. publications. I was a manager! I'd be managing people. Uh-oh. Who exactly would I be managing? I hadn't thought to ask, but Petra answered my question in the form of an e-mail describing the new hierarchy in our department. Bobby, Rachel, and Elaine—along with two writers who occasionally freelanced for us—would all report to me. The company was also going to hire another writer, apparently to replace me.

I'd been so distracted that I hadn't even realized Petra had copied all of my new underlings, for lack of a better word, until Bobby sidled up to me.

"Why, you little go-getter bitch!" he teased. "So, you're now my boss, huh? How'd you pull that one off?"

I shook my head. "I have no idea."

"Have you heard from Elaine? She is going to freak."

"Huh-uh."

Rachel joined us. "Hey, boss," she said, twisting her long hair in her left hand. "Do you want me to start calling you Ms. Elder now?"

"No, it'll be Fearless Leader," said Bobby. "Or she who must be obeyed."

"Enough. It's no big deal, really."

"And are they compensating you well for this new responsibility?"

"Ummm . . . yeah, I guess." Suddenly I felt uncomfortable. Neither Bobby nor Rachel knew what I made. Talking about salaries was frowned on at the Coddled Cook, which just made them the subject of endless gossip and speculation.

Bobby started rearranging my pushpins. "Let's see, you're getting, what, fifty? More than that?"

"No. No!" I lowered my voice. "Not nearly that much."

Bobby looked surprised and glanced around before he spoke. "But you've got to be making more than me, aren't you?"

"I don't know." Before I could say more, Chrystal, one of the designers, appeared, holding the marked-up copy of next month's newsletter. "Trina, I need your final proofing on this so we can get it out." She handed it to me. "And I hate to say it . . ."

"But you need it right away," I finished for her. She nodded.

Bobby was now aligning the comic strips on my cube so they were perfectly parallel. "Rachel went to lunch. You want to grab something?"

I knew he was dying for the whole story, but I waved the newsletter. "No, I'd better not." Lunch would have to wait. I'd grab a Snickers later. I was on the last page when my phone rang. I glanced at it.

"Hi, Jess."

"So? What happened?" I could hear her chewing something—an apple, it sounded like.

"Well, I didn't get fired."

"Told you!"

"No, actually I got promoted."

"That's great, Trina! See? You were worried for nothing."

"I guess," I admitted.

"So, what's your new job?"

"I'm a manager now. Manager of U.S. publications."

"That's great. More money too?"

"Yeah." I left it at that, and Jessie didn't press.

"OK, then. I'll let you go. I hadn't heard from you, so I wanted to check in before I head out."

"Thanks. I'll talk to you later, OK?"

"Oh, wait. I forgot. How about you and Pete come over Saturday for dinner? Ethan and I thought it'd be fun."

Double-dating with my sister. This would be new. "I've got to check with Pete."

"Come at six-thirty. We'll do drinks and dinner."

"Let me check with him, OK? We're not at the making-plans-without-consulting-each-other place yet."

"OK, OK. But hurry up and let me know by tomorrow."

"You have to know by Tuesday if we're going to be there on Saturday?" I had to laugh. It wasn't even worth getting into. "I know, I know. I'll call you tomorrow."

Chapter 21
The Page of Wands, Inverted

Unpleasant news.

I was in the shower, shaving my legs, when I noticed it. I had one leg propped on the side of the bathtub and was carefully maneuvering the razor up my thigh. My "timber line" was looking rather untamed and I didn't have time to use Nair, so this was a stopgap measure. I felt the bump with my fingers before I saw it.

It felt like a big raised mole. I traced it with my fingers, and then squinted down at my crotch for a better view. It was a whitish lump about the size of a pencil eraser. I poked it. It didn't hurt, but I didn't think I'd had it before. No, I knew I hadn't had it before.

My heart sped up and I felt dizzy. What was this thing? Some weird vaginal cancer? An overgrown skin tag? I gulped and turned the shower off.

Fifteen minutes of examining the lump did nothing but fuel my panic. I sat naked on the toilet with a mirror between my legs, angling for a better view. I had another one, too—a smaller one on the lip of my vagina. What were those things? Why had I not paid more attention to my vagina before? I tried not to cry. I tried to remember everything I'd read about STDs. Wasn't that the whole reason I insisted on condoms?

I spent the rest of the day vacillating between blinding fear and chastising myself for being ridiculous. I'd always been careful. It was nothing. It had to be nothing. It was probably nothing. It was probably herpes. Oh, God, herpes. There's no cure for herpes.

It couldn't be HIV. I couldn't even wrap my mind around that idea. It was simply unreal. Once again, I racked my brain for the symptoms of HIV. I was a child of the eighties, after all. I grew up with safe sex drilled into my head. Rick was the only guy I'd gotten to the stage of not using condoms with. It had seemed like such a commitment then. The act of taking him into my body with nothing between us had been terrifyingly sweet and trusting and powerful.

"Oh, Trina. You feel incredible," he'd whispered as he slid inside me that first time. We'd been dating for four months. We'd both been tested and we were exclusive. Even then, the idea of having sex sans condom seemed like the biggest risk I'd ever taken. But I wanted it. I wanted him.

It did feel incredible. There was no hasty interruption, no crinkle of the package, no artificial latex smell, no cool, slippery condom. Just warm, smooth skin.

He'd risen up on his arms and looked at me. "I love being inside you with nothing between us."

I'd felt a rush of emotion so strong I'd had to blink back tears. It felt like my first time. No, better than my first time. Much better. I knew I loved him that night. Not just because of the way he made me feel but because of what I was willing to do for him.

But I hadn't had unprotected sex with anyone else, I reminded myself. By the time I drove out to Jessie and Ethan's, I'd managed to calm myself a bit. I'd been careful. More than careful. Exceptionally careful. This had to be nothing—just some weird little growths. Maybe an allergic reaction to wearing a thong, for God's sake. Who knew? I'd go in and my doctor would tell me it was nothing, and I would have spent hours freaking out for no reason at all.

I forced myself to put it out of my head, and tried to enjoy Pete and Jess and Ethan. She'd made an incredible spread of tapas, and we had three different kinds of wine on top of it. Ethan and Pete started telling stories on each other, and I had a sudden flash. If I married him, we could do this all the time. It would be kind of cool. Jess caught my eye and grinned at me. I knew she was thinking the same thing.

But I begged off going home with Pete that night. When we finally left, it was close to midnight. "You gonna follow me home?"

"You know . . . I'm really beat. I think I'll just head back to my place."

"You serious?"

I wasn't about to get into the reasons with him. And if I spent the night, he'd want to have sex, and I couldn't bear to do anything with those whatever-they-were down there. I begged off, kissed him good-bye, and drove home. Forget my earlier calm. Now I was convinced it was some sort of vulvar cancer. This is what I get for not taking better care of my vagina! I wondered briefly again if it had something to do with thong underwear. I'd never had anything like this before.

Four days later, I was spread-eagled at my gynecologist's office. I'd called the office first thing Monday morning from my car—there was no way I was going to make that call from my cube.

I explained to the receptionist about the bumps and begged for an appointment right away. When she said she didn't think she could get me in until next week, I started to cry.

"Can you please see if you can fit me in? I'm a little freaked here," I admitted. I felt like an idiot, but it also nabbed me an appointment that Wednesday.

I stared at the Magic Eye print that hung on the ceiling. "What is that, anyway?"

"Supposed to give you something to look at so you won't get bored." I could feel her gloved fingers examining me. There was a scrape, and she put her hand on my knee.

"You can sit up."

I sat up, pulling the crinkly white sheet over my lap. My doctor peeled off her gloves and wrote on my chart.

"I want to test it to be sure, but it looks like HPV. Human papillomavirus."

"H-P-V?"

"That's right. Not HIV. HPV is very common, actually. There's more than a hundred different strains, but some cause raised warts that look like the ones you have. They show up on your genitals—the lips of your vagina, around your anus, places like that. You can get them inside as well."

"Are you sure that's what it is? I'm really careful."

"Have you had unprotected sex recently?"

"No! Condoms are a woman's best friend! I believe that."

"That's good, but unfortunately condoms aren't foolproof. You may have been exposed to the virus regardless. If your partner had the virus around the base of his penis, for example, a condom wouldn't offer much protection."

"I can't believe this. This is so gross." I looked at her and she put her hand on my arm.

"This is very common, especially among young women. Millions of women have HPV, and many don't know it because there can be no symptoms. You're lucky. You only have two warts, and they can be removed easily. I didn't see any inside your vagina. We'll freeze them off, and if you have no recurrences, you're fine." She described the freezing process, but I was hardly listening. I was trying to figure out who I should blame. It had to be Javier or Pete, but I didn't know which one.

I scheduled my wart removal for next week. My OB-GYN had made it sound like the procedure would be no big deal. But I kept picturing that Arnold Schwarzenegger character from *Batman* with his giant freeze ray, and envisioning a giant, pointed device that would be aimed at my vagina, for God's sake. The thought made me queasy. It made me want to never put *anything* into my vagina again.

Just as well. At the moment it looked like there was a slim chance of that happening. My doctor had told me I could have had HPV for years. But she admitted that it was probably a recent exposure, which narrowed it down. Certainly it couldn't be Rick, could it? He was the only person I hadn't used condoms with, after all.

A terrible thought struck me. What if Jill wasn't the only woman Rick had been seeing besides me? What if he'd been sleeping with other people all along? I could have been exposed to every germ, every virus, AIDS, herpes, syphilis, chlamydia, gonorrhea, you name it. My doc had suggested that I be tested for a host of other venereal diseases, and I'd been relieved to come up negative on all counts, but I also realized how fortunate I'd been.

"I'm going to stop having sex," I'd announced to Jane, who had laughed.

"Tell me that again in a few weeks, honey."

"I'm serious." We were out for a walk on Saturday morning despite the fact that it was the middle of November—a gray, blustery day. Jane had decided that her larger-than-average appearance was directly responsible for her recent lack of roles. She'd been dieting and had started walking every day. I couldn't simply lie on her couch and drink wine with her like we had before. Now every talk became a joint exercise session.

"Uh-huh." A heavy woman trudged by us, burdened with two shopping bags. "Tell me," Jane said quietly, nodding her head at the woman. "Am I that fat?"

"No! She's got seventy-five pounds on you, easy."

Jane looked down at her body. "I don't know. I think we're about the same size."

"No. You're much smaller." I took a few steps. "Especially recently."

She grinned. "Thank you, sweetie!" She patted at her stomach. "Eleven pounds. It's hard but it's working!"

"You're a walking skeleton."

"That's what I like to hear." One of those maniacal runners jogged past, wearing only shorts and a long-sleeved T-shirt. He did have a very nice pair of legs, which I commented on.

"Uh-huh. And you're giving up sex."

I checked behind us. "Look, this whole thing scared the crap out of me. I thought I was being so careful! And I could have gotten something. I could have gotten AIDS, you know? And I have no one to blame but myself."

"Did you figure it out?" Jane swung her arms harder. Her face was shiny with sweat.

"What, you mean who gave it to me? Nope. Do you even think he'll admit it?"

"You haven't said anything? What are you waiting for?"

"I don't want to bring it up," I admitted. "But I think it's Javier. At least that's what I'm thinking."

"Why?"

"I don't know. " 'Cause he's obviously been around. I guess he has more opportunities to catch something than Pete."

"What about Rick?"

"I don't know. I think if I'd got it from him, I would have had one of those gnarly warts before now." I shuddered. "I can't wait to get it over with. I want them gone!"

"True. You need to say something, though, Trina. Either— or God, both—of them may have it and not even know. That's not fair to them."

Tuesday, I took a personal day and went in for the appointment. It stung momentarily, but it wasn't as bad as I'd feared. I was now wart-free and determined to stay that way, but I knew Jane was right. I needed to talk to Javier and Pete. I couldn't bring myself to tell Javier in person. Besides, the only times we'd gotten together had been for sexual encounters. I chickened out and called him. I had to explain what it was and suggest that he get checked out.

"It couldn't be me," he said coldly. "I always use rubbers."

"I know, but that's not enough. I guess you can be exposed regardless."

"Well, that's fucking great. So now I've got to go get checked out because you've got some warts?"

"I only had two." Not that that helped. "Don't be mad at me! For all I know, you gave them to me!"

"I was whistle-clean before I met you. Don't try to dump this on me."

I figured that that was the end of Javier. Oh, well, it had been fun, right?

I couldn't tell Pete over the phone, though. Him, I had to do in person. As soon as I got the words out, I knew I'd made a mistake. Not in telling him. In not suspecting him.

His face flushed and he looked away from me.

"What? Pete, what's wrong?" We were sitting on opposite ends of the couch in my living room.

He cleared his throat. "So, you've got them, then? Those warts?"

"Well, yeah. That's why I'm telling you."

He leaned forward and rubbed at the sides of his head. "Aw, shit. Shit. I'm sorry, Trina."

"You're sorry?" I stared at him. "Pete, you knew! You gave me this! How could you do this?"

"Look, we're using condoms, aren't we? I just figured it'd be all right. I haven't had one in ages. I just figured I was OK."

"You figured. Have you even been treated?"

"No." He looked at his hands. "But my old girlfriend had a couple of outbreaks."

"I do not believe this." I stood up. "What if you had AIDS? Or herpes? Would you have even told me?" I folded my arms across my chest. "You know what? I think you should go home. I really don't want to see you right now."

"Trina, if I would have thought I could give this to you, I would have said something." He reached for my arm and I jerked away.

"I'm sure." I walked into the kitchen and kept my back to him. "Just get out. Get out! I don't even want to look at you."

He took me at my word and left.

Chapter 22
The Nine of Cups

Celebration; over-indulgence in food and drink.

Any single woman knows that there's a window of time during which you can be celibate and it doesn't bother you. That time period begins immediately after you have sex, preferably really great sex. During those first few minutes of afterglow, you're awash with pheromones and the momentary illusion that all is right in the universe. The idea of surviving without sex, at least for a while, seems rational, maybe even easy. A no-brainer.

A few days later, the glow has lessened somewhat, but your body has still gotten that dose of attention, and you're good to go for a while. A week, two weeks, maybe longer—still doable. But at about the three-week point, it starts to build up.

I was at the three-week point and it wasn't pretty. I knew from past experience that if I didn't have sex in the next couple of weeks, I'd start snapping at people at work. I'd miss the feeling of being touched, the desire to be kissed and stroked, and the first sweet moment of being penetrated, the building excitement toward orgasm, the oh-my-God-I-can't-believe-how-good-this-feels moment and the necessary release.

I also knew that if I could make it through the next few

weeks, things would get easier. Sure, I'd have some pretty erotic dreams. I might notice how tightly the vending machine kid's pants fit. I might daydream about old boyfriends, or read the personals furiously, looking for Mr. Possible, but of course never even make one call.

Even with all this, though, I knew my horniness levels, for lack of something better to call them, would in fact start to drop. And two months later, sex would seem like a vacation I'd taken a while ago—a lot of fun, but a lot of trouble to actually get there. Sure, traveling was great, but you had to pick a place to go, and make your reservations, and pack, and get a ride out to the airport, and deal with the hassles of security and standing in line, and then getting on the flight, and then sitting on the plane, and arriving and collecting your luggage, and finding the shuttle to take you to the hotel, and then, exhausted and dehydrated and crabby, you were supposed to go out and have fun.

"That's nuts," said Jane after I'd shared this insight with her. "The journey is the destination, right?"

"You're missing the point. What I mean is that sex is the destination, but you have to deal with all this other stuff to get there. Finding the right guy, first dates, trying to figure out how much baggage the guy has and if you even want to deal with it . . ."

"That's the fun part, though," said Jane. "You never know what's going to happen."

"I guess." We were driving to my parents' for Thanksgiving. I'd invited her along, and she'd surprised me by accepting. Her mom lives in Miami, her dad in New York, and she doesn't see either of them very often. Her parents divorced when she was nine, and both of them remarried. Her mom has three little boys with her second husband, and Jane says her mother wants her to come home only to baby-sit.

Jane's dad is some big financial whiz who made money on Wall Street, then started his own consulting company. He re-

married, too, to a woman who's just a few years older than
Jane. "Total princess," Jane had said. "Doesn't have a brain cell
in her head."

"What does she do all day?"

"Spends all her time getting her nails done and shopping
and wrapping her thighs to prevent cellulite. I can't believe my
dad would marry someone like that. I mean, my mom is a
flake, too, but at least she's got a brain. Sheila is just a vacant,
empty bag of hair."

"Ouch."

Jane shook her head. "It makes me wonder about my dad. I
mean, even when I was little, I knew my parents weren't happy.
They were always yelling at each other. I thought once I grew
up, my dad and I would see more eye to eye on stuff. But I just
don't get him. He's all about money and having the right kind
of wife to go with it now that he has it."

I didn't say much when Jane talked about her family. Just
thought how lucky I was to have a relatively normal one.

"Anyway, it will do me good to hang with a nondysfunc-
tional family," Jane said cheerily. "Give me hope for the future." She pointed at an Amoco sign looming over the next
exit. "Hey, pull over, will ya? I need a pee break and a smoke."

"Don't forget, you cannot smoke in my parents' house. My
mom will have a cow."

"No problem." We stopped and gassed up the car. I went
inside for a bottle of water and a bag of pretzels. Jane was leaning against the car, smoking, when I came out. Her hair was a
freshly minted blond, and she had on bright pink lipstick. She
was wearing a mint green bowler's shirt with FRED tattooed
over the left breast, and black-and-red-plaid leggings. People
stared at her as they got out of their trucks and walked into the
food mart to buy cigarettes and lottery tickets. I smiled to myself. She'd never be mistaken for a local.

"How much longer?" Jane didn't drive and was suspicious
of car travel. She preferred train and el trips, where every stop
and destination were announced in advance.

"Twenty minutes 'til Bloomington, and then an hour after that." It was our turn to pick up little sis. Jessie and Ethan were driving down first thing in the morning, and Melissa had to work at the college library until 3:00 P.M. today.

We found her dorm and picked her up along with two bulging backpacks, and got back on the road. Missy was excited to meet Jane. She'd heard me talk about her before.

"So, what are you in now?" she asked. "Have you got any movie roles yet?"

"Movies? Please." Jane twisted in the backseat to look at her. "I'm in the theater, my dear." She pronounced it "thee-ah-ter," and Melissa and I both laughed.

"What's the difference?"

"What's the difference? Theater is real. Movies are not." Jane bit her lip and thought for a second. I could tell she was itching for a cigarette, but she knew not to ask me. I hated her smoking in the car, and I wasn't too thrilled about her smoking in my apartment either. Which was why we usually hung out at her place.

I shook my head.

"All right, all right." She sighed and then turned back to Melissa. "You see a movie and every shot, every camera angle, every line of dialogue, the background music, the lighting, everything is prearranged. They might do twenty, thirty takes, even more, to get just the right one. They coat the actors with makeup. They use body doubles. They add emotional music. They use camera angles to manipulate you. It's all make-believe." She paused. "But theater is real. It's live. It's right there in front of you. You don't have the luxury of a camera angle or a close-up to express emotion. It's all your voice and your expression and your body."

"I guess I never thought about it like that," said Melissa. "But don't you get nervous up there?"

"Sure!" Jane reached into the bag of pretzels and handed us each one. "But you can feel the audience. It's almost sexual, it's that powerful."

"Jane!"

She looked at me. "What?"

"Well, that is my baby sister."

"Oh, please. You're just saying that because you're the middle child," said Melissa. "You feel like you don't get the attention of the oldest child or the love of the youngest."

"What does that mean?" I asked. A few psych classes and now she was a big expert.

"It just means that you're only comfortable when people are playing their assigned roles. Jessie is the superachieving oldest child. I'm the baby, never supposed to grow up. And you're the middle child."

"And what does the middle child do?"

Melissa reached for another pretzel. "You're the mediator. You're the one who fixes things, smooths things over, makes things right."

"Sound like psychobabble to me."

We arrived at my parents'. The garage was open, and my dad was sweeping it out with a long-handled broom. He had the little black-and-white TV set out there to keep him company.

"Two of my girls!" He dusted off his hands, and hugged us both. "And Jane, right! An actress in our home, for Thanksgiving." He bowed. "We are honored."

I rolled my eyes and looked at Melissa, but she just grinned.

"Thank you, Mr. Elder." Jane had on her sweetest personality. "It's nice of you to share your holiday with me."

"It's Marty, hon. Come on in. Can I getcha something to drink?"

We went inside. My mother was on the phone, but she waved at us. Melissa pushed past me, dragging two of her bags into her bedroom.

My mom hung up and smiled at both of us. "Happy Thanksgiving!" She hugged me, then Jane. I saw her wrinkle her nose a moment, and I thought of saying something, but then figured Jane was on her own. She'd handle it.

Mom put us to work, chopping vegetables for homemade

stuffing. She'd start cooking tomorrow morning at seven to get the turkey into the oven and we'd sit down to dinner at two. Thanksgiving routine never varied.

After dinner, Jane nudged me. "So, what's the plan for tonight?"

"We'll go out. Probably hit the Hole." For some reason, the Watering Hole, a bar in downtown Urbana, had become the gathering place of choice for returning townies.

"Hey, I want to go!"

"You're only twenty, remember?"

"They won't card over the holiday. Besides, a couple of the guys I know bartend there." She twitched her hips. "It'll be no problem."

We headed out a little after eight. Jane had changed into a low-cut black sweater and straight black skirt, black hose, and black knee-high boots. I was wearing black hip-huggers and a tight green turtleneck that gave me the illusion of much bigger boobs. (The push-up bra didn't hurt.) My sister flounced out in low-slung hip-huggers that barely covered her butt crack and a green spaghetti strap top that left six inches between her breasts and crotch bare.

"Hello? Isn't it winter?"

"Everybody dresses like this at school." She preened in her mirror. "You're just jealous." She wiggled her butt at me and I laughed.

"Yeah, you're right. I wish I were twenty again."

"Me too!" Jane walked in, running her fingers through her hair. "Great outfit. You've got the body for it, kid."

Melissa grinned. "You look pretty hot yourself."

"Do tell." Jane vamped in the mirror. "OK, ladies, let's go break some hearts!"

The Hole looked the same as ever—a long room with a bar on one side, booths on the other, some pool tables and dartboards in the back near the bathrooms. I grabbed the last pair of barstools together. "Here." I motioned at Jane and Melissa. "You guys sit. I'll stand."

"No, that's OK," said Melissa, shrugging off her coat. "I'll stand." She flipped her hair, surveying the room. Every guy within spitting distance eyed her, some more obvious about it than others.

"Hey!" She waved at a pair of guys who could barely be legal and scampered off without a word.

"Suddenly, I feel very old."

"Oh, come on." Jane waved at the bartender and ordered a cranberry and vodka for herself, a glass of chardonnay for me. "She's fun. All that youthful enthusiasm."

"Now I really feel old."

Jane lit a cigarette and looked around. "So this is the central Illinois scene. Boy, people like to eat around here."

"What do you mean?"

"They just seem to be built on a bigger scale than the city." She brightened. "Hey! That makes me appear even thinner. I could be their queen."

"Please. You know you look great."

"Thank you, dear." She tossed her head. "Not much competition in here, anyway."

I never failed to be amazed at Jane's unflappable confidence. The fact she had twenty, maybe thirty, pounds on most of the women in here didn't faze her at all. I remembered one night when some drunk Cubs fan had bumped into her at Bar Louie, spilling her drink.

"Hey, watch it!"

He had swayed backward, his face red, his eyes at half-mast. "Was your fat ass bumped me, bitch."

"I don't think so. I know exactly how fat my ass is," Jane said. "And you'd have to pay me to bump you or, God forbid, touch any part of you."

He had stood there for a moment, then wandered off, no doubt in search of another drink.

"Dumb prick." Jane wiped at her hand. "Why do guys think fat is such an insult, anyway? Like I don't know I'm fat. What do they expect? Do they think I'm going to fall apart and say, 'Oh my God, I'm fat!' Give me a break." She had grinned at me. "A fat girl can do anything a skinny girl can. Usually better."

I didn't see anyone I recognized in the crowd. Everyone looked very young, though. This looked like a college crowd, not a townie crowd. Jane nodded at me.

"You know him? He keeps looking over here."

I followed her gaze. It was Matt. "Oh my God, it's Matt Jacobsen. You know, the one I ran into at that wedding down here."

"That's him? Oh, Trina, he is adorable. Get him to come over. Never mind. He's coming."

He pushed through a knot of girls, oblivious to their appreciative stares. "Trina! I thought it was you." He smiled at Jane. "What's up? Couldn't get enough of C-U?"

"Home for Thanksgiving. The parental thing, you know how it goes." I tried to match his breezy delivery. "This is Jane. She's a friend of mine from Chicago."

"Hey, Jane." He nodded but didn't reach to shake her hand. "You guys up for some pool?"

I looked at Jane, who shrugged. "Sure, why not?"

We followed his slender back through the crowd. Two other guys were already racking the balls, and Matt indicated us with a nod of his head. "That's Trina, and Jane."

"Hey." Skinny, with one of those minuscule strips of hair attached to his chin.

"Yo." A head nod from the other, who had kinky dark hair to his shoulders. Soul Patch—also known as Allen—said he'd sit out, and Jane and I played Matt and his friend, who was introduced as Brian but referred to only as "BD" or "Dude." They beat us the first game, but the second was closer. I made a difficult bank shot on the three and Dude whistled.

"Nice."

"Thanks." I got that familiar flush of pleasure. Don't get

me wrong—I don't mind losing when I play pool. I do mind playing poorly. And I still knew of no better way to impress a guy than by nailing a difficult shot with a lot of green.

We barely lost the second game—Jane scratched on the eight ball—but by the third I was in the zone. Playing pool requires just the right amount of alcohol. Too little and your nerves might cause you to miss a shot. Too much and your coordination starts to go. But in between the two, you can play with absolute confidence. I was in the zone, and I could feel it. I sank the twelve on the break, then kicked in the ten, leaving a perfect setup for the fourteen.

Two more balls, and I barely missed a long shot on the fifteen. "Shit."

"Great run."

BD nodded. "Dude can play."

Matt squeezed by me, so close I could feel the heat coming off his body. "Smart, hot, and a pool shark. What a combo."

Jane looked at me, but I ignored her "what's up" expression.

"I've got talents you haven't even imagined," I teased Matt.

"Oh, baby, tell me more."

"Well . . ." I bit my lip and looked at him, my head lowered. "I write really, really provoking articles about Cook's Helpers."

"Whassa Cook's Helper?" BD again.

"You know, cooking tools. Pots, pans, spatulas, that kind of thing. Pretty much anything you'd find in your kitchen." I could hear my voice give its practiced response. So much for flirting with the babe. And I mean babe in both senses.

"Oh, OK." BD nodded and Matt laughed.

"That doesn't mean anything to him. Dude has nothing in his kitchen except pizza boxes and maybe some roaches."

Jane interrupted this fascinating discussion. "Trina, I'm going to go buy some smokes." BD offered her one of his, but she shook her head. "Salems? What's a kid like you doing smoking Salems?"

"I know, I know. My gramma smoked 'em and I got hooked on the menthol sneaking them out of her purse."

"Stealing smokes from your grandmother?" Jane raised her eyebrows. "How classy." She gave me another significant look. I had a feeling she'd take longer than five minutes to return.

Dude wandered off, and Matt and I started another game of eight ball, and I leaned over to make a difficult shot on the seven ball. I flipped the cue around so it was behind my back and balanced against the side of the table, but my arms wobbled and I was afraid I'd miss. "Shit, there's no way."

"No, you got it. Here, go like this." He slid over to me and positioned himself in front of me to straighten the cue. Our genitals were perfectly aligned, and he was only inches from me. He caught me looking at him and grinned. I could see those appealing little crooked teeth on the bottom. He leaned toward me and I couldn't help it. We kissed.

"So that's why you were trying to suck his tongue down your throat? Because he had cute teeth?" Melissa shook her head. "He's a total stoner, Trina. He's smoked enough pot to kill all his brain cells, and then some."

"I'm not going to marry the guy." We were driving home. Or rather Melissa was driving and Jane and I were giggling in the backseat, treating her as our personal chauffeur.

"Good thing *one* of us can drive us home."

"Hey, you've got the Jewish mother guilt thing down cold! And you're not even Jewish!" snorted Jane.

"Or a mother!" For some reason, this struck us both as hilarious.

"Still, though, Trina. You were making out with him in front of half the bar."

I sat up straighter, shoving Jane, who had been leaning against me tipsily. "I. was. Not. Making out. With him."

"You were! God, how does that make me look? You're like practically a decade older than him!"

"Lighten up, babe." Jane reached around and messed with her hair.

"It's just so embarrassing. You're my sister, you know." She turned around to glare at me. "My *older* sister." The car swerved.

"Hey! Eyes on the road, girl." Jane pointed at her. "You're the Designated Driver, remember?"

"Yes, I know." She sighed. "This is great. Now I've got *two* drunks for sisters."

The remark would have caught my attention if I hadn't been rummaging around for my Cherry Chapstick. "Found it!" I smeared it on my lips and passed it to Jane.

"Yum, cherry, yum." It wasn't until the next afternoon that I remembered what she had said. Jess and Ethan had shown up about noon. He produced some cigars—those awful Swisher Sweets—and he and my dad went out to the garage to smoke them. Which left me, Jane, my mom, and both my sisters.

Missy had been helping Mom in the kitchen all morning while Jane and I wandered in and out, picking at bits of vegetables. I had a hangover but I acted like nothing was wrong. Jane ducked out to join the guys. I was impressed. It was her first smoke of the day, and I knew she'd been dying for one.

"What, is she going to join them for a cigar?" said Jess, a little nastily.

Melissa made a puffing motion with her hand. "Oh, that's right, a smoker." Jess poured herself another glass of white zinfandel and reached for my cup. "I can't believe you let her sleep here, Mom! Shouldn't she be relegated to outside, or at least the garage?"

"Jane's Trina's friend and of course she's welcome."

"I'm just surprised you haven't started in with your usual litany. Lung cancer. Heart disease. Yellow teeth. Stinky hair. Emphysema." Jessie rolled her eyes. "God, you'd think smoking is the biggest sin in the world."

"What's your problem?" Melissa glared at her. "You're an even bigger bitch than usual today."

"Missy!" My mother shook her wooden spoon at her. "Language!"

"Well, it's true," Melissa mumbled, but she bent her head

and didn't say anything else. My mom brushed off her hands on her red apron and came over to give Jessie a squeeze.

"How are you doing, sweetheart? Anything new?"

I could see irritation cross Jessie's face. "I'm fine, Mom. And of course there's nothing new. Or I wouldn't be drinking, would I?"

"That's not what I meant," my mom hastily added. "I meant other things. How's your job? The house? Ethan?"

"Job is the same. House is the same. Ethan is, well, ask him yourself." She stood up and walked to the living room, plopped herself on Dad's recliner, and began channel surfing.

The three of us looked at each other. "She seems so unhappy," said my mom.

"And she's a bitch," Melissa added helpfully.

"That's enough!" My mom's voice was sharp, and Missy and I were both surprised.

"Sorry." Her voice was sheepish.

"I know she's difficult, but we can't understand what she's going through or how painful it is for her. It was so easy for me, with you girls. I just wish there was something I could do."

"I think the best thing is to leave her alone, Mom." I reached over for a cookie.

"Well, I try to talk to her, but she's so short with me it never gets anywhere. I just wish I could help."

I felt an uncomfortable twinge but I didn't say anything. Should I offer to help? Was this what this was about?

Jane rejoined us. I could smell smoke on her hair and clothes.

"You have a very nice husband, Mrs. Elder. How long have you been married?"

"You can call me Bonnie, Jane. Thirty-two years."

"Wow. That's great. What's your secret?" Jane helped herself to a cookie.

"I don't know that I have one. Marriage is hard work. You have to decide that you want to stay married to each other and make it work."

"That must be my problem. I have yet to meet someone I'd want to marry."

"Because you haven't met the right person yet, honey." I knew my mom must smell the smoke on Jane, but she didn't say anything. I thought again how lucky I was.

We all piled into the dining room for dinner. My mom had made the usual—turkey with stuffing, mashed potatoes and gravy, corn, green beans, rolls, and cranberry sauce. Missy started to reach for a roll, and my mom lightly slapped her hand.

"We're going to say grace first, please."

Missy complained under her breath, but lowered her head.

"Lord, on this day we thank you for the food before us, for our family, and for our blessings. Help make us truly grateful for these gifts. Amen."

A chorus of amens followed, and Dad reached for the carving knife. "All right, who wants dark meat, and who wants light?" He carved and loaded up the plates with the turkey while we took turns passing the side dishes around.

"This looks amazing, Mrs. Elder—I mean, Bonnie," said Jane, who was sitting next to me. She took a bite of mashed potatoes. "I've never had a real Thanksgiving before."

"What? What do you mean?" my mom asked.

"My family was never into traditional holiday-type stuff," said Jane. "Plus my dad traveled a lot, so it was usually me and my mom. We'd get Chinese food or something."

"Chinese on Thanksgiving?" Missy took an enormous bite of turkey. "That's like sacrilege or something, isn't it, Mom?"

Mom waved her hand at Missy. "Every family does things differently, honey."

Missy shrugged. "I don't know. I think it sounds cool." She handed her plate back to my dad, who piled more breast meat on it.

"You know, there are other people who might want some of that, too," said Jessie pointedly.

"So what? It's like a thirty-pound turkey," said Missy. "Lighten up."

"I'm just saying that it might be nice if you waited to see if everyone else wanted seconds before you eat half the bird."

"Oh, you're right. You were planning on polishing it off, right?"

My dad had tuned out, I could tell. He was shoveling food into his mouth, making happy noises of appreciation. Ethan did the same. I wondered if it was really true that the way to a man's heart was through his stomach. It hadn't worked with Rick, but then again, I hadn't done a lot of cooking for him, either.

Jessie glared at Melissa. "You always get everything you want, don't you?"

"Oh, give me a break. You need to take a chill pill. For real."

My mom shook her head. "That's enough, girls."

But Missy and Jessie continued to glare at each other. I didn't get it. When she was little, Melissa had idolized Jess. Sure, she followed both of us around and drove us crazy, but it was Jessie who she hung on the most. About the time she hit puberty, though, she'd switched allegiances. Part of it was Jessie leaving for school—Missy and I spent more time together after Jess went to college—and part of it was they were so different. Jessie was a control freak, we all knew that, and Missy was . . . I don't want to use the word *slacker*, but it was pretty much understood in our family that she wasn't seething with ambition. And me? Once again, I fell somewhere in the middle.

"Hello! It's a turkey, guys," I said. "A turkey."

"I'm full anyway," said Jess, pushing her plate away. She poured herself more wine. "It was good, Mom," she added, glancing at my mother.

My mom looked at her with concern. "Sure you don't want any more?"

"No, I'm done."

Ethan offered his empty plate to my dad. "I could handle some more dark meat. And Bonnie, will you pass the mashed potatoes?"

My mom handed him the potatoes. "Oh, you know who I saw at the store the other day? Jenny Dorning. Remember her? She was in your class, wasn't she, Trina?"

"No, Mom. She was a year older. Between me and Jess, remember?"

"Oh, that's right. Well, I ran into her at Kohl's. She was shopping with her little girls—she has the cutest twins! She asked about you girls."

"Oh yeah?" My mom seemed to keep tabs on every single classmate any of the three of us had ever encountered in school. It didn't matter that we didn't particularly care about any of these people, I'd learned.

"Were you friends with her, Jess?"

"No, Mom. I just knew who she was, that's all." Jessie leaned back in her chair. "So, she's got twins, huh? That's super."

"Oh, honey, I didn't even think. I'm sorry."

"Whatever."

Then my dad spoke up. He reached over and squeezed Jessie's hand. "It'll happen for you. Hang in there." No one else said anything. Ethan looked at my dad, and then at his wife. Jess stared at our dad for a moment, and then slowly brought her other hand up to her face and began to cry. My dad kept his grip on her hand. "Everyone at this table is rooting for you. And Ethan," he said, nodding at his son-in-law. "Don't forget that."

"I know." Her voice was small. "Thanks, Dad." Jess looked up, then looked at the rest of us. "Sorry. Sorry, Mom."

"Oh, honey, you don't have to apologize. Your dad is right. Don't forget that we all love you."

"Yeah. Even though . . ." started Missy.

"Melissa Susan," my mom said, and there was no mistaking her tone.

Missy bit her lip and grinned. "Never mind!"

Jane had watched this whole scene without comment, and I couldn't help wondering what she thought. The last year or so, Jessie's unhappiness had colored every holiday, every get-together. We all walked on eggshells around her—well, except Missy—and to be perfectly honest, I was a little tired of it. But I wasn't about to admit that fact to anyone in my family since it made me sound like the most selfish person on the planet. Jane's a big fan of being open about your emotions, even (or especially) the ugly ones, but I wasn't going to share this with her, either. Sometimes you need to believe you're a better person than you know deep down you are.

Driving back early Friday morning, Jane was quiet. "Thanks again for inviting me home."

"You thanked me like ten million times already! Besides, my parents loved you. And it's nice to have a nonfamily bumper there."

"What about Ethan?"

I snorted. "Please. He hardly even participates. My dad's just relieved to have another male in the house to make things a little more even."

"How long have they been having problems?"

"Who?" I looked at her and she raised her eyebrows.

"Jess and Ethan. Geez, Trina, didn't you notice? They hardly spoke to each other all day."

She was right, actually. Now that I thought about it, I couldn't think of them even looking at each other. Jessie had consumed at least four glasses of wine at dinner, but instead of lashing out like at Easter, she'd simply gotten quiet, and then gone to take a nap.

"Pass out is more like it." This from Melissa. But Ethan didn't even go to check on her. Several hours later, she joined us watching the football game.

"You want to go?"

"After the game." Ethan was drinking a Coke. "Aw, crap, look at that!" he said to my dad.

"Bad pass," my dad agreed.

Jessie stood there for a moment. "I thought you wanted to leave by six," she said.

He waved her off without looking at her. "After the game."

Jane's voice brought me back. "So? Is it the fertility stuff?"

"Probably." I thought for a minute. "They seemed so happy when they got back from their cruise."

"Yeah," said Jane. "But vacation isn't real life."

"I guess." We drove in silence for a few minutes, then Jane spoke again.

"So what was that whole thing with you and that kid, anyway?"

"What, Matt?" I laughed. "Nothing. Just having fun." I glanced at her. "Why? God, you're as bad as Melissa. Did I embarrass you, too?"

"Hardly." She looked at me and then out the window. "You can do whatever you want, sweetie. I wonder if you're trying a little too hard, that's all."

"What does that mean?" My tone was defensive. "I was just having fun! It's not like I was going to have sex with the guy or anything." I gripped the steering wheel tighter. "You're the one who always says I need to take more chances, after all."

"Sure, but that doesn't mean making a fool of yourself." She saw my face. "I'm not criticizing you, sweetie. Maybe you need some more time to forget you-know-who instead of jumping into these other relationships."

"Hmm. Whatever." I changed the subject, and Jane let it drop.

Chapter 23
The Ten of Cups, Inverted

Betrayal; chance of a family quarrel.

I decided to skip the post-Thanksgiving shopping nightmare that weekend. This year, we'd agreed to do minimal gifts for each other, and I'd already found presents for my parents, Missy, and Jess. I just needed to get something for Ethan and Jane. I went to Borders on Saturday and stocked up on some new books including the latest Sue Grafton. I spent the night curled up on the couch, reading most of *O Is for Outlaw*, and then finished it the next morning. I was antsy, so I decided to clean the apartment.

I reached under the sink to get the Comet and a roach scurried out.

"Argh!" I hate those little shits. No matter how many traps I put out, they never gave up. I'd heard that for every roach you see, there are a hundred more. The thought made me queasy.

I tossed the Comet back under the sink. Screw cleaning. I sat back on my heels and looked at my kitchen. The linoleum was worn to a faded gold, and gray in places despite my efforts to scrub it. The stove was ancient, the cabinets some sort of cheap wood pulp prefab design that hadn't been hung quite plumb. The doors hung slightly open no matter how many times I took a screwdriver to the hinges.

I'd given up my bigger place in LaGrange for this ground-floor apartment. The bedroom and living room were on opposite sides of the hallway right off the front door; the narrow hall led to a small dining room, the kitchen, and a bathroom with the charm of a claw-foot tub and the annoyance of weak water pressure. I'd done what I could—cute curtains, blue-and-white-striped towels, and a matching shower curtain—but the age and wear of the building depressed me.

Add to that the fact that this building seemed constantly in flux. I saw people I didn't recognize every month or so, and lately I'd been coming home to the unmistakable aroma of lingering pot. I didn't care if people got high, but I really didn't want to have to deal with a drug bust ten feet from my door. Or a gang shooting.

OK, calm down, there's not going to be a gang shooting. I stood up and walked into the living room, noticing the peeling paint on the radiator and the scuffed wood trim. Why had I chosen this apartment? I'd spent almost two years marking time here and I didn't even like the place. But it had been affordable, and I'd had this idea that living in the city would be so much more fun. I'd met Jane—she'd been living upstairs—when I was carrying in boxes, and that had made it worthwhile. And then I'd met Rick, and he'd been only a short drive away. In the back of my mind, I'd thought that we might move in together, so what was the point of looking for a better place? Now I had this dreaded commute and half the time I couldn't find a place to park on my block, and for what?

I needed to get a place of my own. I needed to buy a house. Oh, wait. House meant a yard to take care of. Not quite as appealing. A condo, then. A condo with a built-in lawn service. That would work. A place that was finally my own.

Even a few cursory looks through the *Trib*'s real estate ads immediately crushed my dreams. There wasn't any better news in the *Reader*. For a one-bedroom, even a studio around here, we were talking mid-six-figures. Lakeview, Lincoln Park, and the Loop were even higher. How did people do it? Even if I could scrape up a down payment, I probably couldn't qualify for a loan for that kind of money.

I considered my options. I could buy a place and find a roommate. Or I could buy a place with someone. No, the whole idea was to have my own place. And who was I going to do that with, anyway? Crap. I couldn't afford to buy anyplace that was in a decent neighborhood.

Unless. Unless I moved out to the 'burbs, the real burbs, where the minivans ruled and no one knew—or had to know—how to parallel park. Did single people live in the suburbs? Obviously they did. They had to. It couldn't all be apple-cheeked children, soccer moms, and white-collar dads.

Funny how you can change your mind about things. Last week, I'd been horrified at the mere thought of moving out of the city. Now, as I sat in traffic during yet another interminable drive home, I decided it wouldn't be so bad if I lived in Wheaton or Lisle or Lombard, or somewhere nearby the office. A ten-, fifteen-minute commute? How cool would that be?

Jane thought I was crazy. "Um, Trina, I don't know how to tell you this, but moving to the suburbs is what you do after you get married. And get a kid. And a minivan."

I moved my chair closer to the table to make room for a tall girl in her early twenties, carrying an enormous backpack. We were sitting outside the coffee shop so Jane could smoke. It was unseasonably warm and sunny for late November, but I still sat bundled up in my coat. "There are plenty of single people in the suburbs." I'd decided this was the case even if it wasn't true.

"No, there aren't, don't you see?" Jane drank some of her latte with skim. "That's why they all come into the city every weekend to try to get laid."

"Look, I can't base this decision on the likelihood of meeting men! What do I do now? Go to work. Go to movies. Go to dinner. Go out with you. I can do all of those things just as easily *in the suburbs*," I intoned. "And I could have my own place, and not have to do this damn drive five days a week."

"But that's just for now, Trina! What happens when you get another job?"

"I don't know. It's not that bad."

"Oh, come on. You tell me constantly if you have to come up with another kooky-yet-cute party idea, you're going to, and I quote, 'Poke my eyes out with the long-handled barbecue fork.' I didn't imagine that, did I?"

"Yeah, well, but . . ."

"But what?"

I sighed and leaned my head back. "Well, I got that raise, and it's not that bad, really. Besides, do you know how tough the job market is right now?"

"That's an excuse, not a reason." She shook her head at me, but she smiled. "You're starting to turn into a little corporate drone, you know."

"I am not."

"You are. Working at a job just for the money. What about your spirit? What about your soul? What about following your bliss?"

I mimicked her tone. "And what about paying the bills? And what about eating food? And what about paying the rent?"

Jane shook her head again and lit a cigarette, ignoring the woman at the next table, who scowled at her.

"Smokers have no consideration for the rights of the people around them," said this woman, ostensibly to the fortyish woman sitting across from her.

"If you don't care to smoke, then you shouldn't sit outside," Jane spoke just as loudly, and I tried not to cringe. See, if that were me, I would have shamefacedly crushed out my cigarette and left, probably in tears. I knew Jane would light up until the woman was forced to leave first. The wind blew the smoke away from me and toward the building and their table.

I was right. The pair got up a few minutes later, but the woman wasn't defeated.

She leaned a bony hand on our table, and a row of silver bracelets clanked. "Have you ever seen someone dying of lung cancer?" she said, her flinty eyes focused on Jane. "It's a horrible death."

Jane looked up at her. "Have you ever seen someone who didn't give a shit?" she answered conversationally.

The woman flushed, exhaled loudly, and left.

"Nosy bitch." Jane ground out her smoke. "I'm sick of these fucking antismoking Nazis. They're as bad as the pro-lifers."

"Mmmm." I didn't comment. I didn't care if Jane smoked, but I didn't want her doing it in my car or my apartment. So I came down somewhere in the middle of the smoking/no-smoking debate. Besides, there were those occasions, usually fueled by alcohol, when I simply had to have a cigarette. Middle of the road, that's what I am. I sighed.

"What now?" she asked.

"I don't know. I'm depressed."

"Why, sweetie?"

"I just feel like I have an existential black cloud hanging over my head. What do I have to look forward to? I go to work, I come home, I eat dinner, I watch *True Hollywood Story*."

"So what do you want? What would make you happy?" said Jane, ogling a pair of guys walking by.

I didn't even bother to look at them. "Gay."

"I know, but you can still look." She smoothed her hair, which was now chestnut brown. The blond had lasted only a few weeks. "You like?"

"I told you, it looks good. Listen, I'm tired of living in a box. Having a place of my own will make me feel . . . I don't know, like a grown-up, you know?"

She made a face. "And you want to be a grown-up? What's so great about that?"

"Well, I'm tired of the whole rental lifestyle thing."

"Trina, if you move out to Geneva or Batville or whatever it's called, I will never come visit you."

"It's Batavia."

"Batavia. Bumblefuck. What's the difference? It'll be a bunch of upwardly mobile, or struggling to be upwardly mobile, yuppies and their offspring."

"So what's the difference? Isn't that Lincoln Park, Lakeview, and just about every other Chicago neighborhood?"

"Maybe. But it's not the suburbs. The suburbs! They have *corn* out there!"

"Yes, I'm aware. I did grow up in Champaign, remember?"

"So this is an attempt to return to your roots, metaphorically speaking."

"I don't know. Enough, OK?" I was starting to get annoyed. I love her confidence but the flipside is that she never, ever thinks she's wrong.

On the other hand, Jess thought it was a great idea. "I don't know why you haven't done it sooner," she said. I could hear her shuffling papers on her desk. "It will save you money tax-wise, too."

"Yeah, I guess." I don't know what it is. Just hearing that Jess thought it was a good idea was almost enough to make me reconsider. I doodled an arrow on my sticky note. "So, what's new? How's Ethan?"

"He's fine, I guess. I've barely seen him the last two weeks. I'm in the middle of getting a case ready for trial. It's in Omaha of all places." She sighed. "And I get to go."

"That's kind of cool, though. Are you, what's it called, second-chairing?"

"More like third-chairing. Two partners have the case. We're talking millions. I'm there to be the prime document handler, keeping track of the exhibits, labeling them correctly, having deposition transcripts indexed, stuff like that."

The thought of having to be that organized would make me want to strangle someone, but I didn't say anything.

"So, how long will you be gone?"

"Eight or nine days, though who knows, it may settle at the last minute." She changed tones. "I almost forgot. We're going to do our holiday party when I get home. Two weeks from Saturday. Bring someone if you want."

"Can't I come alone?"

"Sure, if you want."

"Is Pete going to be there?"

"God, Trina, I don't know. He is Ethan's friend, you know. Are we supposed to cut him out of our social circle because you decided he's boring?"

That was the story I'd told her. I didn't want to get into the whole wart thing. I knew she'd tell Ethan, and it was only a matter of time before everyone in their social circle knew. "No, of course not. I was just asking."

"I'll send you an invite." I heard her say something else. "Trina, got to go. I'll talk to you later."

"OK. Bye."

I didn't hear from her the next week, so I assumed she was out of town. Friday night a group of us from work went out to Max & Erma's for beers, and then decided to head to another bar near there. I'd had a glass of wine and then switched to Diet Coke because I was driving. Rachel rode with me, and we agreed to meet the others at the bar. She was giggly. I'd seen her down several Jack and Cokes at Max & Erma's.

"Didcha think that guy was cute?"

"Which one?"

Rachel dug in her purse and came out with a box of Starbucks mints, which she offered to me. I shook my head. She popped two in her mouth and then pulled down the visor on the passenger side of the car to scrutinize her hair.

"The guy playing pool at the table next to us. Tall, khaki pants, blue shirt . . ."

"Rachel, half the guys in there were wearing khakis. Casual Friday, remember?"

"Come on, you saw him. About six feet, thin, dark hair . . ."

"That guy? Come on, he's way too skinny. He needs about forty pounds on him."

"No, I like that look. Thin, dark, intense. He's probably really deep."

"What's the logic of that?" I checked the rearview and signaled right.

"You know, he's probably an intellectual. Maybe he's a writer, and he gets so caught up in what he's working on, he forgets to eat. That's so romantic."

"What's so romantic about being a writer? You're a writer too, after all."

She made a face. "No, a *real* writer. Writing because he can't help but write. He's tortured by the need to get his deepest feelings down on paper, to fully express himself, to live his art, you know?" She twisted a piece of hair around her finger dreamily. "Or maybe he's a musician."

"He's more likely some skinny kid who just doesn't eat much. Probably spends his nights on PlayStation or Xbox. That's why he forgets to eat."

"Don't ruin it for me!" She started brushing her hair. "He just looks like he's one of those shy guys who would never talk to you, but who would treat you so wonderfully. Love you and be faithful to you and appreciate everything you do." She sighed.

"Rachel, you'll meet someone else, really." I knew she was thinking about her latest beau, Willie, who worked in the shipping department. He'd taken her out—twice—and then dumped her. She'd confided that they'd slept together on the second date.

"Should I not have done that?" Rachel had asked me a week after he'd begun pointedly ignoring her in the lunchroom. "He doesn't respect me, right? I blew it."

"Rachel, I don't think it has anything to do with respect." Willie was one of those guys who was too good-looking for my tastes. He wasn't that tall, but he had a lean, muscular body; dark, shoulder-length hair he wore in a ponytail; and good fa-

A-P22

108

cial bone structure. He looked like a slightly rattier Rob Lowe, or maybe a Rob Lowe who hadn't gotten a lot of sleep and had to buy his clothes from Target. From what I knew, he'd also managed to screw half of the single women at the Coddled Cook since he'd arrived about three months after I did. I didn't have the heart to tell Rachel, though, and apparently no one else did, either.

We passed the bar. "See anyplace to park?"

Rachel turned her head left and right. "Nope, but look—there's a parking garage over there."

I parked and we walked the short distance to the bar. The crowd was a little older, a little heavier, and a little better dressed than at Max & Erma's. In addition to the requisite groups of guys and twenty-something women, there were several knots of men in their thirties and forties, and some obviously married couples as well.

I scanned the crowd. "Do you see anybody?"

"Yeah, look, there's Howie and Mike." I followed her through the crowd. Music was playing in the background, but I could barely make it out over the noise of conversation and laughter. I headed for the bathroom and was coming out of the stall when something caught my eye.

It was Ethan. He was wearing a white shirt, and a blue-and-yellow-patterned tie was loosely knotted around his neck. He had one hand on the wall of the bar and was talking with a woman who was leaning against the wall. It was loud, so he had to position his face close to hers to make himself heard. He spoke to her and I saw her throw her head back in response. I could see but not hear her laughter over the noise of the bar. She reached over and pushed his chest lightly, and he grabbed her hand, pulling her toward him. She laughed and ducked her head.

He let go of her hand and glanced around the bar. Shit! I ducked back into the hall. My heart pounded guiltily, and I felt sick. I knew what I had seen, but I didn't want to admit it.

I found the rest of the gang and stayed another hour or so,

but I couldn't relax. I had another Diet Coke and spent the entire time scouting for Ethan from my vantage point. I wanted to get a closer look at the woman he was with, but I didn't want him to see me.

"You looking for someone?" Rachel asked.

"What? Huh? No, no. Just checking out the crowd," I said lamely. It was a relief to drop Rachel off at her car and drive home. He wouldn't. He couldn't. Shit. What was I going to do?

Chapter 24
The Moon

May mean bad luck to those you love.

Monday morning rolled around and I was still replaying what I'd seen in my mind. Maybe they were just good friends. I might laugh like that with Bobby.

Nope. There was something about their body language that gave them away. They'd been standing just a little too close, even considering the din in the bar, engaging in serious eye contact. You only stood that near someone you knew intimately. Or wanted to.

I hadn't said anything to anyone. I talked only to Jessie and Jane about anything of importance, and in this case, Jessie was out. Finally, I called Jane.

"Hey, it's me."

"*Hola!* What's new in the world of tomato slicers and stainless steel whisks?"

"Not much. You?"

"I'm just getting dressed. Got a proofreading gig downtown. Some law firm."

"How'd you get that one?"

"I'm not sure. It's another temp thing, but it's twenty-five dollars an hour and shouldn't be too bad." She named the firm. It wasn't Jessie's.

"What time do you finish?"

"Eight. Weird hours, huh? It's noon until 8 P.M."

"Do you want to do a late dinner after?"

"Sure, why not? Want to be a real sweetie and pick me up? It's supposed to snow and I am not ready to deal with that."

I'd agreed. I could stay at work later than usual and finish the draft of the editorial calendar for next year.

As usual, everyone around me began powering off their computers and gathering their belongings by four forty-five. I knew from editing the HR manual that turning off your PC before 5:00 P.M. was grounds for discipline, but I didn't say anything. Rachel and Bobby both stopped by to say good-bye.

"Working late again? I can see you've got VP dreams, don't you?" said Bobby.

"Get out of here. Go home and stop harassing me."

"Trini, I forgot to ask. I need to take Friday off. Is that all right?"

"Like I'm going to say no to you."

"Thanks." He blew me a kiss. I watched him walk away, realizing I should have double-checked his vacation days before I agreed that he could have Friday off. This managing thing took getting used to.

When my phone rang, I jumped. I looked at the clock—5:29 P.M. The caller ID said "Unknown," in case I didn't already know that.

"Thank you for calling the Coddled Cook, this is Trina, can I help you?"

"Oh, Trina, you're there!" It was Petra. She laughed. "I was expecting to get your voice mail."

"Nope, it's the actual me. What can I do for you?"

"I'm so glad you're there. I'm going to need a proposal pulled together on our web redesign for a big meeting first thing Wednesday. I was going to leave the details on your voice mail so you could start on it first thing."

I spoke carefully. "Isn't the website more Elaine's responsibility?"

"Yes, but I have her working on some other projects for me. I'd be grateful if you could take care of this. I know it's last minute." The words were apologetic, the tone was not.

I thought of my neat list of meetings scheduled for tomorrow and groaned inwardly. I knew it would be another late night. "Why don't you tell me what you need, and I'll get started on it tonight."

She didn't waste any time suggesting that I'd already put in a full day. "Excellent. Here's what I need." She sketched her idea out and I took careful notes.

"Do you understand what I mean?"

"Yes, I think so. I'll work on it tonight and have something for you tomorrow afternoon."

Pause. I could hear the static of her cell phone. "Before noon would be better, so I can make any changes and get it back to you."

"OK," I said. "Of course." I hung up and looked at my notes. Might as well start on it now. I hammered out a rough outline about the current state of the website, omitting statistics such as how many Cook's Helpers visited the site and the like. I could get that from Elaine in the morning. I sent her an e-mail to give her the heads-up, then saved it on the network drive. It still needed a couple of hours' worth of work, but I could finish and polish it tomorrow morning. I grabbed my bag and trotted out to the parking lot. This time of night, it should take me only about thirty minutes to get into the Loop.

I met Jane outside the building. She was bundled up in a heavy brown coat and had a scarf wound around her head and shoulders. "My hero!" She opened the door and slid in, rubbing her hands together. "Can I just say how much I hate Chicago in the winter? Thanks for coming to get me."

"*De nada.* How's the proofing business?"

"Kill me now. I'm reading these legal memoranda, and half of it doesn't make sense to me. But I just look for spelling, grammatical, punctuation errors, stuff like that. At least the money's good." She started to pull out a cigarette and then glanced at me. "Crap. OK, where are we going?"

"I don't care." Snow was falling hard now. Even with the wipers going full-tilt, I could barely make out the street ahead of me. We were just crossing Randolph.

"Take a right. There's a Giordano's just down here," said Jane. Better yet, there was a parking spot just in front of the door. "Come on, it's a sign. Maybe it will quit while we're in there."

I would have preferred someplace closer to home, but I was hungry. A waiter seated us in a booth, and we both looked at the plastic menus.

Jane ordered a Diet Coke and scanned the menu. "Screw it, I'm having pizza. You?"

"Yeah, I'm starving." We settled on a spinach pie with onions and mushrooms on her side only.

"How long is this job for?"

"A week. I'm covering for someone on vacation, I think." Jane took a sip of her Diet Coke. "I'm reading for a new play over at Goodman on Thursday."

"What's the role?"

"It's about a dysfunctional family, and it all takes place during a wedding. I'm reading for the part of the black sheep of the family—the youngest daughter who's never done anything right and shows up unexpectedly."

"She wasn't invited to the wedding?"

"Right. She's kind of the pivotal character." She leaned forward. "It's a great role, sort of that Angelina Jolie thing in *Girl, Interrupted*, but not quite as crazy."

"I hope you get it."

"The cards look positive, anyway." She reached for a napkin to wipe the table. "I don't want to dwell. You know how I get."

"Uh-huh. I'm up for avoiding that." After auditions, Jane could—and often did—overanalyze every single aspect of her performance. Had she come on too strong? Were her clothes right for the role? Should she have worn brick red lipstick instead of the softer coral? It was the type of self-obsession that she chided other actors for, but she seemed incapable of stopping herself. Part of being her friend was having the good grace not to point that out.

"So, what's up with you? How's work?"

"Let's not even go there. I thought this promotion was what I wanted, but I don't know. I seem to have become Petra's personal whipping boy."

"Or whipping girl."

"You know what I mean." The waitress refilled my water glass and I nodded. "She keeps dumping these things on me at the last possible minute. I'm almost starting to wonder if it's intentional."

"I'm sure she has better things to do than make your life miserable, Trina."

"You'd think. But like this thing tonight. The website—the content anyway—is supposed to be Elaine's responsibility. But I'm the one who winds up with it." I sighed. "I don't know." I leaned my head back against the wooden booth. "There is something else going on that I need to bounce off you, but you cannot say anything to anyone."

"Who am I going to tell?"

"I mean it. Swear."

"God, Trina, take it easy. OK, I swear. What is it?"

I filled her in on seeing Ethan, limiting my description to what I'd actually witnessed and leaving my suppositions, theories, and fears out of it. She lit a cigarette ("Pizza won't be out for at least ten minutes!") and listened thoughtfully.

I expected some kind of smart-ass retort, but Jane was quiet. "That sucks," she finally said.

"So you think he's cheating on her?"

"You've got minimal evidence at best, but what does your gut say?"

I felt that familiar twist. "That he is. It just looked . . . well, wrong."

"Are you going to tell Jessie?"

"I don't know. I don't know what to do."

"Well, think about the possible outcomes."

"That's easy. I tell her, she explodes, they get a divorce, and it's all my fault."

"Take it easy! Is that really what you think will happen?"

I rolled my eyes. "I don't know. I just have no interest in being the messenger here, you know? And I think that no matter what I say, it will end up blowing up in my face." The waitress served our pizza, and we paused to lift our plates so she could serve us.

Jane dug into her slice, using her hands. She made an appreciative noise. "I'll get back on the diet tomorrow, really."

I didn't say anything, just picked up a slice, picking off a few onions that had drifted over onto my half. "So?"

"So? OK. I think you're exaggerating. I can't imagine you'd be the one to get blamed here."

"You don't know, Jane. She's on these drugs and they mess with her head. She's swamped at work, she can't have a baby, and now I'm going to tell her I think her husband's cheating on her? Oh, and by the way, do I need to remind you that you can't have my eggs?"

"That wasn't right of her to ask you in the first place," interrupted Jane. She pointed her pizza at me. "I officially forbid you to stop feeling guilty about that."

"Whatever. It's still there. I know it's in the back of her mind." I put my fork down. "Shit! And I have to see him next week at their party! What am I going to do? What am I going to say?"

She snapped her fingers. "That's perfect! Go to the party, get him alone, and tell him instead."

"Tell him what?"

"That you know what he's doing and he's got one chance to knock it off. Otherwise you'll tell her."

I shook my head. "This whole thing is making me sick. I'm serious, Jane. I can't handle this on top of everything else at

WHITE BIKINI PANTIES 187

work." I twisted my napkin. "I wish I'd never gone out that night. I wish I hadn't seen them. I wish I could just forget the whole thing."

"OK, let me change tactics. If you were Jessie, and she were you, would you want her to tell you?"

I thought a minute, remembering the abject horror of discovering Rick in his apartment. "Um, yeah. Definitely."

"Don't you think she'd feel the same way?"

"I don't know. They're married, Jane. This isn't just some loser you can dump and then continue hunting for the right guy. He's supposed to *be* her right guy."

She looked skeptical. "Signs are pointing to no on that theory, sweetie."

"*I* know that. *You* know that. My sister does not."

"So, maybe she'll never have to know. Maybe it was a one-time thing. Maybe he was just drunk and flirty. Who knows? I say, give him the heads-up, see what he says, and then decide what to do."

I thought about how I'd approach Ethan as I dressed for their party the next Saturday.

"Hey, Ethan, how's it going? By the way, are you screwing around?"

"Hi, Ethan. Hey, I just read an article in a magazine about the increasing incidence of infidelity among married couples today. What do you think about that?"

"Hey, Ethan, do you ever worry about getting an STD?"

Of course, nothing sounded quite right. I gave up on the idea of planning and decided to go with the flow. If the situation presented itself, I'd say something—otherwise, I wouldn't.

Chapter 25
The Ace of Cups

Love, joy, fertility.

Their house was ablaze with lights when I pulled up. Little white lights dripped from the eaves, and multicolored bulbs festooned the bushes outside. Ceramic luminaries lined the walk from the drive to the front porch. There were at least two dozen vehicles parked in front of the house, evenly divided between slick Mercedes and Beemers and those monster SUVs. My poor little Honda looked like the country cousin among her more well-heeled relatives. Must be mostly guests from Jessie's office. I wasn't crazy about all of Ethan's friends—Pete came to mind—but I preferred them to the snotty future-partner set from her firm.

At least Jessie had said that she didn't think Pete was coming. "Well, was he invited?" I'd pressed her earlier this week.

"I told you, we had to invite him, Trina. He's Ethan's friend."

"And I'm only your sister."

"He probably won't come. He hasn't RSVPed, anyway."

"Uh-huh." We both knew that men didn't even know how to RSVP. Only women did that.

Another thought occurred to me. "What about Javier?"

Jessie snorted. "OK, sis, I have a suggestion. Quit sleeping with Ethan's friends."

"I believe Javier was your idea," I lied.

"He was? Are you sure?"

"Uh-huh."

"Well, I certainly didn't suggest that you do some crazy *9½ Weeks* deal with him now, did I?"

"Point taken." God, sometimes I hate having a lawyer as a sister. And I really hate it when she's right. Oh well, I'd probably be too busy trying to wrestle Ethan into confessing his adulterous affair and swearing that it would never happen again to worry about making small talk with the man who had given me venereal warts or the man I thought had given me venereal warts.

I rang the doorbell, and when no one answered, I opened the door and let myself in. Most of the noise was coming from the kitchen.

There were probably ten people in the kitchen, and everyone seemed to have a drink. Another cluster of a dozen or so sat scattered throughout the great room. Jessie herself was bending over the oven, pulling something out. A gaggle of women stood around her, rearranging various trays of food without actually eating anything.

"Hi there." I smiled and held up my big contribution, a bottle of Asti. "Happy holidays!"

Jessie came over and hugged me. "Hi, sis." She was wearing a blood-red scoop-neck dress that flared around her ankles. Her face was shiny and pink, and her hair was pulled back in a red-and-black scrunchy. "You look great."

"Really?" I looked down. I already felt underdressed. Most of the women there were sporting either extremely expensive-looking designer blouses and skirts, or horrible multicolored holiday-themed sweaters, no doubt equally expensive. I felt quite plain in my simple dark green sweater and black velvet pants.

"Here, let me get your coat." Jessie followed me upstairs.

"Are you sure? Don't you want to attend to your guests?"

She made a face. "They've all got drinks. They'll be fine for the moment."

"OK." I dropped my coat on their king-sized bed and checked my hair in their mirror. Jessie watched me.

"You look great."

"You, too."

"Please." She fiddled with her dress. "I feel like a cow. This is a twelve, and it's tight."

"Please, yourself." I stroked the fabric. "You look fantastic."

She smiled and hugged me. "Thanks, Trina."

"So, any single men here?" She was just opening her mouth to respond, but I interrupted. "I'm kidding! It's a joke, OK?"

"Very funny." But she grinned. "Are you going to tell me what really happened with Pete? Ethan tried to get it out of him, but he wouldn't crack."

I pointed at her. "You know, there is something worse than having one lawyer in the family. Having two."

"But are you sure you won't get back with him? We had so much fun at dinner, you know?"

"I know, but it just wasn't there. I never got the love thing."

"Maybe you didn't give him enough time."

"It's not just that." I sighed. "Can you keep a secret from your husband? I really don't want Ethan to know this."

"Is it something juicy?"

"I'm serious, Jessie. This is sister-only kind of stuff."

She looked at me, twisted her mouth, and then nodded, raising her right hand. "I won't say anything. I swear."

I checked the room and then pulled her close to me to whisper in her ear. "He gave me warts. You know, venereal ones."

"What? Pete did? You're kidding." She sat down on the bed. "I can't believe that. He made it sound like you dumped him for no reason." She looked at me. "Wait, Trina. Are you sure it wasn't Javier?"

"Pete as much as told me so. His girlfriend gave him the gift that keeps on giving, and he gave it to me."

"I can't believe him!" She scowled and made a fist. "I'd like to kill him. What a total weasel! I should have known not to trust him."

"How could you have known?"

"I don't know. I'd just like to think I know people better." Then she touched my arm. "What about you? Are you all right?"

"What? What do you . . . oh, yeah. I had to go to the doctor and she froze them off. But I should be fine."

"I'm so sorry. Why didn't you tell me? I could have gone with you." She held my hand for a minute. "I'm your sister, you know?"

"I know." I squeezed her hand. "But I'm fine, really." I tugged at her. "Come on, you have a party to throw."

"All right, I'm coming." She smoothed her dress. "And I'm not going to tell Ethan!"

"Thank you." We walked down the oak staircase together, and I followed Jessie into the living room, where she was accosted by an attractive woman with perfectly white hair. I crossed through the kitchen to the bar at one end of the great room. Ethan was standing behind it, mixing what appeared to be a margarita.

"Hey, glad you could make it." He leaned over and kissed me on the cheek. "You look very festive."

I didn't feel festive, though. Just seeing him made me feel sick to my stomach. I nodded at the blender. "Margaritas?"

"I know, Jessie's bent out of shape, thinks we should all be drinking wassail or egg nog." He nodded his head at me. "So, what will it be?"

I hesitated. "OK, make it a margarita." Maybe I'd soften him up a bit by choosing one.

"Coming right up." He salted the glass, turning it upside down so salt stuck to the rim, and then poured the sludgy mixture into it. He added a lime wedge on the rim with a flourish.

"Mmmm." I took a sip and the tequila bit my tongue. It wasn't very Christmasy, but it was very good.

Three guys in their early thirties drifted over and hit Ethan up for a pair of Heinekens and a Jack and Coke. They greeted Ethan, then formed a small circle, animatedly talking about one of their cases.

I gestured to the room. "So, where are your coworkers?"

"Sean's coming. Bill. Deidre can't make it." He thought a moment. "Oh, and Javier won't be here either, in case you were hoping to get lucky."

"What do you mean?" I looked away. "OK, so I have no pride."

He spread his hands. "No biggie. Nothing wrong with getting a little from a guy."

"Please stop right now."

Ethan laughed. "Trina, relax. I'm not going to say anything. We're family, right?"

"Right." I sucked at my margarita and thought about how to phrase what I wanted to ask him. I was just opening my mouth to speak when one of their neighbors—a big, beefy guy named Frank—strolled over.

"Gimme a brewski, barkeep, and be quick about it." He grinned at me and offered his hand. "Trina, right? Saw you around when you were house-sitting."

"That's right." He launched into a discussion about invisible fencing with Ethan, and the moment was lost. I'd catch up with him later, I thought, relieved to be able to forget it for the moment.

Jane called the next morning. "So?"

"So what?"

"So, what did he say?"

I rolled over in bed, holding the phone next to my ear. "He didn't say anything."

"What?"

"No, I didn't get the chance to ask him. There were always people around, and I couldn't get him alone."

"Oh, rats. I wondered what he was going to say."

I lifted my head and picked up the alarm clock. "Why are you calling so early, anyway?"

I heard her light a cigarette. "If you must know, I just got home a few minutes ago, so I thought I'd call."

"It's barely eight."

She laughed. "Come on, come on! Ask me why I just got home."

I sighed. "You're always so chipper when you just got laid, I don't even have to ask."

"But who! You have to ask who?"

I sighed again, but obliged. "Who?"

"Steve. Steve Busleigh."

"Refresh my memory. Which one is he?"

"You know who he is. That tall, gorgeous black guy who was in that production of *Eleventh Night*. Remember that Shakespeare farce?"

I did. I'd gotten only about half of the references in the play and had walked out thinking that my U of I education hadn't done much in the way of schooling me about the Bard. But I was sure I remembered Steve—his smooth black head had gleamed, and he'd been funny, too.

"How did that happen?"

"We were all out, and he showed up." She exhaled. "Trina, he is the most physically beautiful man I have ever been with. His body! Oy vey. You've never seen anything like it."

"You're not even Jewish. What's with the yiddicisms lately?" I could hear the annoyance in my voice.

"Somebody's jealous," she singsonged in my ear. "Come on, you know you want details."

"Why? So I can feel doubly bad about my lack of a sex life?" My phone chirped. "Hang on."

"Oh good, you're up." It was Jessie. "I didn't want to wake you."

"Jane beat you to the punch. She's on the other line."

"Oh, OK. Will you just call me when you get off?"

I agreed and clicked back to Jane. "It's Jess; I'll call her back."

"So . . ."

"I don't know. She just said to call her."

"All right, be a good sister. But I'm only going to let you off the hook if you agree to come over later and hang out. We haven't done that in ages."

"All right." I hung up, sighed, and tapped in Jessie's number.

"Recovered from the party?"

"I'm cleaning. Ethan's still in bed."

"It seemed like everyone had a good time."

"Yeah, I think so too. I'm glad you could come."

"Me, too." I wasn't about to tell her that I had been bored out of my skull at the party. Everyone there had been either lawyers, or neighbors, or wives of lawyers.

"So, are you doing anything today?"

I hated it when Jess did this. She wouldn't come right out and say what she wanted; she had to make sure that I'd have no excuses first.

"Jane and I are getting together later," I hedged.

"Oh, all right. Well . . . do you feel like stopping by beforehand or after?"

"Jess, it's like an hour drive, you know? And I was just out there last night, you know?"

"OK, OK. I was going to go into the office for a while anyway. Can I come by your place?"

I squinted at the phone. Jess never offered to visit me—it was always me (the younger, poorer, less successful sister) traveling to see her (the older, wiser, richer, more successful sister). I wondered what she wanted. A sudden thought occurred to me and I bit my lip. What if she knew? Or she suspected? Oh, no, she was coming over to interrogate me about what I knew about Ethan.

"Is that all right? About two?"

"Um, yeah, fine. I'll be here."

I'd gotten up, showered, and gone grocery shopping. I came home and cleaned the apartment. I tried to see it through Jessie's eyes. Too funky, too many candles and piles of books everywhere, furniture that didn't match, a salmon-colored Ikea couch next to an overstuffed cream-colored easy chair. At least it was all paid for, I consoled myself.

She buzzed downstairs a few minutes before two, and I let her in. "Hi!" she surprised me with a hug. I'd just seen her the night before, after all.

"Hi, yourself." I closed the door behind her.

She pulled off her brown leather coat and carefully laid it on the back of my couch. I waited for her to say something, anything, about my apartment—how small it was, or how hard it was to find a parking spot, or how she couldn't believe I paid nine hundred a month for this place. But she didn't say anything, just sat down on the couch, her hands perched on her knees. She was humming.

"You want something to drink? Diet Coke? I've got some of that Diet Orange Crush, too."

"No, no, I'm fine." She smiled a huge smile. "Actually I'm more than fine. I'm pregnant!"

"Are you serious?" I rushed over to the couch as she stood up, and we hugged. "I can't believe it! But I thought—I thought you couldn't! I thought you had bad eggs or something."

"Well, one of them must have been good. I was late but I didn't even think about it—I've been so preoccupied with work, if you can believe that." She laughed. "I hate to say it. We weren't even trying. With the egg thing, we were on hold. We've even started talking about adopting. Then I find this out." She shook her head.

I just stood there. "I can't believe it. Why didn't you tell me last night?"

"I just took the home test this morning."

"Wow." We stood there for a moment. "Oh my gosh, I'm going to be an aunt!"

"I know. And Mom will finally get off my back about being a grandma." She sat down, and I could see tears in her eyes. "I think I'm going to wait and tell them at Christmas. Isn't that perfect?"

"It is." I smiled. A thought occurred to me. "Oh my gosh! What did Ethan say?"

She shook her head and closed her eyes. "I haven't even told him yet."

"What? You mean I'm the first?"

She nodded. "I know, I should have told him first. But I want it to be perfect, you know? We've tried for so long, I didn't want to just spring it on him by waving the test."

"So, what are you going to do?"

"Well, I want to make sure that it's for real, you know? So I'm going to see my doctor as early as I can and confirm it, and then take Ethan to dinner at Everest."

"Oh, come on! He'll know something's up." I'd never been to the famous restaurant, but Jane's dad had taken her there once during a rare visit. He'd dropped four hundred dollars on their dinner without batting an eye, she'd said. "This, while I had to put myself through school," she'd complained.

"I'll just say that I got good news at work or something. I can fool him." She stroked her stomach and then looked at me. "Do *not* say anything! Not even to Jane, I'm serious."

"I won't. Relax. This is your big news. I'm not going to say a thing."

After Jessie left, I walked over to Jane's. It was cold out, but I'd snagged a prime parking spot right in front of my building. Besides, the sun was shining and I could use the exercise.

By the time I'd arrived, I'd decided that I wouldn't say anything to Ethan or Jessie about what I'd seen, or thought I'd seen. Maybe nothing had happened, and I knew if something had, it would end now that they were expecting a baby. I gave Jane a brief rundown on the party as she sat stringing beads together for a new necklace. "I think I'm just going to wait and see what happens," I finished lamely.

Fortunately Jane was too distracted to pester me about it. Her hair was pulled back in a silky ponytail and she had no makeup on except some lip gloss. Personally, I thought she looked prettier like this instead of with her full battle regalia of makeup. She looked up from her beads. "Sounds good. Do I get to talk now? Do you want to hear about *my* night?"

I rolled my eyes. "Go ahead. Make me jealous."

"I hate to say it, but I think I just had the best night of sex of my entire life."

For Jane, that was saying something. "Your entire life?" I repeated. "Come on. What made it so incredible?"

She thought for a moment, pausing with her beadwork. "I don't know. It started out as just pure physical attraction, I know that. I mean, look at him! What a hunk of man flesh. But then when we started having sex, it was like there was this connection there I couldn't explain. I was looking into his eyes, and he was looking into mine, and he felt it, too, I know it." She looked down and threaded a red bead onto the necklace. "I think we've known each other before. You know, in a past life."

"Oh, come on." I found it hard to believe in Jane's tarot cards, much less any of that Shirley MacLaine stuff. "Even if you were reincarnated, what are the chances that, if you did know each other before, you're going to meet again?"

"You have to understand how it works. No one really dies. Their physical self dies, but their soul lives on."

"What about heaven? Isn't that what most of us are hoping for?" Conversations like this made me uncomfortable. I did believe in God, and I tried to be a good person, but I didn't go to church or ponder what would happen when I died. Who wanted to?

"Call it heaven if you want. The belief in reincarnation isn't that radical. Hindus believe that your soul will continue being reborn until you learn the lessons you're supposed to here on earth, you know."

I shook my head. "I don't know, Jane. This whole thing is getting a little too weird."

"It's not. Think about it. Do you believe in ghosts?"

"I don't know." I mean, I'd seen *The Sixth Sense* like everyone else, but I hadn't thought about it much afterward.

"A ghost is just a soul, a soul who's trapped somewhere. Someone who couldn't cross over."

"Oh, here we go. I can tell you've been watching *John Edward*." This was a psychic who claimed to help his audience contact friends and family who had died, oops, I mean crossed over—and he did it all on camera. I'd watched it a couple of times with Rick, but it had never inspired the loyalty that *True Hollywood Story* had.

"Think of it like this. There are souls here on earth, but there are more souls somewhere else—call it heaven, if you want. And everyone up there can decide when they want to return here on earth. So let's say we're up there, and we decide we want to meet again down here. So we might agree to be sisters in this life, or lovers, or father and son."

"You mean souls can switch sexes?"

"It's not a matter of switching. It's just a matter of which body you happen to inhabit."

"And you think the two of you knew each other in what, a past life, right?"

"I do." She looked up at me, her face serene. Then she laughed. "I do, Trina! I'm not nuts. I mean it. I've never had this feeling before, not with any man."

I got up from the couch. "OK, let me interrupt this metaphysical moment for a second. Have anything to drink?"

"Yeah, there's wine and soda in there. Bring me a glass, too."

I located a bottle of pinot grigio, her red plastic corkscrew that hung from a shoelace above the tiny window in the kitchen, and carried them out with two wineglasses. I poured us both a glass.

"Hey, I need it to hear the rest of this," I said.

She just shook her head. "You need to open your mind a little. Why do you think we became friends?"

"Um, because we lived in the same building?"

"It's more than that. How many neighbors have you had that you didn't become friends with? We hit it off from the start. We probably knew each other before, too." She thought for a moment. "And I bet you and Jess did, too. There's so much tension there it would make sense."

"Um, right. We're also sisters! Sisters born two years apart," I responded. "Any armchair psychologist will tell you that there's bound to be conflict between sisters. It's called sibling rivalry."

She shook her head. "Nope, I think it goes deeper than that. Maybe you were lovers in a past life or something, and she wronged you. That would explain a lot."

I reached for the wine bottle. "Janey baby, you're my best friend, but I got to tell you I think you're full of it sometimes."

She just grinned. "Oh, I am full of it, all right."

It took me a moment. "What do you mean? Oh, gross!" I rolled my eyes. "Hello! Please tell me you weren't foolish enough to not use condoms."

She looked away from me. "Well, I didn't have any and he didn't have any," she said. "Besides, we did talk about it beforehand."

"Uh-huh. Do tell."

She scrunched up her face. "Like, as he was starting to get inside me, I said, 'Is this OK, without a condom?' and he said, 'Sure, baby.' " She actually blushed.

"He said, 'Sure, baby.' " I snorted. "Yes, I stand corrected. I can see that you performed a comprehensive examination of each other's sexual health."

"Okay, okay. I know it was stupid." She sipped at her wine. I hadn't seen her pick up a cigarette yet, I realized. "But I *know* him. I trust him."

"I hope so," I said, my voice sounding prissy and strained. "Because you really don't want to go through what I just did, remember?"

"I know, sweetie." She looked at me. "I'm sorry. You don't have to worry about it, OK?"

"OK," I mumbled, tucking my legs under me.

"What's wrong?"

"I don't know. Here you've met your soul mate and Jessie's finally pregnant and I'm spending half my life commuting to work and the other half at work."

"She's pregnant?"

"Oh, shit. *Do not* say anything. I promised."

"Who am I going to tell?"

"I know, but I'm paranoid. She wants to wait anyway, to make sure everything's OK, and then she's going to tell Ethan."

"She told you first?"

"Yeah, this afternoon. Right before I came over, in fact."

"Interesting. Yup, you two definitely knew each other before."

"OK, say we did. How come when people remember past lives, they were always Cleopatra or Mark Anthony or some prince or something? No one is just a poor slob or a slave or anything."

"That's not true."

"It is! Everyone is Cleopatra," I muttered. "It's a load of crap."

"Have some more wine, sweetie." Her tone was motherly and she was right. I was getting kind of buzzed, but I felt irritable and off-balance rather than happy and relaxed.

"I probably need to eat something."

"Oh, let's get a pie. My treat."

"Are you sure?"

"Yeah. That proofing gig is going to continue this week after all, so I'm rolling in money."

I knew that was an exaggeration—Jane usually managed to make just enough to squeak by, to buy drinks, cigarettes, and makeup—but I accepted her offer. Part of friendship is treating each other, whether you can afford it or not. Jessie used to say a friendship was a like a party—you're supposed to show up with something. Maybe it was a bottle of wine, maybe a six-pack, maybe a bag of pretzels. But when you go to a party, you come with an offering. Sure, if it's a good friend and you're too busy to stop and pick something up, you'll be forgiven. But if you always ring the doorbell or stroll in with nothing but your sense of humor, your host will become annoyed.

"It's the same for relationships," Jessie had told me. This was after she'd broken up with Brad, her boyfriend before she met Ethan. Brad had been gorgeous, sweet, and seriously into Jessie. I'd harbored a crush on him the entire nine months they'd dated, and had even had a few sexy dreams about him. I'd been surprised, but a little relieved, when she'd broken up with him a week before Valentine's Day. "He's not that intelligent, he's not that interesting, and he's not even ambitious," she'd said. "All he wants to do is work, come home, and watch sports. That's not bringing much to the party."

"But come on, he loves you! He's nuts about you."

"That's not enough. I want someone who's my intellectual equal. I want someone who will always bring something to the party."

I had to admit that she had a point. I'd lost touch with most of my friends from high school and college. Some had moved from the Midwest, some had gotten married and had kids and were never heard from again. But there were a few others I'd eventually weaned myself from.

Take Marci. She wasn't a terrible person by any means. Our last year of school, she and I and two other girls had shared a four-bedroom apartment on East John Street together. Marci and I were both between boyfriends, and we'd hang out after class, watching *Love Connection* and *Jeopardy* and *Wheel of Fortune* together. She'd moved back home to Evanston after graduating to look for a job in advertising, but had never found a position that had merited her interest. We'd gotten together a few times over the years—I had moved to Chicago, after all—but she never seemed to make any forward progress. She started grad school, then quit, then went back. She'd decided to start her own dog-walking business. She complained about living with her parents but never moved out. This would have been fine, except her attitude got worse as she got older. She whined a lot, and never bothered to ask me about my life. And eventually, I met Jane and had some friends from work, and I didn't want to hang out with someone who did nothing but bitch and moan.

But how do you break up with a friend? At least with a boyfriend, there's a clean break, a recognized transition of some sort. Even if you manage to stay friends afterward like people allegedly did, there was a clear delineation of boyfriend/not-boyfriend. But with a friend, there was no acceptable social practice. There should be one.

"I'm sorry; this just isn't working out," you'd say to your soon-to-be-former-friend. "We just don't work anymore." Hell, you could even steal the George Costanza line from *Seinfeld*— "It's not you, it's me"—but the end result would be the end of the friendship in a nice neat maneuver. No more strained lunches or phone calls or dreading getting together.

"Wouldn't it be great if you could break up with a friend?" I said to Jane.

"What, am I supposed to be worried now?"

"I'm never breaking up with you. You're stuck with me. No, you know, with people you used to be friends with but now you don't have anything in common with anymore except a shared history—but neither of you has the guts to just end the relationship."

"Yeah, so what?"

"So, you'd buy a breakup card and it'd be over."

"Why bother with that? Why not just tell the person that you don't like them anymore?"

"Some of us live in the real world, Jane. Most of us can't run around telling people what we really think of them."

"Sure you can. Anyone can. Isn't that better than having to deal with people you don't even like?"

"Don't you ever feel guilty about anything?"

"Guilt is a useless emotion. It only kicks in after the fact. So if you're going to do something that is going to make you feel guilty, you have two choices." She finally broke down and lit a cigarette. "Number one, don't do it. Number two, do it and resolve not to feel guilty."

"Ethics according to Jane."

"I have ethics, sweetie. I'd just rather choose my own than have someone else's foisted upon me."

I wished I had her sense of independence. I didn't. When it came right down to it, I'd pretty much accepted what my parents had tried to instill in me. Work hard, get good grades, get a good job, and you'd be set. Finding a boyfriend was secondary—you should worry about "taking care of your own self first," as my dad would say. And I didn't know how good of a job I was doing at that.

Chapter 26
The Five of Cups, Inverted

The return of an old friend.

There's a Chinese saying, I think, that goes something like, "Be careful what you wish for—you may get it." Tuesday night I was lying on the couch, eating microwave popcorn from the bag, and watching *THS*. It was a new one—Steven Segal. The subjects they interviewed fell into two distinct camps—Segal supporters/friends/fans and Segal detractors. One of the latter pointed out that the actor "runs like a woman." That was just the kind of thing that would have had Rick and me cracking up.

The phone rang, and I debated answering. If it was Jane, she'd leave a message, and I could pick it up; phone solicitors would just hang up when the machine clicked on.

I heard my voice chirping the instructions, then a brief pause.

"Hi, Trina." Another pause. "It's me. Rick. Um, it's about eight o'clock . . ."

I didn't think. I simply grabbed the phone. "Hi." Then I added, "It's me" inanely. Who else would be answering my phone?

He took a deep breath. "Hi. How are you?"

He didn't ask it the way he usually did—"Hihowareyou,"

rushing the words together, which annoyed me. He spoke slowly, emphasizing the "are." I couldn't help but smile.

"How are *you*?"

I'd bet he was shaking his head, smiling. "How am I? I asked you first."

"I don't know." My heart was pounding. I had forgotten how much I'd loved his voice, somewhere between tenor and baritone, and the way he could mimic the entire *South Park* cast. He did a mean Eric Cartman.

"On a scale of one to ten?" he teased me. I used to come up with scales for him—"one is being called in at three in the morning because the network just went down, ten is the moment right before an incredibly good orgasm"—and force him to choose a number to describe his emotional state.

"I guess I'm a five." Crap. I should have said eight, or nine. Why let him know the truth?

"Better than me. I'm, say, a three. Maybe a two."

I wasn't going to get pulled back into this. He's the one who had been cheating on me, after all. And he's the one who hadn't even bothered to try to get me back.

"Really. Why is that?" I kept my voice neutral.

He swallowed. "Oh, shit. You know what, forget it. Forget I called."

He hung up. I stared at the phone. What was that? I stopped myself, stood up, and walked into the kitchen. I poured myself a glass of water, drank it, and then grabbed the phone, punching in his number by heart. As soon as it picked up, I started spewing.

"What is this? You call me after, what, four months, ask me how I am, and then hang up on me? What the hell are you thinking?" I could feel myself shaking.

"I'm sorry. I'm sorry!"

"That is so weak." I tried to maintain my anger.

"Look, I shouldn't have called you. I was watching *True Bitter Stories* and missed you, that's all."

"You watched Steven Segal?"

"Yeah. Dude's put on some major poundage. What's up with those long coats, anyway?"

I couldn't help it. I'd thought the same thing. "How about the clip of him running like a woman?"

"Yeah, I wonder if he'll go out and kick some ass now that it's aired."

"Maybe." I squeezed the back of my neck with my left hand. "So. . . ."

"So. Wanna start this conversation over?"

"All right."

"How are you, Trina?"

"I'm OK. I'm fine. How are you?"

"Not great. I got, well, shit, I got fired."

"What? No way. What happened?"

"I still don't know. Combination of things, I guess. They cut twelve jobs out of our department, and some of us had to go."

"But you're the most valuable person in the whole department!" I was outraged. He'd worn that stupid pager everywhere he went, and taken calls at all hours of the night, and this was the thanks he got? "Rick, I am so sorry. That totally sucks."

"I'm all right. Just a crappy time to be out of a job. But I got three months' severance, so I'm all right for the moment."

"That's just guilt money."

"It's still green."

"What are you going to do?"

I heard him sigh. "I'm not sure. I found out a couple of weeks ago and I think it's just now starting to kick in. It was like a vacation, you know? I didn't really miss work at first. Now it feels weird."

"Who else got laid off?"

He listed the names. Some I recognized, some I didn't. I didn't ask about Jill.

"Rick, you're so good at what you do. You'll get another job."

"Yeah." He sounded glum. "What about you? How are things at the Cook?"

"They're all right. I got promoted, actually."

"More bucks?"

"Yeah, another five grand a year. I don't know. I'm not crazy about having to be the boss. Oh, guess who's now working for me?"

"Who?"

"Elaine."

"Who is that, again?"

"Remember, you met her. Skinny? Blond hair?"

"Tries too hard? Thinks she's prettier than she is?"

I'd said that to Rick more than a year ago, and he remembered. For a second, I forgot we weren't together anymore. "That's the one."

"You'll get used to it. You've got good people skills."

"Maybe, but I'm not very good at making people do things. I wind up doing it myself instead."

"Give yourself some time."

We talked for a few more minutes. It was both familiar and strange, hearing his voice in my ear, his laugh. I debated. As soon as I'd heard his voice, I'd wanted to see him. I could feel my whole body thrill with the idea of touching him again, feeling the smooth muscles along his back.

"Rick, why haven't you called me?"

"Are you joking? What could I say? I blew it, right?"

"Yeah." I pressed my lips together. "But I'm over it now," I said lightly.

"That's good, I guess."

"So why call me now?"

"Crap, I don't know. I've been thinking a lot. About work, about stuff with you, about stupid shit I've done. I'm sorry, Trina. I know I can't take back what I did, but I never wanted to hurt you."

"I know that." I sighed. I again felt that awful empty sense of loss for what we couldn't have now. "You really screwed things up."

"I'm an idiot."

"So, am I ever going to get the whole story?" I kept my voice calm. This was an important conversation. "About you and, um, Jill."

He didn't say anything for a minute. "It's a long story."

"I've got time."

"You want to hear this? I don't believe that."

"It's no big deal. I'm over you, anyway."

"Oh yeah?"

"Yup. Totally, completely over you. I was just curious."

"Uh-huh. Does that mean you don't want to get together sometime? Maybe do dinner?"

I actually pulled the phone away from my ear to stare at it.

"Are you serious?" My heart was thudding, and I pulled my legs up under me on the couch.

"No, I'm just jerking your chain. Yeah, I'm serious."

"You're jobless. What are you doing, going out to dinner?"

"Told you, I've got three months' severance pay. Besides, anything's worth it to see you again." I heard his voice lower. "I've missed you."

"Well, I haven't missed you. It's been nice talking to you, though."

"What about tomorrow?"

"I don't think so. I've, um, got to work late tomorrow." I scrambled for an excuse. I wasn't ready to see him. I could see him only when my heart had completely healed, when I'd be able to set eyes on him without feeling that little flutter deep in my belly.

"Thursday?"

"Nope."

"Friday?"

"Jane's got a show," I lied. "Saturday and Sunday, too."

"I guess you're busy."

"Extremely."

"All right then. I guess I'll talk to you later then."

We hung up, and I spent the next twenty-seven minutes staring blankly at the television screen, watching a rerun of some reality show. I couldn't keep track of their names anymore. When my buzzer sounded, I jumped. I depressed it, and then waited for him to knock at the door.

Chapter 27
The Fool

A choice must be made.

I was sitting in my chair at work, staring at the Dilbert cartoon stuck on the wall when Rachel wandered over with a piece of paper in her hand. "Will you look at this, Trina? I made those changes but I wanted you to check it again before I pass it up to marketing."

I skimmed it. It was a new product teaser, designed to whip our Helpers into a frenzy over a line of plastic storage containers. I'd made the mistake of referring to it as Tupperware at a department meeting and Petra had shot me a look.

"That's a trademark, you know," Elaine had piped up helpfully. "And this isn't Tupperware. It's Keeperware." She smiled at Petra. "It's important for us to adhere to trademarks in this business, isn't it?"

I'd apologized, hiding my annoyance by appearing to make careful notes on my legal pad, but in my mind I was strangling Elaine.

I handed it to Rachel. "I think it looks great."

"Oh, good." She dropped the piece of hair she'd been twirling. "I hate working with Shelley," she said, referring to the head of the products department. "She's so snappish, you know?"

Shelley had an extremely short haircut and a temper to match. Her whole department was afraid of her, and now that we were officially one department, she oversaw a portion of the work we writers did. "I know." I looked around. "Did I tell you how she yelled at me the first week I was here?"

"You're kidding!" Rachel did the same kind of visual scan, then sat neatly in the chair by the corner of my desk.

"It was the first piece I'd done for her, and I didn't know what she was like. First, she never got back to me and I've still got approvers waiting on it, right?" I shook my head. "So, I stroll over and figure that I'll introduce myself and pick it up."

Rachel watched me closely. "So, I walk on over, and I'm, like, 'Hi, I'm the new writer, I don't think we've met,' and she picks up the story and says, 'Are you by chance the person who wrote this?' " I imitated her nasal voice and Rachel giggled. "And I said, 'Why yes' "—here I made my voice sound high and sweet—"and she looks at it, snorts, and says, 'This is completely below standard. I won't even look at it until you bring me something passable.' "

"Oh my gosh! What did you do?"

"Well, I just stood there. You know when you're thinking, this must be a joke, right?"

"Yeah?"

Bobby came around the corner cube. I had stopped speaking, but when I saw it was him, I continued.

"So, I just stood there like a big moron! And she says, 'Do you have a hearing problem?' "

"Oh no!"

"Yup. And that's when it started to sink in."

"So what did you do?"

Bobby had heard this story before, but he listened again.

"Well, I just ran back here and tried not to cry," I admitted. "I guess that's trial by fire, huh?"

"Wow. I feel better, then. She's never been that bad with me," said Rachel.

"Me either," said Bobby.

We both rolled our eyes. "Because you're a guy," said Rachel. "She wouldn't try that with you."

He'd picked up Rachel's piece and read it quickly. "Sounds good to me, kiddo."

Rachel stood up. "Thanks. And thanks, Trina. For looking at it."

"That's what I'm here for." Rachel trundled off to her cube, and Bobby slid down into the chair she'd vacated.

"What's up?"

"*Nada.* The newsletter's with design, and I'm waiting on some feedback. I need something to do, boss."

I spread my hands. "I can't believe it, but we're caught up."

"What about that project for Petra?"

"The web redesign?" I made a face. "After all that, she decided to scratch it."

"Welcome to corporate America!"

"Yeah, I know. But it's a job, right?"

"Umm-hmmm." He recrossed his legs. "OK, so I have *nada.* Do you want me to offer myself to marketing?"

"No, don't do that. I'll dig up something for you to work on." Three days ago, all three of us had been churning out work; now there was nothing to do. The feast or famine nature of the work was one of the most frustrating parts about it.

"Whatever you say."

I turned in my chair and tucked my foot underneath me. "Hey, what's going on with your screenplay?"

He signed and leaned his head back. "I don't know. Some nights I look at it and think it's pretty good, and then I'm convinced it sucks." He grinned. "But Marcus thinks it's fantastic."

"I'm not even going to try to keep up with you anymore."

"Still no luck in the love department?"

"No. Not like you're thinking."

"Please don't say you're back with that little sex monkey attorney."

"No. No!"

"Who then? That nice suburban boy?"

"OK, I tell you way too much. No, not him either." I hadn't told him about my little STD encounter, nor would I, though.

"Who then?" He looked at me intently, screwing up his eyes. "Oh, oh, I've got it. What, did he come back begging for forgiveness?"

"Who?" But my voice was weak. I'm a terrible liar.

"Your little geek boy. So, what did he say? Was this just a booty call or are you back together?"

"I don't know." My phone rang and I checked the caller ID. Petra. "Gotta take this."

He sat and waited until I got off the phone. "So?"

"OK, you do need to find something to do."

"Give me a nugget of information and I'll be off."

"All right. He called me. He apologized. He came over last night. And we had a huge fight." I looked down. "I don't want to talk about it." I looked up at his face. "OK?"

He didn't say anything for a minute.

"Can I say one thing?" he said. "If you had a terrible fight, there's still something there. The opposite of love—"

"Isn't hate, it's indifference," I finished for him. "I'm aware." I tried to smile.

"All right." Bobby reached over and squeezed my shoulder before getting up. "If you do want to talk, you know where to find me."

The thing was, I didn't want to talk about it, not with anyone. When I'd opened the door and saw him standing there, I'd felt like all the air had been sucked from my chest. Neither one of us said anything, and then he simply stepped forward and hugged me. I hugged him back, my arms around his neck, my face pressed against him. He smelled so good.

"You smell so good," I said, without moving my face.

"You feel so good." He tightened his hold and I thought, God, I've missed you.

But then, when he bent to kiss me, something sharp and ugly twisted in my brain. I had a sudden flash of his face when

I came marching out of his bedroom that night and I pulled away from him.

"What? What's wrong?"

I crossed my arms over my chest. "Why did you come over here?"

"I couldn't help myself." I didn't say anything. "I wanted to see you." I still didn't answer. "I wanted to see you, Trina! I've missed you!"

"This isn't fair. This is like a sneak attack, showing up like this." I fiddled with my watch and looked up at him. "I suppose you think now we'll jump in bed and all will be forgiven."

"Aw, hell, Trina, I don't know. Don't make more of this than it is. I wanted to see you. Does it have to be complicated?"

"Well, I think it does have to be, yeah. This isn't like we don't know each other, you know? We do have a history, don't we?" I was trying to keep my tone casual, conversational, logical. I was failing. "Now, you just show up here and . . . and . . ."

He reached out for my arm. "And what?" His voice was gentle but I tore my arm away from him.

"And I'll forgive you and everything will be fine, and we'll be right back where we were."

"Trina, is what I did so terrible?"

I stared at him. "Are you joking?" I marched toward the phone. "Do you want me to take a poll?"

"Look, we're not married." His tone was reasonable.

"So? Dating doesn't count for anything?"

"Will you sit down for a minute?"

I sat stiffly, and crossed my arms, glaring at him. He tugged at his hair, leaned his head back, and spread his arms open.

"Look. We had a great thing going. Seriously. I didn't even know how great. But I don't remember ever telling you that I'd see only you."

"See? You mean fuck, don't you?"

"See, fuck, what's the difference?"

I didn't laugh, and instead continued to stare at him. My

face felt hot and dry, and I could feel tension snap along my
back. I just wish he didn't look so good with that razor stubble
and that black sweatshirt that had long since faded to dark
gray. I'd loved to wear it around his apartment, and sneak it
home with me to bum around in. Had he chosen it on purpose? Had she worn it? I shut my eyes.

"Am I right?"

I thought. He was wrong. I knew that at some point, we'd
agreed to be exclusive, to be faithful. Maybe we'd never said
anything specifically about not seeing anyone else, but we
were grown-ups, for God's sake! Or supposed to be, anyway.
After a certain amount of time together, couldn't you assume
you didn't have to worry about your boyfriend finding someone he liked better? Wasn't that a safe assumption even if you
couldn't recall the exact conversation when he'd guaranteed
you were the only one for him?

I didn't say anything. "Come on," he teased. "You know
when I'm right."

"Argh!" I made a supremely unattractive noise and covered
my face with my hands. "So the whole time we're going out,
you were fucking other women?"

"No." He sat down on the coffee table and grabbed my
hands. "No," he said, his eyebrows raised and his expression
that of a sweet six-year-old. "But I never thought that I couldn't,
either."

I just stared. Since I'd met him, there hadn't even been another man on my radar screen. Who was going to make me
laugh like he did? Who would watch *True Hollywood Story* with
me? Who would be content to go to Borders with me and
spend three hours in the café, reading, so I had the wonderful
sensation of slipping into a private world in a public place,
alone but not alone because he was there only inches from me?

I'd been so in love with him that I hadn't even noticed any
other guys, let alone considered going to bed with them. I
clenched my teeth. And I was *not* going to admit this to him.
I'd be as cool about it as he was.

I shook my hair back away from my face. "I'm sorry. You were saying . . ."

"I didn't fuck anyone else when we were together, Trina. I didn't particularly want to. Then I met Jill and . . . well, I wanted to." He looked away.

"Oh, I see. That was big of you, giving up all those possible fucks for me for what, a year and a half! Thank you." Like I said, I wasn't doing the best job of being casual.

"I wasn't giving anything up. That's what I liked about you, Trina. You're smart, you're funny, you're sexy, you're fun—come on, I was satisfied with that. I loved it! But just because you're happy with what you have at the moment doesn't mean you're going to give up your freedom. Forever."

I got up. "I'm getting a glass of water." I walked to the kitchen, and something occurred to me. I turned.

"This whole thing started up after I asked you about getting married, didn't it?"

"What? What are you talking about?" said Rick.

"You know. When we went to my parents' for my dad's birthday, and Jessie got drunk. We were driving home and I asked you if you ever thought about getting married."

"No. That's not it."

"It is." My voice rose. "And you're so afraid of making a commitment—of even thinking about it—that you went out and screwed someone else. This stuff is just a smokescreen."

"I told you, I didn't screw her."

"Not at all."

He hung his head slightly. "Well, not until after . . ."

"After I found out about her. Well, thank you very much!"

"Look, why are you so angry? Admit it, I never promised you I'd be 'faithful.'" He emphasized the word with a mocking tone. "So why are you so upset about it?"

"Because I think you're full of it. I don't believe this crap about you always having the license to go out and bang anyone you wanted. I think you liked the way things were with me, but you got freaked out, so you had to blow it."

"You're crazy."

"Nope, that's it." I was pacing now, nodding to myself. I felt like a combination of Dr. Joyce Brothers and Angela Lansbury, pulling together the clues to explain the story. "So instead of being a man and telling me—admitting to me—that you're scared, you do something to make me—force me to break it off. That way you don't have to be the bad guy. Classic male behavior." I don't know where I came up with that one. Jane would have been proud of me.

Rick threw up his hands. "Whatever! You've obviously got me figured out, so why bother?"

"So, my problem is—or I should say, my problem was—that I was expecting too much from you. I was expecting more than you are able to give." I paused. "But I was blind to it. I see it now."

He stood up. "You know, I came over because I wanted to see you. I miss you. But this shit is over the top." He strode to the door. "Later."

I heard him clomp down the stairs, and I stood there for another minute before I let myself cry. I'd almost torn after him, and then steeled myself. He was the one who had started this whole thing, after all.

I considered talking about it with Jane, but she would probably just cheer me on. She seemed impervious to getting hurt. After breaking up with a guy, she might rake him over the coals a few times, but then she was on to the next conquest.

Jessie might get it. No, I didn't want to share this with her. Let her enjoy the excitement of being pregnant without me butting in. Besides, there were some uncomfortable similarities between my situation and hers. She might not know that, but the idea of discussing it with her made me nervous.

Wait a minute. Here I am, twenty-eight years old. I've got a good job, I'm fairly intelligent and insightful (at least I like to think so), I'm able to pay my bills on time and act and think rationally. Who says I even need to discuss this with anyone? I needed to be more of a lone wolf, I thought, the kind of person who makes a decision without a thought of what someone else might think. Someone like Jane.

My phone rang, drawing me back to the present. I glanced at the display. It was Rick. I took a breath.

"What, are your ears burning?"

"What?"

"Nothing." I shook my head though he couldn't see me. "Forget it."

He didn't say anything. "I'm sorry about that scene last night."

"Are you really? Or are you just saying that?"

"I'm sorry. I'm sorry for that and sorry about what I did before. How many times can I say that? What do you want? I fucked up. I did some stupid shit. I thought maybe if we saw each other, we could talk, work things out."

I sighed and held the phone closer to my mouth. "How come every emotion a guy feels gets expressed as anger?"

"What do you mean?"

"I mean, you keep saying you're sorry but what you really sound like is pissed off."

"Point taken." I heard him exhale. "I'm frustrated. And I am pissed, but I'm more pissed at myself. I want to set things right with you, and I don't seem able to do it."

"You do?"

"I do. So how do I do that? What do I say?"

I took a swig of water. "You know what I want you to say?" I whispered. "Something like, 'I'm really sorry I hurt you and lied to you and screwed up a really great relationship.'"

"Well, I am." I pictured him holding his cordless phone. I knew he'd have his hand in his hair, absently tugging at the roots. I'd seen him do it when he was puzzling over his computer at home, trying to solve a problem. "What do you want, anyway? What do you want from me? Why does this have to be so complicated?"

"We're right back where we were last night," I said. "Look, I've got a lot to do here." A lie, but he didn't have to know that.

"Wait, wait. How about if you come over to my place

tonight. I'll get us some food and we'll watch *THS*. Come on. I think it's the *Baywatch* one."

I didn't say anything. I'd be crazy to go over there.

"Come on, Trina. No strings. Come over. We'll talk. That's it."

"All right," I said finally. "But this isn't a date."

"Nope, not at all."

I drove straight to his apartment after work. I wasn't going to go home and shower and put on makeup and nice under-wear. This was come as you are, and it *wasn't* a date. I'd blasted Linkin Park all the way into Chicago to toughen me up, refus-ing to think about what I was doing.

When I got there, I trotted up the steps to his walkup and knocked on the door.

He opened it. He was wearing a faded maroon T-shirt and old Levis that hung off his hips. He'd shaved, and his hair was still damp from a shower. We looked at each other for a minute.

"I don't want to start with 'hi' again," I said. "That doesn't seem to be working too well for us."

"True. How about, 'thank you for coming,' " he said, mo-tioning me in with his arm. I was surprised. His apartment was spotless. The newspapers that were usually piled on one end of the couch were gone; there weren't any sweatshirts or running shoes scattered throughout the small apartment. It looked sterile somehow.

"Can I get you something to drink? Glass of wine?" He showed me three bottles on the counter. Chardonnay, merlot, and white zinfandel.

"Trying to get me drunk?"

"I didn't know what you'd feel like."

So he bought three bottles. I accepted a glass of chardon-nay. He was drinking a Beck's Dark. I sat down at the tall kitchen counter in his apartment that doubled as a table.

"You look great," he said. "I meant to tell you last night I like your hair like that."

I touched the back of my head. "Really? You don't think it's too short?"

"No, I like it. It's cute."

I made a face, and he quickly amended, "I mean, it's pretty." He knew I hated being called cute. Puppies are cute. Babies are cute. Women are pretty.

"Thanks."

We talked about other inconsequential things for a few minutes. I had that sensation of watching the scene from outside my body. It was like acting in a bad play, where the dialogue was wooden and the acting was worse. I didn't want to sit and talk about the weather with him or why the Bears were sucking so bad. I wanted him to tell me why he had invited me over, but I wasn't going to cave and ask him.

We'd been talking in the kitchen, but it was ten minutes before I realized I didn't see any evidence of cooking. No utensils, no delicious smells, no spatter stains. I got up and checked the oven. It was cold.

"I thought you were making dinner."

"I said I'd get us some food. I'll make it appear, how's that?" He shook his head. "I don't know what I was saying."

"So, what do you do all day now?" I waved my hand. "Besides clean?"

"Now that I have no job? Let's see. The first week was spent being pissed off," he said. "The second, I questioned my manhood."

"Please."

"It's been rough. I know lots of guys who have lost their jobs, but I never thought it would happen to me." He opened the refrigerator and got himself another beer, and poured me more wine. "Shit, I forgot." He took out a can of cashews and pulled off the red plastic top. "Bar snacks."

I took a small handful. They were my favorite. "Why would you think it wouldn't happen to you?" I thought about the anxiety I'd felt when the reorg had started up at the Coddled Cook, how I'd been sure that I'd be one of the ones to be axed.

In fact, everyone I'd spoken to about it had had the same awful anxiety.

"You know how it is. Thought they couldn't run the firm without me." He tugged on his hair. "I, of course, was proven wrong."

"Well, I'm sorry. I know how much you liked your job." Is *she* still working there? I wondered.

"I'll be all right. I'm in the third week now."

"And what happens then?"

"Figuring out what I want to do next."

"Have you interviewed for anything? Sent any résumés out?"

"Nah. The job market's so lousy I don't know if it's worth it. I've talked to a few recruiters and they'll let me know if they come up with anything. I told them I'm willing to move."

"Oh, you are? That's good." Listen to us. We sounded like we were making small talk at a very small party. A boring one.

"What about you? What's happening in your world?"

"Well, I already told you about work. It's going OK. I'm still getting used to the idea of being someone's boss, though. I think I liked it better when I was only responsible for myself."

"How's Bobby, and what's her name, Rachel, doing?"

He'd remembered. Well, it'd been only four months, after all. "They're both good. He's writing a screenplay, actually."

"No shit? For work?"

"No. For himself. He's the same, you know how he is." They'd met several times, and I'd been surprised that they hit it off. Both were *Godfather* addicts—Rick had seen I, II, and III at least ten times—and Rick had commented on Bobby later.

"He's all right. Not a flamer or anything." Not that Rick was homophobic, but like most straight men I knew, he was the tiniest bit uncomfortable around any gay man. You could see it in their faces, as if their underwear were suddenly pinching just a little bit too tightly, minute little shifting motions of the body, the attitude that, if touched, they might suddenly fly apart.

"And Rachel's the same. Living with her parents, looking for Mr. Right." We smiled an avuncular smile at each other like we were her grandparents or something. Yeah, right. I had a mere four years on her and I wasn't having any more success in my love life than she was. But at least I knew more.

"And what about Trina?"

I played along. "Trina is . . . Trina is thinking about buying a house. Well, a condo probably. But something."

"Where?"

"Closer to work."

"The burbs?" His tone said it all.

"Please, now you sound like Jane. In any decent neighborhood in the city, I can't afford to buy. There I can get a place with parking and everything."

"But why buy?"

"I'm sick of renting. I want something that's my own. And it makes more sense for taxes and everything."

He nodded. "I guess. Have you looked at anything?"

"A few places." Well, I had. I didn't need to say that I'd just driven by them. On one occasion, I'd parked in the visitors' lot and watched the cars driving in. Could I live here? Would I be happy? A condo was so much more permanent than an apartment. It scared me a little.

I didn't want to get into all this with Rick, though. "We'll see," I said. "I'll keep you posted."

"So."

"So."

He reached over and picked up my wineglass out of my hands. "I had an idea today. What do you think of starting over with me?"

"Starting over how?"

"Wipe the slate clean, start over. Like we have no past."

"But we do have a past."

"Yeah, and I fucked that up."

"I thought you said last night it was my fault for expecting too much from you, you know, like fidelity."

"Wait. I don't want a repeat of last night." He grabbed the bottom of my barstool and pulled me toward him. "Can we agree that maybe you were thinking what you wanted to think, and that I was thinking what I wanted to think, and that didn't work out?"

"I thought we were supposed to have no past." I pulled away from him and crossed my arms.

"How do you want it, Trina? Do you want to try again? Maybe I should have said something to you, all right?"

"Maybe?"

He refused to cave, to admit that I was the one who was right, that I was the one who had been wronged. But I might be able to forgive him for that, over time. He did say he'd like to start over.

"We'll lay out the ground rules from the beginning so there's no confusion," he said.

"OK, then. Rule number one is no other women. Period."

"That's fine. I can live with that," he said mopily. He saw my face. "I'm kidding! I mean, that's great!" he said in a bright voice, shaking his fist in the air. "That's what I want!"

I had to laugh. "All right, give me one of your rules."

"I don't have any. I just want you."

Come on. You've got to admit that's a killer line.

Chapter 28
The Ten of Cups

Family happiness.

I didn't realized how easy it would be to slide back into the same comfortable routine. I stayed at Rick's that night, but we didn't have sex. I still felt off-balance with him, not completely comfortable. I told him about the whole wart thing—how embarrassing—and his reaction surprised me.

"You mean, you slept with someone else?"

"What did you expect? That I'd give up on men entirely because of you?" I didn't mention that the whole idea had been to exorcise him from my heart. Or that it hadn't worked.

Rick's mouth twitched. "No, I guess not." He didn't say anything for a moment. "So what's the deal? Were you serious about this guy?"

Guys, I mentally corrected, but I'd left Javier out of this conversation. Rick didn't need to know everything, after all. "If I didn't know better, I'd say you were jealous." Rick tugged at his hair but didn't answer.

I felt a small thrill but without the jubilation I'd expected. I'd wanted him to suffer the way I had. Or least I'd thought I wanted him to suffer. The truth was I didn't want him to hurt. "It wasn't serious," I said. "It's not like I loved him."

Still, though, I needed to keep Rick at arm's length for a

while—I knew if we made love, I'd be right back where I'd been emotionally. I wasn't ready to fall in love with him again. Or so I told Jane a few days later.

"That's nuts," said Jane. "You're in love with him already."

"No, I'm not," I said. "It's like layaway love. He won't get it unless he pays the balance."

"OK, forget what I said. *You* are nuts," said Jane.

I lowered my voice. Another memo had recently circulated about the ban on using the telephone for anything other than work-related calls. We'd all cheerily ignored it, but that didn't mean I wanted to get caught, either.

"More nuts than, say, thinking that you knew someone in a past life?"

"That is not nuts, sweetie. That is karma."

"Uh-huh." She and Steve were still together. He'd practically moved in at Jane's. I liked him. He was slow in his movements, and you could feel him weighing things, considering his words carefully before he spoke. I could sense him watching people, but I never felt that he was doing it in a judgmental way.

"He's very aware," Jane had confirmed. "He has the most amazing insights! He'll watch someone and just know all about them!"

"Like what?"

"Well, like with you. He says you're a little mouse, sticking her nose out of your mouse hole but afraid to venture outside."

"Really. How flattering." But the remark stung. A little mouse? Thanks a lot. "And what are you?"

"A tiger on the prowl, all pent-up energy, looking for how to spend it," said Jane. "And that is so true! That is me!"

Sure, why not. She got to be a sensual tiger; I was a trembly little mouse. I told Rick about it later. "Isn't that ridiculous?"

He was thoughtful. "I don't know, Trina. Maybe he's right."

"Thanks a lot!"

"Don't get pissed. Come on, you know you tend to err on the conservative side," he said. "Nothing wrong with that."

"So what am I supposed to do? Get drunk, flash my tits on one of those *Girls Gone Wild* videos?"

"Ooooh, yeah. Would you?" I kicked him in the thigh. We were sprawled on my couch, watching some *TechTV* show about computer games. I'd learned to talk to him during commercial breaks, compressing conversations into succinct three-and four-minute windows.

"I'm serious. Do you think I'm a scared mouse, too afraid to take risks?"

"Maybe." I kicked at him again, but he grabbed my foot. "Don't knock it. I like that about you. You're nice and sweet"— he paused and grinned—"and mousy. Yeah."

"Shut up." I grabbed a pillow off the couch and tried to smash it into his face, but he took it away from me easily and pinned me on the couch.

"Look what I caught," he said, holding my hands above my head. "A cute little mouse."

I squirmed. "Shut up!"

He smiled. "I love it when you get all mad like this."

"I am not mad. Let me go. You're hurting me." He was holding my wrists carefully, though, and he shifted his weight so he wouldn't crush me.

"In a minute." He kissed me, a very nice soft delicate little kiss. "Mmmmm." He kissed me again and let go of my hands. I could feel the warmth of his lips, the familiar scratch of his stubble, the downy softness of the hair at the back of his neck.

"I don't want to push you, but are you, uh, ready?" he whispered after a few minutes. I'd told him I didn't want to jump right back into bed with him, and he'd respected that.

"What do you think?"

There was only one problem, one fly in the ointment. Namely Jessie, and Jane, and my parents, and even Rachel. Bobby knew enough of men's hearts not to offer his opinion, but I knew that no one was going to give Rick the benefit of the doubt. I'd said too much when we'd broken up, especially to Jessie. I'd have to break the news that we were back together carefully.

But I had prepared a scripted speech for nothing. "Really? That's great."

I didn't say anything. I'd heard of pregnancy hormones, but I hadn't expected this softer version of Jessie. She was distracted, dreamy even. She didn't look pregnant yet, but she'd taken to resting one hand protectively over her stomach. It would have been annoying but I realized it wasn't conscious.

I hadn't seen Ethan since their party, and I was relieved. I knew from Jessie that he was happy about the baby, and hoped that that would be the end of his, well, whatever. I'd stopped calling it an affair in my mind. Just an innocent little flirtation, and there was nothing wrong with that, even if you were married.

Christmas had snuck up on me—now it was only a week away. This was the Coddled Cook's busiest season for the delivery department, but things were slow in marketing/communications. Our work was already done—now it was up to the Cook's Helpers to capitalize on the holiday season this month, and sell, sell, sell.

The season also meant it was time for the office "holiday" party. We'd been sent a memo reminding us not to call it a "Christmas party" in an effort to be sensitive to non-Christians, Jews, Muslims, Buddhists, you name it. This was the first year it was being held off the premises. To accommodate everyone, the party would be held on two different nights.

Shipping, order fulfillment, facility operations, and the other blue-collar departments would have their party on Friday; the office-type employees including marketing, communications, sales, information services, and other departments would have ours on Saturday. That, of course, meant we got stuck with the managers, vice presidents, and all the suits as well. The twin sisters who had founded the company attended both parties so no one would feel snubbed, but traditionally these things were a rather sedate affair.

Until this year, that is. Just add alcohol and see what happens. The party was held at a big hotel in Oak Brook, and dress was "business formal," the invitation had read.

"What does that mean?" Rachel had asked.

"I don't know. Maybe a dress instead of pants." I'd decided on a black skirt, black turtleneck, and black boots. I added a silver belt and silver earrings. I looked polished, I thought.

I knew when I arrived that I'd made an error. I'd parked, and checked my coat before stepping into the ballroom. The room was decorated with hanging lights and lots of greenery, and white-gloved waiters strolled around offering little hors d'oeuvres on platters. I'd been expecting something more along the lines of construction paper cutouts and popcorn strings, but obviously I'd been wrong. The other women were wearing cocktail dresses that exposed more flesh than I'd seen since the summer months. Rachel hurried over. She was wearing a green corduroy jumper over a long-sleeved green-and-red-striped T-shirt.

"Look at everyone's dresses!" she hissed. "I look awful!"

"No, you look fine." I grabbed her. "Come on, let's get a drink."

The theme of the party seemed to be, "If you've got it, flaunt it—and even if you don't got it, flaunt it all the same." There was a lot of skin on display. Even Petra sported a clingy sapphire blue dress slit down to her butt cleavage. Her bony shoulder blades jutted out like tailfins on a fifties car. I nudged Rachel.

"I know! I saw it." Rachel looked down at her jumper. "I'm a total frump."

"You and me both."

"No, I love that outfit. You look very . . . warm."

I laughed.

"How long do you think we have to stay?"

"At least an hour or two. The sisters will make some kind of speech; don't dream of leaving beforehand."

"Who should I talk to?"

"What do you mean?"

"I just read in *Cosmo* that these parties are the perfect place to network to further your career. You know, network and make contacts and everything."

"In *Cosmo*? Well, I don't know that you can further your career here. You can probably hurt it a lot, though." I made a tiny movement with my head. Several of the women from sales were standing in a tight little knot, laughing a little too loudly. One—Teresa, I think—threw back her arm and slammed it into the head of the new products division.

"Oopsie! So sorry!"

Rachel was talking to Anne, one of the designers, and I was listening to their conversation halfheartedly. Mostly I was watching the party unfold.

I'd like to see this on time-lapse photography, I thought. People went from standing about stiffly, taking small polite sips of their drinks, making muted small talk. Fast-forward to an hour later, a sizable increase in the blood alcohol levels of most of those present, and the noise level had grown. Another thirty minutes, and the clamor hurt my ears.

I was bored, but I consoled myself with the thought that I'd soon be home. I asked the bartender for another Diet Coke, and sat down at a table, watching the crowd. Elaine saw me and waved. Don't come over here, I thought, but she didn't get my psychic message.

"Too much partying?" she asked.

I forced a smile and pointed at my drink. "Not exactly. Not unless you consider Diet Coke a wild drink."

She sat down and we watched a few brave souls attempt to dance to "Who Let the Dogs Out." This was worse than a wedding. At least there you could usually sneak out after a decent time without the bride and groom noticing or even caring. Here, I felt I should stay long enough to prove my dedication to the company. I just wasn't sure how long that was.

"Can I ask you something?" said Elaine suddenly. "How well do you know Bobby?"

I looked at her. She knew we were friends. "Pretty well."
She said nothing, and I shook my head. "Why?"

"I heard a rumor about him." She fluffed her hair with her
fingers. "A rumor that could get him fired."

I couldn't believe the company was *that* conservative.
Would they really care if he was gay? Could he even be fired
for that? But I bit. "Cut to the chase. What's the rumor?"

She leaned toward me. "I'll tell you this. It doesn't have
anything to do with what he's doing at work. At least not for
the Coddled Cook."

I squinted at her. "I have no idea what you're talking
about."

She sat there for a moment, then stood. "Well, all righty
then. Just thought you'd want to know."

"Elaine, you haven't even told me anything. What do you
want me to say?"

"Forget it. I thought as his boss, you'd know what he was
up to."

I watched her walk away. Bobby hadn't even bothered to
come to the holiday party. I'd reminded him how bad that
looked, but he'd waved me off. I wondered what Elaine was
talking about, and whether this was just another one of her
ploys to get me stirred up. I'd ask him about it on Monday, I
decided.

After the requisite speech by the sisters, about a quarter of
the people there headed for the door, home to husbands,
wives, and children. The higher-ups and the singles stayed on.
I didn't see Elaine anywhere, but I found Rachel.

"I'm getting ready to take off," I told her.

Her face was shiny, and strands of her curly hair had
worked themselves free from the loose bun. "Oh, don't go!"
She grabbed my arm. "It's just getting fun."

"Yes, but I've got that long drive ahead of me." Sometimes
I appreciated the excuse.

"Okay!" She grinned at me. "I'll give you a full report on
Monday."

I drove toward the city, worrying about Bobby. Then I switched gears and worried about Rick instead. Should I invite him home for Christmas with me or not? Jessie knew we were back together, but I didn't know if she'd said anything to Mom or Dad. Probably not. Her head was full of baby right now.

It was a strange situation. After all, if we had dated for only a couple of weeks, I wouldn't have dreamed of inviting him home for the holidays. But then again, we had a history whether we pretended to or not. I didn't think he'd have any plans; at least he hadn't said anything about it to me.

I decided to check it out with my parents first. I knew I could show up with him, but I didn't want any free-floating hostility circulating to ruin the day. Christmas was my favorite holiday. My parents had never been big on the church part of it, but we'd always gone all out with decorating the tree, making and decorating Christmas cookies, listening to old Elvis holiday classics, the whole nine yards. My dad would put on Christmas albums and sing along. Jessie and I would be helping Mom decorate stocking-shaped cookies with red-and-green icing and those hard little silver balls that hurt your teeth when you ate them, and he'd be blasting out, *"I'm dreaming of a white Christmas,"* and Melissa would be crawling around under our feet.

Jessie would spend at least fifteen minutes on each of her cookie stockings, using a toothpick to draw elaborate designs with the colored sugar. My method was simpler—I took a teaspoon of sugar, dumped it on a cookie, and moved on to the next one.

"Chestnuts roasting on an open fire . . ." my dad boomed. "Come on, girls, sing along!"

"Dad, that song is for old fogies." Jessie sniffed and tossed her ponytail before returning to her meticulous work.

"I like it." I ate one of my less successful creations. "Besides, Dad isn't an old fogie."

"Thank you, sweetie pie." My dad grabbed my mom. "Hear that, hon? I've still got it."

"You've got it, all right." But she was smiling, and he wrapped his arms around her from behind. He kissed her neck.

"You guys are gross! Not in front of the children!" said Jess. I just watched. I hoped that someday my husband would be as nice and funny and handsome as my dad was.

"How do you think we got you children, anyway?"

Jessie was mortified. "Mom, please. Tell him to quit."

"Relax, Jessie. Part of being a teenager is being embarrassed by your parents." My mom took another sheet of cookies out of the oven. Dad scooped Melissa up from the floor.

"You're not embarrassed by your old man, are you, baby doll?" He hung her upside down for a moment and she squealed with delight.

"I'm not embarrassed!" I said, but he hadn't heard me—he was making Melissa laugh. It wasn't a big thing, anyway.

I called my parents late Sunday afternoon to prepare them. "Hi, Mom," I said. "It's me."

"Hi, Trina. What are you doing?"

"Nothing. I just wanted to ask about Christmas."

"Yes?"

"I'm wondering if you'd mind if I brought someone with me."

"Of course not. We'd love to see Jane again."

"Well, it's not Jane." I felt a twinge of guilt. I hadn't even asked Jane about what she was planning for the holidays, but she'd probably be with Steve. They were practically joined at the hip. "It's Rick, actually."

"Rick? Really? Are the two of you back together?"

"Yes. But," I hurried on, "it's not a big deal. We just agreed to give it a try again." The less detail involved, I figured, the better.

"Well, I'm glad to hear it. Bring him. Oh, what should I get him? Is he a sweater guy? I saw some gorgeous turtlenecks at Kohl's."

"Mom, you don't have to buy him anything. And please don't get him a turtleneck."

"Well, of course I do. He's going to be here for Christmas and I want him to have something to open."

"All right. But no turtlenecks, all right?"

"What's wrong with turtlenecks? You wear them all the time."

"Mom, I'm not a guy. No guy is going to wear a turtleneck."

"Well, never say never," said Mom. "When will you get down here?"

"Probably afternoon, Christmas Eve. Is that OK?"

"All right. We'll see you then."

Chapter 29
The Eight of Cups, Inverted

Joy, feasting, merriment.

Rick and I left for Champaign just before noon. I'd told him if he didn't have other plans, he was welcome to join us downstate, and he'd agreed. "That sounds good," he'd said.

"Really?"

"Yeah." He saw me looking at him. "I like your family, Trina. Relax. All right?"

"All right." Since we'd been back together, I'd been trying not to expect too much. We had a great time together, we made each other laugh and we still had that same sexual bond. And I knew he loved me. I didn't need to ruin things with traditional expectations like getting married. I'd take things one day at a time.

Besides, he still hadn't found a new job. Not that he was working that hard at locating one. As far as I could tell, he spent most of his time during the day playing *Soldier of Fortune* or some other computer game where you could kill your opponents and their bloody limbs would go flying off. He said he had recruiters looking for him. "Besides, the market's so bad, it's not even worth looking right now," he told me.

When we arrived at my parents', Jess and Ethan were already there. My dad immediately ran off to the garage with Rick and Ethan. I headed into the kitchen, where my mom and Jessie were sitting.

"You want coffee? Coke? Glass of wine?"

"Herbal tea," said Jessie, lifting up her cup. "No caffeine for me."

I checked the coffeemaker. "I could go for some coffee." I motioned to Mom to sit down. "So, what's going on?"

"We're just talking about the baby's room," said my mom. "Jessie's thinking of a Winnie the Pooh theme."

"Who?"

"You know who Winnie the Pooh is," said Jessie. "I told you about this."

I didn't remember, but I tended to glaze over when she started rambling about baby things. I'd thought her talking about the law was bad. I'd had no idea.

"I've already seen the perfect crib and it has a matching bassinet," Jessie was saying. "And I've found some of the most adorable newborn outfits!" She rubbed her stomach. "I've got six of them already."

"Oh, I know. Those little rompers are so tiny," my mom said. "I remember before you were born, I'd hold up a T-shirt and think, how can a baby possibly be small enough to wear this?"

They continued on in this vein, and I found myself feeling invisible. Of course I was excited about the baby too—I'd be an aunt! But talking about baby clothes wasn't my idea of a good time.

My mom said something to me, but I didn't catch it.

"I said, how is Rick doing?" she repeated.

"Well, he's here. Ask him yourself."

"Someone seems to have a case of the crankies," said my mom, unperturbed. "More coffee?"

"Please."

Jessie stood up, stretched, and sat down again. "Yes, fill

us in before the men return from the garage. What's the deal?"

"I don't know." I lowered my voice. "I told you he lost his job."

"Oh, that's right. Has he found anything yet?"

"No, Mom. He's working with some recruiters, though. I'm sure he'll find something soon," I said.

"What's he looking for? I can ask around at work if you want. Maybe the firm needs someone," said Jessie.

"That's a good idea, but I don't know what kind of position he's looking for," I said lamely.

"I'd think if he doesn't have a job, *any* position would be a good one," said my mom. "He can always find something else eventually."

"I guess. It's up to him, though. I'm just trying to be a good listener. And besides, it's not really my business. We're not married or anything."

My mom and Jessie exchanged a look.

"What? What does that mean?"

"Nothing, honey," said my mom. "How was your work party? Is everything going well there?"

We talked for a while, until the guys came stomping in from the garage, rubbing their hands together and smelling of cigars. Melissa and her roommate, Amy, arrived a few minutes later, dragging their backpacks with them.

"Good, the whole family's here," said Dad. "Now we can eat!"

My mom had set the table for eight, with her at one end, Dad at the other. Jessie sat at her right, then Ethan, then Melissa. Rick and I were sitting on the other side of the table with Amy, a tiny brunette with long straight hair and smooth skin. She was wearing a tight little T-shirt that stretched the word ANGEL across her disproportionately large breasts. She didn't say much during dinner, but she was polite, complimenting my mom on the dinner several times.

"My parents are in Spain for the holidays," she explained. "It's so great that Miss invited me."

"That's what the holidays are all about," said my mom.

"Well, it's so great."

"What are you majoring in?" I asked.

"Well, I started in sociology, but then I got interested in psych. But then I took a poetry class and it was so fascinating! So I changed majors to English. The written word is so incredible."

"Trina's the writer in our family." My dad spoke up between bites.

"Oh, that's right! So, do you like to write short stories or novels or what?"

"Not exactly. It's more business writing, writing ads and newsletters, and stuff like that."

She made a delicate face of disgust. "Well. That sounds so, well, boring!"

"It's not that bad."

"Isn't that kind of writing kind of selling out, though? I mean, you're not expressing your true self doing that kind of work."

I took a sip of wine. "*Well*," I said, though she didn't appear to notice, "it's really hard to get paid to write poetry full-time, you know."

"But I don't care about material things. I just want to be able to work on my art when I get out of school and not worry about having a nice house or a nice car or any of that material stuff. Follow my bliss, you know."

"I know," chimed in Melissa. "It's like people only go to college now to get a job so they can make money. What happened to broadening your mind and expanding your horizons?"

"Why'd you switch out of sociology?" asked Ethan. "That's what I majored in, before I sold out to the man and went to law school."

Amy smiled at him. "I don't mean that *everyone's* a sellout. If you're following your bliss, if you're doing what you want to do, that's wonderful. But too many people simply do what they think they're supposed to do, and follow the path of least resistance."

"Uh-huh. That's true," said Ethan. "I never thought of it but you're right."

"Oh, please. You always wanted to be a lawyer," said Jessie.

"But why? Because I chose the profession or because I thought it was the easiest path to follow?" said Ethan. "That's what Amy's saying, isn't it, Amy?"

She nodded vigorously, and Jessie made a small noise in her throat.

"I have to say that I always knew I wanted to be a network administrator," announced Rick. "Ever since I was little, I dreamed of connecting servers and routers and hubs." He said this in the voice of a wistful child and we all laughed, even Amy.

After dinner, Melissa dug out the board games. "Oh no," groaned Rick. "Anything but Pictionary, please."

"How about Taboo?"

"I refuse to play that game," said Jessie. "It's too frustrating." The idea of Taboo was simple—you split into teams and then took turns. One person from each team tried to get his teammates to guess a certain word—without using the best words to describe it. It was like language charades. But the way to win was to put people who thought the same way on the same team. Having the same point of view, the same frame of reference, made it much easier to win.

"OK, who else doesn't want to play?"

"I'll skip it, too," said my mom. "Jessie and I will be cheerleaders."

"OK," said Missy. "Let's do boys on girls, then. Me, Amy, and Trina take you guys on."

"You're on," said Rick. "We're going to mop the floor with you girls."

We started playing, sitting in a circle around the floor of the living room. "We have to sit on the floor?" complained my dad. "What's the point of having all this furniture?"

I was sitting between my dad and Rick, buzzing Dad whenever he said one of the taboo words. "Ah, shit," he said, hitting his forehead. "You shouldn't be allowed to play this game after a couple of beers."

"Come on, it's my turn," said Amy. She came up with obscure clues, but Missy got most of the words after only a couple of guesses.

"No fair. Married couples and roommates shouldn't be allowed on the same team," said Ethan. "Unfair advantage!"

She laughed. "Come on, are you afraid to lose to a girl?" She pushed against his arm.

"Maybe." He, Amy, and Rick were all leaning against the couch; me, my dad, and Melissa were facing them. My dad got up. "Got to put some new tunes on."

"Oh, no. Not any of that old stuff."

"Shows what you know. I've got some new ones here." He held up a handful of CDs. "Celine Dion, Garth Brooks, *Very Special Christmas Volume 3* . . ."

"Oh, play that one, Dad," Melissa said. He put it in and we returned to the game. We drank more boxed wine and, after another hour or so, were laughing more than we were playing. It was close to eleven.

"When do we open presents?" said Amy.

"That's Christmas morning," said Melissa.

"Yes, and I'm going to go to bed," announced my mom.

"Me, too." Jessie got up. "You coming, honey?"

"I'm not tired," said Ethan. "I'll be there in a while."

My dad got up, too. "I guess I'd better get some sleep, too, if I'm going to get up and make that turkey tomorrow." He'd be up by six, basting the bird on the hour until we ate. Thanksgiving and Christmas, we always had turkey, stuffing, mashed potatoes, scalloped corn, and rolls. The menu never changed. Dad did the turkey; Mom did everything else.

Melissa picked up the remote control. "Maybe there's a good movie on." She got up and turned off the lights. "For the full movie theater experience."

It turned out that "good movie" meant *Tommy Boy*. I'd seen it before, but I didn't mind watching it again. Rick and I were curled up in the loveseat, his arms around my waist. Melissa, Amy, and Ethan were all slumped on the couch, their feet propped up on the coffee table.

I must have fallen asleep. I opened my eyes. The volume on the TV was turned down, and the room was lit only by flickering images. I could feel Rick's breath against the back of my neck, and I shifted carefully so I wouldn't wake him.

Melissa had her head propped on her arm. Her eyes were closed and her mouth was open. Amy and Ethan were sitting close together. He was speaking in a low voice, and she had her head close to his. She started to laugh and then clamped her hand over her mouth.

I squinted, trying to see better. Why wasn't Ethan in bed with his wife, where he was supposed to be anyway? For God's sake. I yawned loudly, stretching my arms, watching for their reaction through slitted lids.

They jerked apart spastically. "You scared me!" hissed Amy.

"Huh? Oh, really?" I stood up and pushed Rick's shoulder. "Hey, sleepyhead. Let's go to bed." Ethan and Jessie had the queen bed in the guest room; Melissa had offered to let Rick and me sleep in her room.

"What about Mom and Dad?" I'd asked earlier that day.

"Amy and I will probably want to stay up late anyway. We can sleep in the living room."

"No, I mean, I don't think they're going to go for that." On other trips home, I'd slept with Melissa, Rick on the couch.

She shrugged. "Mom said it was fine with her."

Hmmm . . . maybe there was progress. I pulled Rick to his feet and shepherded him into Missy's room.

"Um, I should probably get to bed, too," whispered Ethan, glancing at me. "Night, Amy. Night, Trina."

"Good night."

Rick collapsed on the bed without taking his clothes off.

"Don't you want to get undressed?"

"Too tired."

I looked at him. One arm was thrown up over his face, and I could see the pale skin on the underside of his arm. His shirt had come untucked, and a sliver of dark belly hair showed above his jeans. I got undressed, pulling on an extra-long T-shirt to sleep in, and got into bed next to him.

"Could you believe that?"

"Huh?"

"Didn't you see them?" I whispered.

Rick was already asleep. I strained in the darkness, but I didn't hear Ethan. Had he gone to bed or was he still in the living room?

Gradually I became aware of sunlight, and the smell of coffee, and noises from the living room. I heard Jessie's voice, and then heard my dad laugh.

"Mmrfh," Rick mumbled behind me, and then rolled over, pulling me against him. "What time is it?"

I glanced at the clock radio. "Seven-seventeen."

"What the hell." He rearranged his pillow and yawned. "What is it with your family, man? It's a holiday. We should be sleeping in."

I pulled the blanket up over my shoulder and nestled against Rick.

"Would you tell me why I still have clothes on?" he asked, kissing my neck.

"Because you were too drunk to get undressed last night."

"Wasn't drunk. Was just tired. Am still tired." He pulled me closer, and I could feel his erection through his jeans against my ass.

"Uh-huh. You can forget about that."

"Come on." His voice had that too-early-in-the-morning rasp. "We could do it in here while they're out there drinking coffee and opening presents."

"No way! This is the first time I've been allowed to sleep in the same bed with a boy under their roof. If only they knew how safe I was last night."

"You're not safe now," he said, sliding his hand around to my breast. I grabbed his hand.

"Don't even think about it."

Knock, knock, knock. "Merry Christmas!" sang Jessie, opening the door. "Time to get up!"

I pulled away from him and sat up, but Rick just grabbed a pillow and threw it over his face. "You know, Trina, your sister is entirely too fucking cheerful in the morning," said Rick.

Jess wasn't fazed. "Good morning to you, too!"

I slid out of bed, pulling the covers off with me. Jessie saw his clothes.

"What, don't you believe in undressing before bed?"

"Too tired," he grumbled. "Need coffee."

I grinned at Jessie. "You know how men are in the morning."

"Ethan's worse. I'm going to roust him out of bed now. How late did you guys stay up, anyway?"

I pulled on a pair of sweatpants. "Geez, I don't know. One A.M.? One-thirty?"

She laughed and shook her head. "I can't do that anymore. I'm so tired all the time now."

I reached for a sweatshirt. I'd shower and get dressed later. "Come on, sleepyhead."

Amy and Melissa were still lying in their sleeping bags on the living room floor, but Mom and Dad were both up, drinking coffee in the kitchen. Mom was cutting up bread to make stuffing. Elvis was singing Christmas classics in the background.

"Coffee. Coffee." I hugged both of them. "Merry Christmas."

"Merry Christmas, Trina." Mom set another handful of bread chunks in the casserole dish.

"Can I help?"

"I'll tell you what you can do. Get that lazy little sister of yours off the floor so we can use the living room."

"Mom, I'm recovering from finals! I need my rest!" I heard her call from the living room.

"And we need the space to open gifts. Get up, and roll up those sleeping bags." When I came out into the living room, Melissa and Amy were both out of their nests, stretching and yawning.

"Come on, we can dump these in my room," Melissa grumbled. They trudged off, their arms full of pillows and bedding. I heard Jessie come downstairs and greet them. Ethan trailed down a few minutes later. His hair stuck up all over his head, and his beard had started coming in.

He came over and scratched his face against the back of Jessie's neck. "Oooh, itchy!" She pushed him away. "Nice hair."

"Huh?" He reached and touched his head.

"I think it looks cute. Kind of like Jimmy Fallon's." Melissa bounced into the kitchen, followed by Amy.

"Yeah, it looks good," agreed Amy. I glanced at her. She was wearing pajama bottoms, that same T-shirt from last night, and no bra. And her nipples were hard! I saw Ethan notice. Rick did, too. Dad didn't appear to, but who knew. Maybe he'd figured out a way to do it without his eyes popping out of his head. Rick and Ethan had not.

But could I blame them? She had big boobs, and no bra, and apparently it was chilly in the kitchen. I expected guys to look. That was part of the package. Rick knew enough, though, to glance at me after Amy sashayed into the kitchen. He caught my eye and grinned like a naughty child.

Rick came and grabbed my arms. "It's cold in the kitchen," he whispered.

"Yeah, I noticed you noticed."

"Hey, what do I want with a twenty-year-old?"

"The same thing every man wants with a twenty-year-old."

"Good point," he said, but I shoved him.

"Just try not to ogle her so obviously, OK?"

"Yes, boss." He all but ignored Amy after that. Ethan did too. The rest of the morning was spent drinking coffee, eating cinnamon rolls, and opening presents. My parents—well, my mom, actually—had gifts for all of us. She had always made sure that we had an equal number of gifts, and often bought the same thing for all three of us, whether it was socks or sweaters or gift certificates.

Despite my warnings, she'd gotten Rick a dark blue turtle-neck. "Oh, thanks, Mrs. E!" He pulled it out. "It's great."

She beamed. "I thought it would look good on you."

"I'll wear it today."

I stared at him. "Do you really like it?" I hissed.

"Yeah, I do." He looked at me. "Why?"

"Because it's a *turtleneck*? And you're a *guy*?"

"I like it." Rick pulled it out of the box. "In fact, I think I'll try it on now." He stood up and left the room. When he returned, he had it on with the jeans he'd been wearing last night.

"I like it a lot," he insisted.

My mom looked at him and started laughing. The sweater was much too tight. You could see the planes of his chest and the fabric straining over the outline of his ribs and stomach.

He looked so ridiculous we all started laughing. "I'm sorry," my mom managed. "It's too small. I'll get you another."

He walked over and kissed her cheek. "It's the thought that counts. And I love the color."

I saw my mom do a little preening gesture as she resettled herself in her chair.

"My mother loves you," I whispered in Rick's ear when he sat back down next to me.

"I know," he whispered back.

Chapter 30
The Ace of Wands, Inverted

The new beginning may not materialize.

Is there a workday any more depressing than the Monday after Christmas? People are recovering from holidays that didn't meet their expectations (were there any other kind?), and now that the paper had been torn off the gifts, the only thing to look forward to other than the drunkenness of New Year's Eve was the bills arriving next month. Rachel had asked me about my new year's resolutions, but I didn't have any.

"Come on, you must have some," she insisted.

"No, I don't. I never make them. What's the point? People say they want to lose weight or get in shape or whatever, and within two weeks, they've given up. I'll just skip that whole step."

"Well, I've made five." Rachel pulled out a piece of paper from her pocket. "Read more. Take classes toward my master's. Get my own apartment. Lose twenty pounds. And find a boyfriend," she added.

"That's one of your resolutions? Come on, Rachel. Your other ones are good, though," I quickly added. "Except I don't think you need to lose twenty pounds."

"That's what my mom says, too," she sighed. "But everyone else is so skinny!"

"Who's skinny? Look around!" We were sitting in the lunchroom, surrounded by Coddled Cook employees. There were a few twigs here and there, but there were just as many normal weight, overweight, and a few really big people as well.

"Yeah, but all the actresses are so skinny. I want to look like Cameron Diaz. Or Gwyneth Paltrow."

"Rachel, those women are sticks! They're also tall, and blond, which you are not."

"I know, but I can dream, can't I?"

I thought about it. Sure, I wouldn't mind being a little thinner. But my body had pretty much looked the same since high school. Average. I was average height, average build, medium-sized breasts—34B, nothing to be ashamed of but nothing to be excited about either. I wore an 8 or a 10, depending. Sure my stomach stuck out, but didn't everyone's? Jane had told me I had no body awareness once. I'd thought it was an insult.

"It's a compliment, Trina. You don't think about the way you look or how you carry yourself or anything," she'd said.

"Thanks a lot. You make me sound like a big ape or something."

"I don't mean it like that. I mean, you don't obsess over your body or your clothes or your makeup or anything girly. You're not really a girl at all."

"Geez, these breasts had me fooled."

"You're not a girl deep down. You're more, I guess, just yourself."

"I don't get it."

"OK, how many diets have you been on?"

I frowned. "I don't think I've ever gone on a diet. I mean, in college, we always said we were going to quit eating so much pizza, but that usually lasted a day or two."

"No diets. See, you're not a girl."

"Lots of women don't diet."

"OK, point two. What kind of underwear do you have on?"

I thought. "I don't know. Cotton?"

"What color?"

"Shit, I have no idea. Blue? Green?" I thought back to that morning. "Pink." I pulled the waist of my pants away from my stomach. "Pink."

"Again, not a girl. A *girl* always knows what kind of underwear she has on, what color, and whether it matches her bra."

"Jane, that's retarded."

"OK," she thought a moment. "Navy blue thong, pink lace demibra." She tugged at her bra strap to show me. "See? Girl."

"I still don't get it."

"Don't you see? Some writer said, 'The world is made for those who aren't cursed with self-awareness.' And that's you."

"I think I'm self-aware."

"Not in the sense that I'm talking abut. You don't second-guess yourself or worry about whether you're pretty enough or dressed the right way or making the right impression. That's the price of being a girl."

"I think about that stuff. I do!"

"But you don't obsess over it. That's what I like about you."

I didn't know whether I agreed with her or not. Jane had a theory for everything, and it went without saying that her way of thinking was the right way. Jessie was pretty much the same way—she was so certain about everything.

I asked Rick about it later. "Do you think I'm a girl?"

"You've done a good job of fooling me if you're not. This isn't going to be some *Crying Game* thing, is it?"

"No. I'm just thinking about something Jane said."

"What's a girl?"

"You know, someone who's worried about her body and her looks and her underwear and her clothes . . ." I let my voice trail off. "Well?"

"Under that definition, then, no, you're not a girl."

"But I do care about that stuff! I want to be attractive and everything."

"Yeah, but you're real, Trina. Guys say they want some

knockout with huge tits and a killer body, but they're high maintenance. Most guys want someone nice. Pretty but not *too* pretty. Funny. Someone to hang out with."

"So I'm pretty but not too pretty?"

"You know you're pretty. Beautiful even."

"Not as pretty as Jessie."

"Apples and oranges. The two of you hardly even look like sisters. You have more of a natural look. I like it. Obviously."

"What about Jill?" I felt my stomach clench as soon as I asked.

"You really want to know?"

"Yeah." We had scrupulously avoided the subject of her for the past six weeks. I'd been thinking that, as time went on, she'd fade from my thoughts, but I couldn't help thinking about her. I'd realized that this particular boil would have to be lanced if we were going to continue.

"I mean, yeah, if you want to tell me," I amended.

"She's high maintenance. Very high maintenance."

"How so?" I tried to keep my breathing calm and even.

"The girl had a freaking to-do list she followed every morning, right down to seven minutes in the shower, sixty seconds to brush her teeth, you name it."

"No way."

"Uh-huh. She was uptight, big time. I couldn't deal with it after a while."

"How long's a while?"

"I don't know. A month?" He saw my face. "Trina, I'm sorry. You know that 'you don't know what you got until it's gone' thing? That's what I kept thinking."

"But according to you, you felt free to screw around when we were together before."

"Yeah, but I didn't, remember?" I moved away from him, pulling my legs up under me. "You started this," he said gently.

"I know. I say I want to know, but it makes me angry all over again."

"Are you going to stop being angry?"

WHITE BIKINI PANTIES   249

"Eventually."

He sat there for a moment, then got up and came back from the kitchen with two bottles of water. "Thanks," I said, unscrewing the top.

"I didn't tell you. I got a call from a recruiter today."

"That's great! What kind of job?"

"Network stuff. It's a consulting firm. Decent money, good benefits, it sounds like it might be a good gig."

"Well, that's great! When do you interview?"

"On Friday. I'm flying out there—the job's in Seattle."

"Seattle, Washington?"

"Yeah. You know, Microsoft's out there in Redmond and there's a lot of tech companies out there. It may be the right place to be."

"So, you'd move there?"

"If I get the offer, yeah, maybe."

"Oh. Oh, OK." Don't worry, I thought to myself. Maybe he won't get the job.

And if he did? What would I do then? I guess we'd have to break up, wouldn't we? I couldn't see us doing a long-distance relationship. Besides, I didn't *want* to have a long-distance relationship. I wanted to have more than what we'd had before, not less. If he got the job, our relationship would go backward, not forward. I didn't think I could handle that.

Great. So getting back together had been a huge mistake. I felt a weight crushing my chest. Why was I so stupid? Why couldn't things just be easier for me? Why couldn't Rick just get a job here in Chicago? I thought about picking up the phone to call Jane, but she'd tell me I was catastrophizing— making the worst out of a situation that hadn't even arisen yet. Calm down, I told myself. Maybe he won't get the job and this will all be a completely moot issue. Hey, sometimes there's a fine line between practicality and denial.

In the meantime, I had work issues of my own to deal with. Bobby had had four weeks off, and I hadn't had a chance to follow up on that whole weird Elaine thing. I'd asked him to lunch, and after we'd run through our usual catch-up-on-our-sex-lives banter, I'd changed subjects.

"Okay. I need to ask you something."

"Sure. What's up?"

I fiddled with my napkin. "This is probably nothing. But Elaine said something to me about you at the holiday party."

"Let me guess. She's in love and wants to get into my pants."

"No. She said there was some rumor that you were doing something that could get you fired."

"Oh, shit." He looked away.

"What? What is it? It's not because you're gay, is it?" I pointed my fork. "God, I can't believe them! What jerks!"

"What? Get ahold of yourself. No, I bet I know what it is." He stared at his plate. "I've been doing some freelancing."

"So what? What's the big deal?"

"For the Perfect Kitchen."

I stared at him. "The Perfect Kitchen, as in one of our biggest competitors? Are you kidding?"

"Look, I need the money. My screenplay's almost done but I need to get out to L.A. to sell it. And I can barely pay my bills on what I make here." He gestured at his hamburger. "When was the last time you even saw me eat out?"

I had noticed that he'd been bringing sandwiches from home, but I figured that was because he'd been working on his screenplay over lunch. "I didn't realize money was so tight."

"I feel like I've got a shot with this script, Trini. But it's all about getting out there and making connections. I've been try-ing to figure out a way to make enough to spend some time out in L.A., and I heard the Perfect Kitchen needed some free-lance copywriting, so I sent my résumé in."

"Don't they care that you work here?"

"I guess not."

We sat in silence. "Bobby, I don't know what to tell you. You can't do it anymore. It's in the employment agreement. You could get fired."

"I know." He rubbed his eyebrow with his fingers. "It was a stupid move. What should I do?"

"I don't know. But if Elaine knows something, you'd better figure something out. I can't believe she'll keep it to herself. You know how she is."

"Like a dog with a bone," he said, and then pushed his plate away. "Are you going to say anything?"

I looked at him. "I don't know."

"Trini, we're friends."

"I know that. But I'm also your boss."

That's what made it so difficult. If I would have been Bobby's supervisor from the outset, we wouldn't have become such good friends. I mean, I don't think it's really appropriate to discuss your sex life (or lack of such) with your underlings. You need to be on equal footing to do that.

But we were friends—there was no escaping that. If this were a few months ago, I would have still been worried and upset for Bobby. He was violating a company rule—a big one—after all. That was a stupid, potentially dangerous thing to do. But I would have never dreamed of saying anything about it—that's wasn't my job, after all.

Was it my job now? Was ratting on my closest friend at work included in my job description? I felt suddenly, unspeakably depressed. This is not what I wanted. Bobby made work bearable—better than that. He made it fun. I needed to have at least one simpatico person at work. Without him, this job would be one long eight-hour drudge every day, five days a week. But even a drudge job was a heck of a lot better than no job. I was pretty sure Rick would feel the same way about that one.

Chapter 31
Nine of Swords

Pain, misery, suffering.

Rick called me at work on Tuesday.

"Hey, babe, guess what? I got it! Just got off the phone with the head of HR there. They're offering sixty-five thousand dollars and will throw in extra for moving expenses."

"Oh, that's great. Great!" I forced some enthusiasm into my voice.

"I figure the cost of living should be about the same as here. It's not a bad city, Trina. You'll like it."

I closed my eyes, already envisioning the long-distance relationship we'd have. I'd see him once every two months or so, maybe more frequently. We'd talk on the phone, e-mail, instant-message each other. Within four or five months, though, we'd get tired of the distance and we'd break up. I rubbed my forehead. I shouldn't have gotten back with him; I knew it. I'd tried to keep a firm grip on my heart. I didn't allow myself to fantasize about the future. I forced myself to be grateful for any time I had with him. It was only temporary.

"Yeah, I'm sure I will. Isn't it like really rainy out there, though?"

"Sure, but you don't get the snow and ice like you do here. I've been thinking, though, that it would be tough to do the long-distance thing, especially when we're used to seeing each other so often."

I steeled myself. I'd known this was coming. But did he have to tell me at work? I will not cry. I will not cry. Why hadn't I gone and gotten more thong underwear? He wouldn't be dumping me then.

"That's why I think you should come with me." He paused. "If you want to."

"You mean to help you move?"

"No, babe. Come with me. Move out there. We'll get a place. You can get a job there and we'll see how we like the Pacific Northwest. Do it together."

I sat perfectly still.

"Are you still there?" He laughed. "Don't say anything yet. We can talk about it later."

We hung up the phone and I stared dumbly at it, my hand still on the receiver. Rick sounded so happy. The past two months he'd had a vague sense of unhappiness lingering about him. He said he didn't mind not working, but I knew that wasn't true. This was the first time since we'd gotten back together that he'd sounded completely confident again, like the guy I'd first met.

I knew that losing his job had been hard on him, and it had made me absurdly grateful for my own. I couldn't imagine having nothing to do all day, especially with no money coming in. That idea had stopped me from buying a place of my own. In the back of my mind, I thought, what if I lose my job or something happens and I can't make the mortgage? I'd have to sell my condo and move back home . . . God, it would be awful. I supposed the same could happen with the apartment but losing a place you *owned* seemed so much more humiliating.

What was I thinking? And was what I going to do about Bobby? If I didn't tell Petra about his freelance gig, and she found out, I might get fired as well. It was possible, probable even. Bobby had agreed to not do any more work for the Perfect Kitchen, and I was hoping the whole thing would blow over. I still wondered how Elaine had found out, but I wasn't about to ask her.

Ethan called me later that afternoon. His voice sounded funny.

"Oh, hey. How are you? You getting a cold?"

"Trina, Jessie had a miscarriage. She's at Northwestern Memorial. They're going to keep her overnight, make sure she's stable, before they release her."

"What?" I clutched the phone tighter. "Is she OK?" Of course she's not OK, I thought. What an idiot.

"She lost a lot of blood. The doctor said when you're that far along, they want to keep an eye on things."

"Oh, God, I am so sorry, Ethan. What happened?"

"She'd been bleeding some the last couple of days, and then she started having bad cramps at work this morning. She called me, but I was in court." His voice broke. "She took a cab over here and they called and finally got me. She'd already lost it by the time I got here."

Tears welled up in my eyes, and my throat hurt. "Oh, that is so awful. Poor Jessie. Can I do anything?"

"I don't know. She's sleeping now. She's bad, Trina. She was hysterical. They gave her something to calm her down. I don't know what to do."

"I'll come out after work."

"You don't have to."

"No, I'll come. What's her room number?"

We hung up and I reached for a Kleenex and blew my nose. Then I called home. My mom answered. I could tell she was crying.

"Hi."

"Hi, honey. Did Ethan call you?"

"Yeah. I'm going to stop up there after work."

My mom began crying, which set me off as well. "I feel so terrible for her. She was so excited about this baby."

"I know. I know." I let her cry, silently wiping my nose with my Kleenex.

"I'm glad you're going to see her. I'll come up tomorrow and see if I can help her at home."

"Does Dad know?"

"I'll tell him when he gets home. I don't want to call him at work and get him upset."

"Will you tell Melissa? Or do you want me to?"

"I'll call her later. Oh, I'm getting a call. That may be Ethan again. I'll talk to you later, honey. Thanks for calling."

I parked in the garage across from the hospital, and stopped at the information desk, where an older woman directed me to Jessie's floor. I found the room and stood outside for a moment, taking some deep breaths. I didn't want to upset her more by crying. I should have brought flowers, I thought, then thought, what an idiotic thought. You lost your baby, but hey, check out these daisies!

Jessie was lying in the bed by the window. A tube snaked down from a bottle of something clear and was taped to her arm. Ethan was sitting in a plastic chair next to her, one foot crossed on his knee.

I looked. She had her eyes closed.

"Hi," I greeted Ethan.

"Hey." He started to get up, but I motioned him down. I came over and squeezed his shoulders.

"I'm sorry."

He nodded.

Neither of us spoke. The room had that sharp chemical hospital smell, but I could pick up Ethan's cologne underneath it. He really was a good-looking guy, I thought. I was so used to seeing him as Jessie's husband, I forgot that. Then I had a surge of guilt. This was worse than the flowers.

"Want to take a break? I'll sit here." I pulled off my coat.

"Yeah, all right. I should check my voice mail anyway."

He left and I sat down. I looked at Jessie. Her face was puffy, but her hair gleamed. I noticed her nails—long, smooth ovals of pearl. I thought about holding her hand but I didn't want to wake her.

She spoke without opening her eyes. "Figures, huh?"

Her voice was thick with sleep or drugs or both, and I had to strain to understand her.

"What?"

"Shoulda known it was too good to be true," she mumbled.

"Shhh." I reached over and stroked her hair. "It's okay. It's all right."

She made a noise, and then fell back asleep. I was relieved. I didn't want to see her awake, didn't want to witness her pain. I felt ashamed to admit it to myself, but it was true. I simply sat there, watching her, until Ethan came back.

"She OK?"

I nodded, and we went out into the hallway. The door closed silently behind us. The skin on Ethan's face looked tight, like it was one size too small for his skull.

"How are you?"

He shook his head. "I don't know. I'm more worried about her."

I told him my parents were coming up, and he nodded. "I know. They're great."

"Have you told your parents?"

He nodded again.

"Do you want me to stay awhile?"

"No, that's all right. Visiting hours end at eight anyway, and I'll head home and shower."

I was relieved to be able to go, then felt guilty for thinking so. "What else can I do?"

"Nothing, Trina. Just check on her when she gets home, I guess. Her doc said she should probably stay home a few days and rest before she goes back to work. I'll take some time off, too, if she wants." He looked away and then down at the floor. "Whatever she needs."

"Sure, no problem. Just let me know." I left the hospital. It was bitterly cold outside, with a wind off the lake that sucked the breath out of me. I let the car warm up for a few minutes, shivering, and then pulled out onto Michigan and took Lake

Shore Drive to Lawrence. I found a parking spot down the block and hurried home.

I'd forgotten that I'd turned the radiator up last night. The apartment was at least eighty degrees. I turned off the dial, opened windows, and poured myself a glass of wine in the meantime.

Rick called a half hour later. "Hey, I wondered where you'd been. Late night?"

I told him what had happened, my voice flat.

"That is the worst. I'm sorry for them. How's she doing?"

"I think physically she'll be fine. Emotionally, I don't know."

"Do you want me to come over?"

"Thanks, but you know what? I'd rather be alone right now. I'm beat and I won't be good company."

"I don't mind. You don't even have to talk to me."

I smiled. "Thanks, but no."

"All right. Call me tomorrow?"

"Sure. Thanks."

"Trina, I . . ." His voice faltered. I heard him clear his throat. "I'm sorry. Tell her that, all right?"

"I will." I hung up, finished my wine, and poured another glass. I could feel a pleasant dampening of awareness. My stomach growled, but I wasn't hungry. I simply sat on the couch, drinking my wine, and staring at the Van Gogh print on the wall. Then I stood up, walked to the bedroom, took off all my clothes, left them in a pile, and climbed into bed.

Chapter 32
The Two of Pentacles

Inability to handle two situations at once.

It had been two weeks since Jessie's miscarriage. The weather was typical of Chicago in January—three days of bitter cold followed by a sunshiny day in the forties, followed by six inches of snow. Jessie had gone back to work a week ago. She seemed to be coping, but with her it was hard to tell whether she was doing OK or not.

I'd taken to calling her every morning. We'd always spoken by phone frequently before, but now I made a point of calling her before lunch. I actually wrote it on my calendar so I wouldn't forget.

Our conversations were always short. I hadn't told her about Rick's job yet. In fact, I hadn't told anyone. I knew once I did, I'd have to make a decision. People would ask if we were still going to see each other. How would I answer that?

"Why yes, we'll be seeing each other every day! At breakfast, and at dinner!"

Of course, that was only if I moved out there with him. Why should I do that? Give up a good job, leave my family and friends, just to follow my man? Gloria Steinem would not approve. Then again, if I were going to follow my man, shouldn't I be married to him? Or at least engaged?

I hadn't told anyone about it, but I already knew what they'd say.

Jane: "Go for it! It'll be an adventure."

Jessie: "Are you kidding? Have you thought about getting a job there? What if you can't find work? What are you going to do then? Your problem is you have no plan."

My mom: "Honey, I just don't know if you should take that kind of risk, without a real commitment from him. We like Rick but you know what they say about getting the milk for free."

Melissa: "Seattle? Cool! Can I come visit?"

My dad:

Here I drew a blank. What *would* Dad say? I knew he liked Rick—at least he acted as if he did—but this wasn't the kind of thing I'd go to him about. I didn't talk to him about the guys I dated except in the most general of terms. Deep down, I thought he'd disapprove, though. He'd side with my mom, embrace the parental party line of "no-living-together-before-marriage."

Rick had already begun packing his apartment. He had boxes of computer accessories scattered about, and a big garbage bag by the front door.

"So you're really going." I cleared some cables from the couch and sat down.

"I'm going to take off on Tuesday or Wednesday."

"OK."

He looked up. "I told you, you've got an open invitation. Come with me."

"I can't just dump my job and run off with you."

"You can look for a job out there now, can't you? Have you checked out monster-dot-com? There are lots of gigs for tech writers out there. I looked."

"I'm not a tech writer. Nor do I want to be a tech writer."

"What do you want to be?"

"I don't know. Happy."

"What does that mean?"

I thought. "It means . . . I don't know. Having friends who make me laugh. Being with you. My family. *True Hollywood Story*. Good sex," I added. "Good books. Good movies. Good food." I sighed. "God, I'm boring, aren't I?"

"The sex part got my attention, anyway." He came over and sat on his scarred plaid footstool. Stuffing was leaking out of three different places. He poked it. "By the way, you'll be happy to know that this particular piece of furniture will not be making the trip."

I'd always teased him about his frat house chic style of décor, but now I felt absurdly sorry for the footstool. "Why not?"

"Come on. It's a piece of crap. I'm only taking the stuff that's important. And easy to move."

"What about all your other furniture?"

"I'm taking the futon. The table and chairs. That's about it."

"Wow. You are traveling light."

"There'll be plenty of space for more furniture, you know."

I twisted my fingers together. "I'm just not sure. I need more time to decide."

"It's up to you." He taped a box. I sat and watched him, unaccountably angry.

"You know, this is easy for you! You've already got a job there! You'll make friends like that." I snapped my fingers. "You don't care where you live. What about me?"

"What about you?"

"Well, I've got a good job, and my family's here, and Jane's here," I said.

"So, stay here. We can do the long-distance thing, I already told you that."

"What if you meet someone else?"

"I'm not looking for anyone else."

"Yeah, you'll meet some cool Seattle babe, some dot-com wonder with huge boobs and a great body and lots of money, and you won't even remember my name. Trina? Who?"

"Tell me more about her!" he teased. "She sounds pretty hot."

"Shut up." I crossed my arms. "I'm serious."

"You're paranoid."

"Even a paranoid has real enemies." I'd read that somewhere and it sounded good.

"Look, I've been straight with you. If you want me, you got me. I'm not looking for anyone else, and even if I met someone, I'm not going to fuck us up again. Lesson learned, all right?"

"So why . . ." I took a deep breath. "Why don't you want to get married?"

"I'm not ready. Look, we've had this conversation. I want to live with you, I want you to come with me, start a new life together! Isn't that good enough?"

"I'm not sure."

"Well, that's all I can offer. It's your call."

I wanted more from him. That was the problem. I wanted him to tell me he really *did* want to marry me, he just needed some time. I wanted him to promise that if I moved out there with him, we'd have a future together. I wanted him to cross his heart, swear on a stack of Bibles, and give me an unbreakable, solid, airtight guarantee that he'd never even imagine going to bed with anyone else ever again.

Jane, of course, thought I was expecting too much. I hadn't seen her much since she hooked up with Steve. They were deep in coupledom bliss, but he had an improv class that night. I was curled up in the corner of her couch, picking at the fringe on one of her pillows.

"There's no such thing as a guarantee, sweetie."

"Sure there is. It's called a ring."

She snorted. "Come on. He could cheat on you just as easily if you were engaged, or married for that matter. Or you could cheat on him. Or you could fall in love with someone else. Or you could just decide you don't want him anymore."

I bit my lip, considering. "I don't see that happening."

She spread her arms. "Who knows? You're twenty-eight years old. Lots can happen. What is it you want? Because if it's some ironclad money-back guarantee, you'll never find it. You can't control the human heart."

I thought about what she said. I hated the fact that she was right. Love by its very nature isn't logical. It would be so much neater, more organized, if I could have simply stopped loving Rick. I could have found someone else by now. Someone who'd be ready to get married. Or at least engaged.

"What? What are you thinking?"

I sighed. "I'm just wondering why my head's not the boss of my heart. I don't like feeling this way."

"What way?"

I teared up. "Angry. Frustrated. Afraid. I'm afraid of him going without me, and I'm afraid to go with him." I punched the pillow. "I'm a big wimp. You'd go, wouldn't you? If it were Steve?"

"If it were Steve, I'd go to Antarctica."

"But that's who you are, Jane. You're a risk taker."

"No, I'm not. You'd never catch me bungee jumping or rock climbing or leaping out of a perfectly good plane to sky dive."

"I don't mean physical risks. I mean emotional risks. You put yourself out there. Every audition, you're putting yourself out there."

"You have to as an actor. It's part of the package. But you get rejected a lot, too, you know." She picked up a cigarette. "You just hope that you'll succeed more than you fail. Or that your successes will carry you through the times when you don't get a callback."

"I suppose."

"Sweetie, you know what I think? I think you know what the answer is." She blew a perfect smoke ring. "Follow. Your. Heart."

"What about you? What about my family? What if it doesn't work?"

"What if it does?"

I didn't answer. I picked up the tarot cards sitting on the end table. "I wish these would just tell me what to do. I want an answer."

"They don't work like that. They can give you a glimpse into your future, but they won't interfere. You still have free will. Unless you believe in that predetermination stuff, where everything we do has already been decided for us. I'd like to think we still control our lives."

"That's the problem. I think I'm waiting for someone to step in and control mine."

Chapter 33
The Moon, Inverted

Storms will be weathered, peace gained at a cost.

I finally told Jessie about Rick's new job. "What does that mean for the two of you?"

"He's actually asked me to move out there with him."

"And do what?"

"I'd get a job. There's plenty of writing and editing work out there."

"How long would you live out there?"

"I don't know. I guess it depends on if we like it. We haven't really talked about that."

Jessie drank some coffee. We were sitting at her kitchen table on Sunday morning. Cold winter sunshine streamed in through the windows, and the sky was clear. Ethan was off playing basketball, and she'd invited me out for brunch.

"It's an awfully big risk to take, especially when he won't commit to you," she said.

Hearing her say what I already thought annoyed me. "Well, of course it's a risk. But maybe I need to take a risk now and then," I snapped.

"I'm just saying, it's a much bigger deal than if the two of you were just moving in together here," said Jessie. "Then if it didn't work out, you'd still have your job and not that much would have changed."

She got up and poured us both more coffee. "But it's up to you, I guess."

"I know that."

We sat in silence for a few minutes. "How do you know he won't do that again?"

"He says he won't." I tried to explain what Rick had said about never having explicitly committed himself to monogamy with me before. "The thing is, I don't remember us ever talking about it," I admitted. "I just assumed that since we were together, he wouldn't see anyone else."

"Marry him and you'll eliminate that excuse," said Jessie. The conversation was making me uncomfortable.

"So, how is . . . everything else?"

She looked down at her coffee cup. "Bad." Then she looked directly at me. "You're not going to believe this. I've started seeing a therapist."

"Why?"

"First I thought it would help me cope better with the baby." Her voice trailed off and she closed her eyes briefly before continuing. "It's not just that, though. I feel like I'm lost. Nothing's going according to my plan!" She forced a laugh. "And you know how I am. I cannot deal with that."

I reached over and put my hand on her forearm. "I think it's a good idea, actually. I think it could only help."

"Ethan says the same thing." She poked at a strawberry with her fork. "You know, I thought Ethan might be having an affair a few months ago."

I choked on my coffee. "What?"

"I know. It's crazy, but something seemed off with him."

I reached for a handful of grapes. "Did you say anything about it?" I couldn't see Jessie keeping a suspicion like that to herself.

"Sure. I asked him flat out, the night of our Christmas party," said Jessie.

"And? What did he say?"

She smiled. "He said he'd never even looked at another woman since he met me," she said, idly stirring her coffee. Then she looked directly at me. "Which is bull. I see him looking. Did you see how he was at Christmas with that roommate of Melissa's? But I know he'd never act on it." She twisted her wedding ring. "I like knowing that."

I opened my mouth to speak, then shut it. And decided to keep it shut.

Chapter 34
Strength, Inverted

Abuse of power, discord.

Rick left on Tuesday morning, planning to spend four days driving to Seattle. He'd advertised on craigslist.com and had found some nineteen-year-old guy to ride along to share the gas expense.

"You're going to spend four days with a total stranger?" I'd asked.

He'd just grinned. "Why not? It'll make the ride go quicker."

Monday night, he'd come over to my place after he loaded his furniture and boxes of computer equipment into a U-haul he'd rented. I didn't get to sleep until after three. I lay there thinking *this is the last time I may ever hear him breathing. This is the last time I may ever feel the warmth of his back against my skin.* It wasn't a happy scene. But when he left the next morning, I didn't cry. I felt hollow, an empty cantaloupe rind scraped clean of feelings.

At work, I was on autopilot. I smiled and said hello as I walked to my cubicle, sat down, turned on my computer, and read through my e-mails.

Bobby stopped by when he got in. "How are you?" I'd told him Rick was leaving today.

"I'm alive. I should just accept that brokenhearted is my usual emotional state. Or lonely."

"But you guys aren't calling it quits. Aren't you still going to see each other?"

"Yeah, but how long will that last? Until he meets some little grunge-rocking, espresso-drinking, poetry-writing Seattle chick. Then I'll be kicked to the curb," I said. "Again."

"Ouch. I thought you'd forgiven him for that whole scene."

"I have."

"Uh-huh."

"No, I have. But there's a difference between forgiving and forgetting. And let's face it, people don't change. If he did that before, he'll do it again."

"Even if he tells you he won't."

"If he felt that strongly, if he was sure, he'd marry me."

"Good thing you're not gay, Trini. You'd never make it."

"What does that mean?"

"How honest do you want me to be? Or do you want me to sugarcoat it?"

"You can be honest." I sighed. "Go ahead!"

"OK. Here's my perspective. Girl meets guy. Girl gets guy. Girl loses guy. Girl gets guy back. Guy wants girl. Guy asks girl to move with him. Girl says fuck off."

"It's a little more complicated than that."

"Not really. So he doesn't want to get married. So what? Does that have to be the ultimate goal of every relationship?"

"If you're straight, then yes." I saw his face. "I know, you think I'm hopelessly boring and conservative. But I want to get married! There's nothing wrong with that."

"So you'd rather marry some guy, just any guy, than be with someone like Rick who you know you love?"

"No! No. I just want to find someone I love who wants what I want." I smiled briefly. "It sounds so easy when I say it, doesn't it? So why is it so hard?"

I thought my day couldn't get worse, but it did. About ten, my phone rang. Petra yet again. Now what? I answered.

"Trina, there's something I need to speak to you about. Immediately."

"Um, sure, I'll be right there."

I pushed back my chair and started toward the hallway. A movement caught my eye. It was Bobby, standing at his cubicle. His head was bent, and as I watched, he pulled on his leather coat. "Where are you going?" I teased.

He raised his face and I knew. "Oh no. What happened?"

He lifted his palms. "Somebody squealed about my freelancing. Petra just canned me." Rory, one of the security guards, walked over in his gray uniform. I looked at him and he nodded at me.

"What? Are you waiting for something?" Then I got it. "What, do they think you're going to steal valuable company secrets or something?"

Bobby was pulling photos off his cube wall and stacking books in a box. "Take it easy, Trini. This is how it works."

"This isn't fair! You're the best writer we have!" And my best friend here, I thought but didn't say.

He stopped his packing and took my shoulders in his hands. "I knew the risk." He opened his desk drawer and scooped out a couple of pens, waving them at Rory. "Brought from home, I swear!" The office seemed strangely quiet. I knew that people were sitting at their desks, fingers poised over keyboards, straining to hear every word. "I'll look at it as a sacrifice for my art."

I shook my head again. "Look, we can figure something out. You're a valuable employee here. Maybe Petra will understand." Oh shit! Petra. I was supposed to be standing in her office as we spoke.

He buttoned his coat and picked up the box. "I wouldn't waste your breath. You can't fix this, Trin. I'll be all right." He lowered his voice. "If I don't leave now, I'm going to cry, and I do not want that. Understand?"

I nodded, and he grinned. He mouthed the words "I'll call you" to me. Then aloud, he sang out, "Ladies and gentlemen!

Elvis has left the building!" turned to Rory and said, "Shall we go?" and paraded out.

I took several breaths to steady myself, then hurried to Petra's office. She was on the phone, but looked pointedly at her watch when I came in.

"Did something come up?"

"I was talking to Bobby."

"Interesting. That's what I wanted to talk to you about. Were you aware that he was violating his employment contract by writing for one of our competitors?"

I stared at her. "Was I aware?" I stalled.

She steepled her fingers and looked at me.

Had Bobby told her? I couldn't believe that. He would have kept it to himself. I didn't know what Elaine knew, or how she'd come about it, but this wasn't the right time to explore that question.

"Um, no. I wasn't aware. Until just now when he told me that's why you fired him," I added. I kept my hands in my lap. Jane had told me it was a dead giveaway to touch your face or rub your eyes when you told a lie.

She stared at me. Stare all you want, I thought, I'm not caving. "I see." She started to say something, then stopped. She picked up a piece of paper and passed it to me. It was an interoffice memo. "Elaine Jurasek will be taking Bobby's position as senior writer. We'll hire someone for the junior position soon."

Elaine? It had been bad enough having her in my department. She lacked basic grammatical skills, for God's sake! How many times had I seen her confuse *your* and *you're*? If I saw one more headline with HAVE YOU'RE GREATEST PARTY YET, I thought I might scream. But I took the path of least resistance.

"All right. Anything else? Because I have to get going on the newsletter," I added quickly.

"That will be it."

I walked back to my desk. I knew Elaine would be dying to find out what had happened, and I didn't have long to wait.

She stopped by my desk on the pretense of checking on a story assignment.

"Did you see Bobby leave?" Her eyes were wide and very blue. Contacts, I figured.

"Uh-huh." I kept my voice level. She wasn't going to know how angry I was.

"Can you believe that? I guess he was working for the competition, but you probably knew that, huh?"

Did she really think I was that stupid? "No, I didn't. I can't believe he'd take such a risk." At least that part was true. "I guess you're happy now that you have his job, though, aren't you? At least some good comes out of it." I smiled and cocked my head at her.

She opened her mouth in disbelief. "What? No, that's not true. I feel awful about the whole thing, just awful." She pushed her hair behind her shoulders. "You must feel awful, too."

"Just awful." I turned back to my computer. "I need to get back to work." I felt her lingering behind me, but ignored her. She walked away a few seconds later.

Chapter 35
Judgment

An awakening, change of position, renewal.

The next several weeks dragged by. I went to work, came home, and distracted myself with whatever was on TV. Bobby had called—he was looking for a job and using his downtime to polish the screenplay. I told him I hoped he'd include a back-stabbing corporate drone who'd do anything to get ahead . . . and name the character Elaine. The in-the-flesh version was her usual suck-up self and had started sitting with Rachel at lunch. I tried not to care. Maybe our new hire would turn out to be someone I could talk to.

True to what he'd said, Rick called me almost every night. He liked the new job, his coworkers were "all right," and he was starting to find his way around town.

"How about the rain?"

"Yeah, it's wet. But not nearly as cold as Chicago. You'll like it, Trina. When are you coming out? Next weekend?"

"I can't. Mom and Dad are coming up."

"For what?"

"They're staying at Jessie and Ethan's for the weekend." I picked up the remote and flipped through the channels. I had the volume on mute. I liked watching TV with no sound sometimes. I'd found that most of the time I could tell what was happening without needing any dialogue. Sure, you missed the punchlines, but most sitcoms weren't that funny anyway. Other than *Will & Grace* and *Friends*, I'd given up on most network television.

"What's the occasion?"

"Nothing. I think they're just coming up for support."

"How's she doing?"

"OK, I guess." I thought about it. "She says therapy is helping a lot. I think she probably should have gone a long time ago."

"What about Ethan?"

"What about him?"

"I mean, how's he doing?"

"I'm not sure. I'll see him next weekend, I guess. I'm going out there for dinner."

I hung up, feeling vaguely annoyed. It was fine for Rick to ask about Ethan, express his concern. What did he care? Ethan wasn't part of *his* family. He was the one who had left, after all. What difference did my family make to him?

Of course he had needed a job. But he could have stayed here and kept looking for one. That thought skittered across my brain. And now he wants me to come and see him!

I told my mom and Jessie about it the next weekend. "He wants you to visit, honey," my mom said. "It certainly sounds like he still wants to see you. Though I don't know how you'll manage that distance," she added.

"Of course he wants me to visit. Why not? I get to spend the money and fly out there, and then I just get to come home and miss him even more."

"But wouldn't seeing him be a good thing?" my mom asked, confused.

"Not if she just wants to get over him. Right? Then it's just delaying the inevitable," said Jessie.

I was standing at the stove, stirring Jessie's pasta sauce. I pointed the wooden spoon at my sister. "Exactly."

"Why do you want to get over him? I thought the two of you just got back together. Don't you love him?"

"Mom, that's not enough."

"Well, absence makes the heart grow fonder."

"Out of sight, out of mind," I countered.

Mom shook her head. "I don't get it. Things were easier for us. You met a man, you fell in love, you got married, you had children. What's so difficult about that?" She saw Jessie's face and reached over to squeeze her shoulders. "Oh, honey, I'm so sorry. I didn't mean that."

Jessie stood stiffly. "No, you're right. What's so difficult about that?" She reached for the wine bottle and poured herself another glass. "Get married, have sex, get pregnant, get a baby. It's not hard at all! Any moron can do it. Fourteen-year-olds can do it. Hell, twelve-year-olds can do it."

My mom tried to enfold her, but Jessie stepped away from her grasp. Ethan came in. "Mmmm, sauce smells good." He stopped and looked at us. Jessie had her back to him. "What's wrong?"

My mom was in tears. "I'm sorry." She hurried out of the room.

Ethan looked at me, then walked to Jessie and put his arms around her waist and kissed the back of her neck. "Hey. Hey. Are you all right?"

She shook her head.

He turned her toward him. I could see she was crying. "It's okay. Shhh. It's all right. I'm here."

I stood there, watching them. I felt like a peeping Tom, witnessing her private pain. I put down the spoon and tiptoed out to the great room, where Dad was watching a basketball game.

"What happened to Ethan? I sent him on beer patrol," said Dad.

"He's in there with Jess." I stood behind him, my hands on the back of the couch.

My dad turned his head to look at me more closely. "What is it?"

"Mom just wasn't thinking. Did she come in here?"

"She walked through a minute ago." I walked into the living room and dining room, but both were empty. I opened the front door. She was standing on the edge of the driveway. I went back in the house, grabbed both of our coats off the rack in the front hall, and followed her.

"You forgot your coat." I handed it to her. "You'll get a cold, you know!" I said, imitating her. My breath came out in little puffs.

"I can't believe I said that. Mothers are always supposed to know the right thing to say."

"That's not true. We realize you're human." I put my arm around my mom. She seemed smaller than usual. "Really."

"I don't know how to help her, Trina. There's nothing worse than seeing your child suffer and not being able to do anything about it."

I kicked at a clod of dirty snow. "Yeah. I forget we're still your kids. When does the mothering license wear out?"

She smiled. "Never. That's what they don't tell you."

We came to a street. A couple my age passed us, walking a golden retriever pup tugging on the leash with his mouth. We both smiled.

"Mom, Rick asked me to move out there with him. To Seattle."

"You didn't tell me that."

"I knew you wouldn't approve."

"You mean the two of you would be living together?"

"Yeah, that's the idea. But it's crazy. I'd have to get a job out there, and move all my stuff, and I don't know anyone except him. And I'd be so far away." I looked down. "You know?"

"What's the worst that could happen?"

"Isn't it obvious? I move out there, and get a new job, and then we break up. And I'm stuck out there."

"You can always come home, Trina." My mom wrapped her arms around herself. She looked at me thoughtfully. "I don't think I've ever told you this, but out of the three of you girls, you remind me the most of myself."

"What do you mean?"

"Well, Jessie's always had her plan." We both smiled. "And that younger sister of yours—well, she jumps into things feet first, no questions asked. But you're more careful about things. You don't want to rock the boat."

"Isn't that the job of the middle child? The peacemaker?"

"Oh, honey, you're much more than that. You're pretty and smart and talented. You could do anything you want, do you realize that?"

I felt tears well up.

"What? What's wrong?"

"Why don't you ever tell me things like that?"

She stared at me. "What do you mean?"

I looked away. "You're always fussing over Melissa. I mean I know she's the baby and everything and she probably needs you more, but still." I gulped. "And with Jessie expecting the baby and everything, you were so excited about that, too." I couldn't look at her. "Sometimes I just feel left out. Like an afterthought."

"Oh, Trina." She hugged me close. "I'm sorry. You're not an afterthought. I guess I just haven't had to worry about you as much." She squeezed me. "Do you want me to start?"

"Yeah. No. I don't know. Just remind me of some of these things sometimes." I smiled and wiped at my eyes. "Sorry I'm upset."

"Don't be sorry. I've been so worried about Jessie I haven't even asked you about your life."

"But she needs you right now. She needs all of us."

"Yes, but that doesn't mean you don't need me, too." She slid her arm around my waist. "I'll try to be a better mom."

"You're a great mom. All my friends are jealous of me. Geez, Jane wants you to adopt her!"

"Yes, but she'll have to quit smoking. No kid of mine is going to smoke."

I laughed. "Yes, Mother."

"Should we go back?"

"Yeah."

We walked in silence. "I feel guilty leaving Jessie," I confessed.

My mom nodded. "I thought so. You know, even when you were little, you were so concerned with doing everything right. You never wanted to disappoint me or anyone else."

I listened to her with the same fascination we all have hearing about our own childhoods from someone else who was there.

"But you need to think about what you want, too, Trina," my mom continued.

"Isn't that selfish?"

She sighed. "Maybe. But only by making yourself happy can you give your best to anyone else." She glanced at me and continued. "I'm not saying I'd be delighted with you two living together. I still don't think it's right. But I don't think you should base your decisions on what you think other people want for you. You should do what *you* want. Provided it's not illegal, of course," she added.

"I don't know what I want."

"I bet you do." My mom smiled.

I didn't answer. I thought of Rick, how scratchy his voice sounded first thing in the morning. When he'd bought me three pairs of socks—"thick and fluffy, like you like"—two months after we'd started dating so my feet wouldn't get cold when I spent the night at his place. The way he'd surprised me by digging out my car last month when we got eight inches of snow overnight, so that when I came downstairs, dreading the chore, I instead found a cleared car and a sticky note that read "Surprise!" The way he made me laugh no matter how crappy my day had been. The way he'd put on that ridiculous turtleneck at Christmas. The way I just felt right with him, like the best version of myself. And how in spite of everything, I still loved him. If anything, I loved him more.

I pulled the door open for my mom. "Let's go in." She stepped in front of me, and I followed.

Jessie, Ethan, and my dad were all watching the game. Dad sat on one of the easy chairs with his feet propped up while Jessie and Ethan were on the couch. He had his arm around her. They all turned toward us as we came in the room. My mom went over and hugged Jessie from behind, whispering in her ear. Jessie nodded, and Ethan watched her. As my mom walked toward the kitchen, I saw Ethan catch Jessie's eye, his brows raised.

She smiled at him. "I'm OK," she mouthed. He nodded.

I watched them for a moment. They might be all right. I knew they loved each other. Maybe that was enough.

I glanced at my watch. It was almost 4 P.M. Seattle time. "Can I use your phone? I forgot my cell."

"Go ahead."

I dialed and he answered.

"I thought you were going to be at Jessie and Ethan's today."

"I'm there, actually. I've been thinking. Does that offer still hold?"

I could hear his smile. "What about the rain? What about finding a job out here? What about leaving the Midwest?" His tone teased, but I could hear the unasked question.

"What about you?"

He didn't say anything.

I took a deep breath. "Well?"

I could hear noises in the background. "I am cleaning up as we speak. Preparing my pad for your arrival."

"I don't care about that."

"Uh, if you saw my place, you might say otherwise."

"Our place."

"Oh, right. Our place," he repeated. "I like the sound of that. Trina, you're going to love it here. There are so many things I want to show you. I found a great Thai place, and you can get a latte on any corner, I swear."

I could feel my heart speed up. Nerves, anticipation, excitement. It felt a lot like fear.

"Can I ask you a weird question?"

"As weird as you want."

"Do you like thong underwear?"

"On you or in general?"

"Um, both."

"I don't know. It's all right. What I really like are those little white bikinis. With the bow in the front?"

I thought of my underwear drawer, jammed with every imaginable color, style, and variety of panties, and laughed.

"You're serious."

"Yeah. Those are my favorites."

I unzipped my jeans and checked. Jane would call that a sign. I decided I would, too.